This is a work of fiction. Names, characters, places and incidents either are products of the author's imagination or are used fictitiously. Any resemblance to actual events or locales or persons, living or dead, is entirely coincidental.

Copyright ©2022 by Emma Bruce

All rights reserved. No portion of this book may be reproduced in any form without permission from the publisher, except as permitted by U.S. copyright law. For permissions contact: youreaglecoach@mail.com

Cover Art by Marie-Louise O'Neill

Formatting by Renee Brooks PA

ISBN:

First Edition

❀ Created with Vellum

Dreams In Pink
Pink Club

Emma Bruce

Acknowledgments

Firstly, I would like to thank my parents Bruce and Sheila for doing such an amazing job bringing me up and giving me just the most amazing childhood and life anyone could ever wish for. Your encouragement with my writing has been what spurred me on over the past five years, putting this project together. Just as you are undoubtedly very proud parents to one of your awesome daughters, I, too, am very proud of you because of how lucky I am to be able to call you my mum and dad! The luckiest woman in the world that's who!

Secondly, I would like to thank my husband for watching our children giving me the time to write when needed and always giving me love and support for all my decisions when investing in necessary people along the way to bring this to fruition. Love you to the moon and back. xxx

I would also like to acknowledge some very special people who have been with me through varying degrees of this journey: Holly—who has pretty much been there since this all began in 2016: Thank you for your wisdom and bringing my attention to the power of self-publishing.

The awesome author, Duncan Falconer, of books such as The Hostage & The Hijack: Thanks for introducing me to the amazing and phenomenal Barri Evins! Without her coming to my rescue and saving my bacon, I highly suspect Pink Club may have become a non-event, and that would have been a tragedy, which I'm sure you—as the readers—will agree with once you fall in love (hopefully) with the story and its characters.

Foreword

If you haven't read Pink Club yet—the first in this series—hop over to Amazon and grab a copy! Hurry before the third book is released! Please leave a positive review on Amazon and Goodreads for these books.

~ Chapter 1 ~

One Week Later...

Presently, I am trying and failing to watch a soppy romance movie while sitting on the sofa with Binks purring away happily on my lap. My mind has been distractedly racing all week, and my sleep patterns are all awry since news of Mimi returning to her family alive and well have been broadcast every day. I've heard nothing from Eva or Pink Club and feel currently on edge about my position within the club and wondering if the spring gala will even be going ahead. If I'm fired, what will I do? Go back to waiting tables? The thought depresses me.

An earlier snow shower has now turned into pouring rain, drumming a soothing rhythmic pitter patter sound on my windows and roof of my building. Intermittently, I'm checking my mobile phone; the silence has been deafening. I've also not left my apartment all week for fear of being spotted, as press have been loitering, knowing that Pink Club's Bella Fitzroy used to reside here. My mobile still shows no missed calls or text messages from Eva about what is happening with dance rehearsals. Everything has gone very 'repetitive' on the media front about Mimi Glass with no new details, which has given way for internet conspiracy theorists to go wild with their imagined scenarios. All anyone knows now is that Mimi has been discharged from the hospital, and the family have asked the press and public for privacy during this very sensitive time.

At the start of the week, Eva had messaged everyone on a group text chat, reminding us to keep *very* low profiles and that more information would come out when it was available.

Having felt too scared to leave my apartment, for fear I may 'blow my cover,' I suddenly feel an overwhelming urge to stretch my legs. Quickly, I make a call down to the main reception of my building and the receptionist kindly informs me no press have been outside for at least two days. Breathing a sigh of relief, I begin to get ready to carry through with my decision to go out, even if it is raining. Gingerly, I move Binks off my lap, sliding him onto the sofa as I stand up, and walk over to my bedroom to change into suitable clothing for the weather.

"Hi I'd like to book a taxi from the megaplex cinema.

That's right, the one on the corner of Pear Grove Avenue."

After handing over the details of where I wish to be collected by my ride, I proceed to put on my new Cath Kitsen floral rain mac, pink scarf with matching gloves and bobble hat. I then grab my yellow umbrella, and lastly, pick up my handbag off the kitchen counter, breathing a big sigh before heading out.

The rain has broken briefly, which makes the walk up to the cinema, thankfully, a dry one. It feels good to get some fresh air and helps my nerves abate a little. Condensation hits my legs where rainwater evaporates from the pavements, the damp warmth seeping through my jeans —not enough to make them soaking wet, just mildly soggy. People enter and exit out of the cinema doors as I wait patiently for my taxi ride to arrive. The temperature, now dropping again, enables me to see my breath flow out of me like puffs of smoke.

Believe me, it's times like these I wish I smoked!

Eventually, my taxi arrives, the driver apologising for being slow to get here, explaining the traffic is not good due to treacherous road conditions.

The journey to my slice of Heaven, *Angel Cake*, is smooth and easy. This driver seems to know the best back roads to escape the huge traffic jams. She wants to give me a discount for being late picking me up, but for having just given me such a quick ride over, I instead tip her the offered discounted amount on top of the full fare price, which she seems very thankful for. As the taxi peels away from the roadside, I walk onwards to my happy place: *Angel Cake*.

Peering through the glass door, I see Vera busy attending to customers as always, and I'm glad to see more staff on hand now to help keep the place ticking over. Entering, the little bell above the door chimes its nostalgic jingle, alerting staff and customers of my arrival.

"Hello there, my name is Serena. Would you like me to take your coat for you?"

"Hi, yeah, that would be lovely, thank you."

"Where would you like to sit? We're quite busy, but there is a booth at the back where the bookshelves are, or that window seat right over there."

"Thanks, Serena. I'll take the booth over at the back if I may."

"Certainly. Let me take your coat and umbrella to the cloakroom," Serena says, relieving me of my gubbins.

Smells of cinnamon, hot chocolate, tea and coffee in the air invade my nostrils as I breathe in the heady aroma. My earlier anxiety is now beginning to melt away.

Vera, spotting me, breaks into a big grin that spreads across her face. Busy making a coffee for a customer, she indicates with her hand that she will be over in one minute. Frank, I notice, is nowhere to be seen.

"Darla, hello, sweetheart! Gosh, it seems to have been forever since we last saw you!" Vera exclaims, walking over to envelope me in a big bear hug. She smells of a stronger scent of cinnamon, chocolate and coffee.

"I know, so sorry. I've just been very busy...you know."

"Mmm-hmm. Mum's the word," Vera says, winking and indicating with a zip motion across her mouth with her hand that she is to be tight-lipped on the subject.

I confided to Vera what my new job role was within Pink Club. Apart from her and Frank, Sarah and Dante knowing, there was no one else from my trusted inner circle who knew of my new dance position.

"Your staff member, Serena, was about to take me to my seat. She's very friendly," I say as Serena approaches us.

"Don't be silly; I can do that. The booth at the back, I'm guessing?" Vera gestures with her hand in the direction of my desired location. "Serena, I will be attending to our guest. Can you man the bar, please?" Vera's statement was not a request. I'm not used to seeing her so authoritarian and in charge.

"How's Frank?" I ask as we walk on to the booth while gentle jazz music plays in the background.

"He is good. We decided it's better he retires now with his dodgy knees. The money you gave us came in very handy. I went on a managerial business course—hence the reason this place runs better than it has in years."

"Wow! Well done, you! I must say, *Angel Cake* does look to be in tip-top shape."

"It's all thanks to you, my dear. Right, what can I get you? Oh, that reminds me. Something else has changed. Here is...our *NEW* menu!" Vera exclaims, producing a nice, cream-coloured menu displaying a lovely photo of *Angel Cake* on the front.

"Gosh, you really have gone upmarket since I was last here. Ok, I'll have a peruse, but to drink, I'd like -"

"A honeycomb hot chocolate with marshmallows and whipped cream?" Vera interjects.

"Oh my God, one hundred percent yes!"

"Excellent! You have a look then at what you might like to eat. I'll be over with your hot chocolate."

Vera walks back to the bar, clicking her fingers and firmly giving orders to staff as she goes, delegating for tables to be cleaned and empty trays to be removed from the bar's surface.

Sinking into the dark brown faux leather upholstered seat, I busy myself scanning the menu for new yummy delicacies. There are petit fours, muffins, cakes, pastries, sandwiches, wraps, soups, and a set menu outlined for light bites or main meals.

Seeing as it is lunchtime, I decide to go for a chicken, bacon and cheese panini with salad. The rain has started up again, but it's more like sleet—not quite rain, not quite snow, just a slushy in-between stage.

Vera, I notice, is now receiving another influx of customers, as the weather has turned into a heavier downpour, so she is busy manning the bar. Serena comes to give me my hot chocolate and take my food order.

"Ok, that's the chicken Milanese panini (the fancy term for chicken filled with cheese and bacon) and salad. Any sides with your dish?"

"No, thanks. Just as is, please."

"Coming right up. Oh, and Vera has a message for you," Serena says, handing me a folded piece of paper before walking away to put my order through to the kitchen.

My note reads: *If I don't see you before you leave, put your mobile number down here or email address so we can stay in more frequent contact.*

Suddenly feeling awful, as I'm not allowed to give any of this information out—not without Pink Club's say so—I console myself in the knowledge that an email address probably wouldn't cause too much of an issue, unlike a phone number might (should it fall into the wrong hands). Before I can change my mind, I quickly get to work setting up a brand-new email address, via my phone, just for Vera. Once it's set up, I jot it down. After all, what harm could it do?

~ Chapter 2 ~

Vera remains too busy to come and see me before it's time for me to make my way back home. Not wanting to have a fuss, after paying for my food, I discreetly pass Serena the folded-up piece of paper with my new email address inside, explaining the note is for Vera. Serena acknowledges this, and without opening it tucks the note safely into her apron pocket before she hands me back my coat and umbrella. Serena then holds the door open for me, letting in a blast of cold air that makes both of us squint in discomfort.

Stepping out into the cold, I momentarily lose my footing, realising the pavements have become icy due to the cold weather snap we are having. The door shuts behind me and I'm glad to see the taxi I called is already here, and it's the same female driver from earlier. To make my walk home shorter with the deterioration in the weather, I ask the driver to drop me off at a post office that's a lot closer.

"There you go. That'll be twelve pounds and eighty-five pence," the woman says, reeling off the price. Settling the fare, I head off back home.

Thankfully, the path I'm walking on has been gritted with fresh salt, so the risk of skidding or falling has been removed. This is of great relief to me. You'd be amazed how many dancers' careers were brought to an abrupt end thanks to accidents on ice.

Riding the lift to the thirteenth floor, checking my phone with still no messages or missed calls from Eva or anyone, that all too familiar sinking feeling returns to the pit of my stomach. The lack of contact with...well, anybody, makes me feel quite lonely and vulnerable with everything seemingly now so 'up in the air.'

"Hey, bud," I call out to my furry compadre on entering my apartment. "What do you fancy tonight? Chicken? Beef? Tuna? Ok, beef it is. Good choice, by the way," I say, pretending I'm a cat translator.

I head to my larder—yes, I'm one of *those* people now with a cupboard full of food for myself, guests and Binks, which is quite ironic when, in my previous life, it was all about living hand to mouth.

I pick up a tin of wet beef cat food and empty the contents into his bowl, which he is very excited about. He meows his approval, walking circles around my legs before pleading for the bowl to be placed down.

As my furry friend tucks into his supper, my mind begins wandering again until, at last, the phone finally rings. My heart rate flutters as I see it is Eva calling.

"Hello, Eva," I answer after a brief pause to collect my thoughts.

"Hi, Darla. Good news. Everyone's being called back to Pink Club. It's business as usual as of tomorrow."

"Great; what time do you need me there?" As I say this, I place my phone on speaker and mute the microphone for a second to let out a big sigh of relief with the breath I'd been holding onto.

"You have been assigned a new bodyguard who will be there to collect you at ten-thirty. Her name is Penny Evermore. Really lovely woman. You'll like her, I'm sure."

"Ok, cool. I'll see you tomorrow then."

"Yes, see you tomorrow. Oh, before I forget, we have a staff meeting, so please dress smartly, as Stella Almasi is chairing it herself."

Gulp!

"S-sure...smartly, got it."

"Ok, then, lovely. See you tomorrow. Can't wait."

"Me too. I'm excited to get back to rehearsals."

"Glad to hear it."

With the conversation now over, with confirmation I still have my job, my heart pounds away excitedly in my chest.

Then I feel sick, bile now rising at a rapid rate as anxiety fuels the adrenaline now coursing through my veins at having just been informed that I'm about to meet the big bitch boss lady herself, Stella Almasi!

Now I am not sure what to wear tomorrow. I head to my walk-in wardrobe which offers an array of fancy outfits and smart casual clothing such as jeans, T-shirts, hoodies, all the sort of *'cool'* street clothing I could have ever wished for, alongside cocktail dresses and outfits that a *'girl next door'* type might wear. One good thing about having had a week off was that it has allowed me to actually spoil myself a little with some nice new designer pieces. Having never owned anything designer in my life until now (apart from gifted dance wear when Blueberry was on tour at *Lucifer's Haven*), the experience of being able to shop for myself for such lavish clothing items has been titillating.

"What do you think, Binks? Nah, you're right; too casual," I say, looking at my Buttercup street dancing designer jeans.

Turning and catching my reflection in my floor-length mirror, it is here that I realise I'm trying to fit into somebody else's expectations. Bonnie always taught me the importance of being myself. Suddenly, an idea pops into my head to do just that. Busily, I start collecting what I'm going to wear that reflects me as a person but is also my version of 'smart-casual'.

Time to make a statement on who the real Darla Pebble is, I think while grinning proudly at my reflection, knowing that Bonnie would be cheering me on with all the ladies back at *Lucifer's Haven*. I'm missing my old friends, and the familiar sense of loneliness envelopes me, breaking my cheerful mood.

~ Chapter 3 ~

Happy with my choice of outfit now hanging proudly in my walk-in wardrobe and feeling at ease with my decision, I spend the rest of the evening vegging out on the sofa before making my way to bed. I'm ready to face whatever comes tomorrow —hopefully putting my best foot forward in front of Stella.

Momentarily, I languish in my comfortable bed, awakening to the sound of classical music playing out of a ceiling light speaker in my bathroom. Eva had shown me how cool the bathroom facilities were when I first moved in. There's the option to change the tone of light with a mini remote control to be either a more soothing amber hue or brighter with more of a blue/white tone.

And, of course, they also have Wi-Fi speakers, which can be paired to mobile phones or other modern-day smart devices. There are also some other mod-cons—which I won't bore you with—such as sensor-activated taps and soap dispensers, as well as underfloor heating so I don't have to suffer a cold floor. I'm not going to lie; I am in love with the underfloor heating.

I take a moment to embrace everything I'm grateful for in my life, then climb out of my bed, which feels like a fluffy cloud. It takes my mind a few moments to fully awaken until suddenly I remember that today is the first day back to work at Pink Club.

"Whoop! Whoop!" I shout excitedly, launching myself out of bed. I head to the bathroom with a more excitable pace to my stride than normal.

My massage shower with pulsing jets works to awaken my body all over while I'm singing along to cheesy pop songs that are more befitting of my excitable mood. Fully cleansed, stepping out of the shower, I wrap a fluffy white towel around my body and another around my head. Confidently marching with an added bounce to my step, approaching my walk-in wardrobe, I carefully choose my clothing for the day, smiling to myself that this is definitely a 'me' outfit.

Once fully clothed, I take a moment to check myself out in my floor-length mirror. I'm wearing a tight-fitting black leotard with short sleeves—a smattering of glitter all over it—a multi-coloured tutu skirt and sheer skin-coloured tights. To finish the look, I'm wearing leg warmers—one neon pink and the other a hot yellow one. On my feet are a pair of white Stiletto heeled ankle boots.

A knock at my door signals Penny Evermore's arrival, and after a sudden moment of panic, I bottle it. "Just a minute," I call out to the person knocking while quickly undressing at lightning speed, grabbing my baby pink dressing gown to wrap around me as I go to answer my door.

"Good morning, Miss Pebble. My name is Penny. I can see you need a bit longer to get ready. Would you like me to wait in the car?"

"Hello, lovely to meet you. Please call me Darla. Come in; it's freezing out there. Please make yourself at home while I get dressed. Tea and coffee are over there on the kitchen counter. Help yourself." I don't wait for a response from Penny, as I'm now hot-footing it back to my walk-in wardrobe, wondering what the heck I'm meant to wear.

In the end, I decide to go for a very modest plain pair of black leggings with a simple white butterfly stitched onto the pocket, a white T-shirt, and over the top of that, a thick knitted pastel blue polar neck. On my feet, due to the recent icy conditions, I decide to don sensible footwear and put on my dark navy blue and grey walking boots; my dance shoes are already in my bag with another change of clothes. Breaking into my brand-new make-up palettes, I put on a very basic fresh look, putting my hair into the stereotypical bun for a ballerina.

"Sorry to have interrupted you in the middle of getting ready," Penny says, standing up from one of my cream sofas and placing her drink on one of the glass tables as I enter the living room.

"Please, don't apologise. Have you eaten already? Do we have time to grab some food? I haven't had a chance to eat breakfast."

"Sure, we have time. What were you thinking?" Penny's face brightens at the mention of food, making me guess she also hasn't eaten yet.

"How about something quick and easy...perhaps an omelette?"

"Sounds great. Would you mind if I have a look around? I promise it's part of the job; you can check with Max for confirmation." Penny's tone holds a slight apprehension to it.

"No problem. Sorry my room might be a bit messy," I say.

Penny smiles before getting to the job in hand. I notice she is very pretty. Her dark hair is pulled back into a ponytail, and she is wearing a charcoal grey suit and dark blue blouse. I spot some handcuffs hanging around her waist and realise I'd never noticed anyone else carrying any such gubbins on them, except perhaps for Max and Co. It's easier for men to conceal such things.

Binks trots lazily into view to see what's happening in the kitchen, licking his chops in hopes of a tiny morsel of the omelette, no doubt. Not sure if he should eat eggs, I give him one of his cat *'yummies'* treats. Apparently, on the advert, cats will do anything for these treats—even run through house walls which I'm yet to see.

"Aww, your cat is beautiful. He or she?" Penny

comments, coming back into view just as I'm putting the omelettes onto our plates.

"*He* is called Binks. Hope you don't mind, but I've made the omelette with onions and peppers. Sorry if it's a bit 'lunchy'."

"Great name for a cat; he's such a sweetheart. The omelette smells delicious. Honestly, I'm so hungry, I could eat a horse."

"Well, I hope it tastes as good as it smells," I say, feeling bad that, had my offer of food not been mentioned, Penny would have stayed hungry for God knows how long. I can't afford not to eat doing such an energetic job; I'd pass out.

"This is so good—just what the doctor ordered," Penny says, sounding thankful.

After finishing our omelettes and putting the plates and forks in the dishwasher, I'm mindful not to leave it running while I'm out. When Mum and I went through the experience of having our old apartment block go up in flames, the fire chief told us that most washing machines, tumble dryers and dishwashers start most housing fires. That time it had been someone's tumble dryer on the fourth floor. I still shiver to think about it.

Penny grabs her duffel coat off the hook, and I put my thicker black and blue tartan button-up coat on, along with a black bobble hat and gloves to keep in with having a low profile.

The journey to Pink Club is slower than usual due to the icy road conditions, giving Penny and I more time to warm up to each other. I learned that she's Greek but grew up in the United States. Her job there was working for the FBI until she met and fell in love with her English husband. Wanting an easier life where she could be closer to him, she hung up her gun and badge, now happy with her current role of being employed by Max's private security company.

~ Chapter 4 ~

My reverie of hearing how awesome Penny is soon breaks as we turn into Pink Club's underground car park. Thoughts of meeting Stella Almasi suddenly flood my mind, bringing me down to earth with a bump—or perhaps that was a speed bump. Knowing I'm about to come face-to-face with the big, bitch boss lady herself, a neat little knot begins forming in the pit of my stomach.

"Ok, shall we?" Penny asks, indicating the way to the lift with her hand after locking the car (a very nice expensive-looking, navy-blue BMW). The number plate reads PE52 NNY, so I'm hazarding a guess this is actually her car and not a Pink Club company car.

Together, we step into the warmth of the lift. It has inbuilt air conditioning, and the warm air brings welcome relief from the biting cold outside. Even with my winter clothing on, the cold still manages to creep in enough, making me shiver. I swear, here in England we don't really have spring; it's more like a very long winter than muggy and sometimes a very wet summer and autumn.

"Ah, much better. I should remember to bring gloves with me from home tomorrow," Penny says, rubbing her hands together.

The lift doors open, and we step out into the corridor, where I'm thankful to be reacquainted with the bouncy pink carpet, faux pink candlelight fixtures attached to the walls, and French boutique pink candy-striped with black, lace-styled wallpaper. It's quiet here, as this is the corridor that takes people through a double doorway and into the hub of Pink Club. I soak up the stillness before the ensuing chaotic, excitable energy that will surely be buzzing through me soon.

We enter the main reception area of Pink Club, where the Pelican Brief bar is situated, as well as the massive reception desk. The pink marble pillars and huge pink chandelier hanging from the high ceiling take my breath away every time.

The day this sight gets old is the day I quit my job, I think as we check into reception. *Odd, I haven't ever needed to check in at reception before.*

"Right, that's us booked in for the day," Penny says, turning and handing me a *guest pass!*

"Err..."

"It's only a temporary requirement until Max has put new security protocols into place. Even though Mimi's perpetrators have been caught and locked up, Stella insisted we tighten everything until after the spring gala."

"That sounds a bit paranoid. Sorry, you said her perpetrators?"

"I can't tell you anything more, but trust me, there is zero risk to any of us here linked to the people who kidnapped Mimi Glass. I have to check in with Max. Speak of the devil. Are you ok getting to the meeting on your own?" Penny asks as Max approaches. He indicates with a nod to Penny that she is to go and join him.

"I'll be fine; I know where to go."

I am feeling confident that there is no way I can get lost now, as Joshua's office is right up the grand Juliette staircase along the corridor, last door on the left.

Penny nods in acknowledgment while going to greet Max. I watch them animatedly chatting as they leave me to head off to the security offices.

While ascending the staircase, it suddenly dawns on me that I wasn't told where this meeting was going to be held. I presumed it was in Joshua's office. It could be in Eva's office or somewhere else entirely. As I've only briefly seen Pink Club in its entirety once—which was on my first and only thorough tour of Pink Club—I wouldn't be able to make heads or tails of where to go.

I am beginning to panic, which makes me feel suddenly very hot all over, and I need to remove my jumper since perspiration is now breaking out all over my body. If I get lost and end up a no-show for this meeting with Stella Almasi, it would look *very* bad as a first impression with her.

I decide to check Joshua's office first anyway, having reached his office door. However, as I am raising my hand to knock, I fast change my mind, instead first placing my ear up against it to make sure there are people inside. Relief washes over me to indeed hear low murmuring voices.

Phew! That was lucky, I think, my earlier apprehension abating a little.

The door opens with Joshua standing on the other side with no one else in sight.

Oh, fudge fingers!

Believe me, I am as stunned as you are that language of a much more colourful nature hadn't flitted through my mind. I mean, *fudge fingers? WTF!*

"Hello, Darla. Is everything alright? You're going to be late for the meeting with Stella," Joshua greets while checking his watch before stepping into the corridor to join me. He closes his office door behind him. "I was heading there myself. Come on; we can walk over together."

"Great, sorry. I had presumed the meeting would have been here in your office. Penny asked if I was ok finding my way to the meeting, and silly me, I didn't even realise I'd not confirmed where it was."

Stop blabbering, woman!

"For future reference, all meetings normally go on inside our conference rooms. We'd better get a shift on before Stella has both our heads on the chopping block."

I'm suddenly aware I've been grinning like an idiot for the past few moments and blushing like a Belisha beacon, so I quickly resume a more serious expression as we head back down the grand Juliette staircase, making our way to a different set of lifts. These are neatly tucked inside another corridor I hadn't even known existed before now, sitting behind a secret screen with a two-way mirror system so staff on this screen can see out, but members on the other side can't see in. As the doors to the lift open, a cool blast of air greets both of us.

"Brrrr! I must speak to maintenance about the air conditioning inside this lift," Joshua comments, making a motion to hug himself. He smiles at me, causing my head to go all gaga again. Joshua mentions using the other lift, but it's occupied, and we are already running late for the meeting.

Spotting my reflection in one of the lift mirrors lining the interior walls, my dreamy state at being in such close proximity to Joshua is suddenly well and truly shattered as I notice my nipples are now standing out erect and proud through my very visible white T-shirt.

Kill me, just please kill me now, I think, hurriedly pulling my pale blue polar neck back over my head.

Something mechanically must have failed with the lift as I do this with my jumper just over my head and my arms in the air. The lift makes a sudden lurching movement, causing me to stumble blindly forward with no control over my limbs before the lift comes to a painful screeching halt. With my head still covered—unable to see, blinded by my jumper and arms still above my head —it is here that I realise I must have fallen into Joshua or he into me, as I can now distinctly feel warm hands over my...bosoms.

"Err, ah...looks like we're stuck," Joshua mutters,

rapidly moving his hands off my ample bosom and helping me with my jumper, finally getting the bloody thing on properly. Thankfully, it now hides my pointy nipples. Even so, sufficed to say I feel my dignity is now in shreds.

We both try the intercom, but to no joy; the electrics have completely gone on the panel. Joshua starts shivering, and I must admit even with what just happened—which made me feel rather *warm,* shall we say—I too am now beginning to feel the cold.

"Are you okay? Have you got your phone with you? I left mine in my office."

"Oh," I utter, looking down at Joshua's feet.

"Oh indeed," he says, bending down to pick up my now shattered phone.

"It must have fallen out of my pocket when the lift juddered to a halt. What do we do? How do we get out of here?" My voice is quickening as I'm beginning to feel trapped.

"Try and stay calm. Max or Penny will be alerted to us missing soon—especially as my sister Mimi is here today."

"She's here? How is she? Sorry, that was completely inappropriate and unprofessional of me to ask that."

Shut up! Shut up! Shut up! Shut up! I think, willing my thoughts to check themselves before they wreck me.

"It's ok. You would have been finding out soon enough in the meeting today, but seeing as now we are both stuck, I guess I can fill you in until we get rescued. Sorry, do you mind if we sit and huddle on the floor? It's fucking freezing in here," Joshua says gingerly, putting an arm around me as we draw in close to one another before sitting on the floor of the lift. I, now—as you can imagine—have more than enough heat coursing through my body for the both of us.

I want to imprint this moment to memory and never let it go.

Now huddled in a corner, cool air still blasting away through the small vents at the top of the lift, Joshua starts to fill me in on Mimi and what happened to her over the past five years.

~ Chapter 5 ~

"Let me get this right: It was Mimi's boyfriend's... ex, who copied a key to their apartment before letting themselves in to live in the attic?!" I echo to Joshua from what he told me, feeling super creeped out. The way Joshua tells the true story about what happened to his sister is bone-chilling!

"Not only that, she surveyed their movements for days, hatching a revenge plot to kill Mimi and frame her boyfriend for it. Needless to say, when it came down to it, the ex couldn't do it. He laced both their drinks with a date rape drug, but once Mimi's boyfriend was out cold, Mimi took a little longer to succumb to the drug's effects. Mimi caught sight of the ex and apparently began screaming. The ex then hit Mimi over the head hard, knocking her out. The woman's brother, a corrupt police officer for the Met, went to help his sister. However, en route to the scene, he ran over and killed a Spanish foreign exchange student. You may remember the name: Milagros Morena?"

"Yes, I remember there was a huge manhunt for her, but it seemed she had just vanished. Good God! I'm so sorry, Joshua. I don't really know what to say. How did it come about in the end that Mimi was still alive?"

"Well, as you undoubtedly saw, there was a media circus when she first went missing. So much misinformation went around with many 'sightings' that turned out to be fruitless, like the story about the boys who saw her in that house in the woods. Just another dead end. That house belonged to an old, retired couple, and the blood stain was nothing but a few drops from one of the homeowners having had a nose bleed. Blame was placed squarely on Mimi's boyfriend's shoulders once police discovered charred remains. The body was that of Milagros Morena, but the corrupt police officer threatened to expose a dodgy dentist he knew didn't exactly do things by the book. For it all to go away, the dentist agreed to match dental records to the corpse to show the body was Mimi's."

"That's horrific. What about the clothing your parents used to identify Mimi?"

"Again, all speculation and hearsay. The press was never privy to the real facts however much they may have liked to have sounded as if they knew everything."

"What about Milagros Morena's parents and family?"

"They have been notified. The truth will all be revealed soon. Our family was issued a week's grace to process everything, as were the Morena's, but police will conclude their investigation soon once dental records of Milagros's body have been properly matched up from the ones on file with police."

"Bloody hell! So what happened to the sister and her corrupt police brother? I take it you can't mention any names."

"It will all be released soon in the press."

"What about Mimi's boyfriend?"

"Things are moving forward for him to be released as soon as possible; my family has the best lawyers working on the case. I was so awful to him. He begged and pleaded for help, insisting he didn't murder Mimi, but I was too angry with grief to listen. The guy is such a soppy git; none of what was being said rang true anyway. But I was blind."

"How did they frame him?"

Easy there, Nancy Drew. The man's still in bits, remember! I think, reminding myself to wait to be handed information instead of trying to plug it out of my new boss.

Joshua takes a long sigh, closing his eyes to recall more of the details. "The ex and her brother stole a pair of his boots and some clothes, placing him at the scene. As it had only been him and Mimi the night they were attacked, he had no alibi."

Annoyingly, and with my heart in my mouth, the lift judders to life, taking us finally the rest of the way to the floor where the doors open with ease. Max and a team of engineers are standing in the corridor, looking at us still huddled in the corner.

Joshua stands to give me a helping hand. Max then helps me out of the lift, as it hasn't quite married up to the floor, so I have to take a bit of a step up to get out.

"Sorry about that, Mr. Glass," one of the engineers pipes up with a rich Welsh accent.

"See to it, please, that all lifts are checked and double-checked. Also, the heating in this one is broken," Joshua says with a clipped tone to the engineer with the accent, who I notice doesn't seem too bothered.

"Will do."

"Mr. Glass, Stella opened the meeting without you due to this unfortunate hold-up. She left Pink Club to return to her apartment, asking that you drop in to see her before she flies back to Spain this evening."

"Thanks, Max. I suppose I'd best go and see the demon queen now and get it over with."

"There is...something else that you should know."

"Go ahead," Joshua says, sighing tiredly again, squeezing the bridge of his nose as if to show perhaps there is the threat of an ensuing headache.

"Stella...well, she took Mimi with her. By the time I was alerted of what had happened, they were already well on their way back to Stella's apartment."

"That *BITCH!* Get my jacket, grab the car, and tell Eva I will be speaking with *her* later. Tell her to expect to work late!"

"Right away. Am I to take Darla to see Eva first for a meeting summary?" Max inquires, as all notion that I am even standing here has been seemingly forgotten by Joshua.

"Get Penny to take Darla home. Eva will be sending out a typed-up email of minutes from today's meeting. Take the rest of the day off, Darla," Joshua says, not even glancing at me before storming off.

There he goes; the real Joshua now locked away again, replaced by the cold hard beast exterior he's been exuding since I started working here.

"I should really follow him, but I'll take you to Penny first," Max says kindly as we head off, using a different lift this time to make our way back down to the main hub of Pink Club.

~ Chapter 6 ~

Max and I step out and evade the busier areas of Pink Club in order to keep my profile low. There is a noticeable increase in activity. Many more people are milling about than I've ever seen here before—both a mixture of guests and staff. I'm guessing various events must be going on in each of the different themed rooms.

"Hi, Penny. I'm dropping Darla to her dressing room. Can you take her home, please? Joshua requests it. I'll be leaving with Joshua very shortly, so please be prompt," Max says through an earpiece.

"It's good to see the place alive and busy," I comment, soaking up the energy and general vibe throughout, as we head to my dressing room.

There are people wearing all sorts of vibrantly weird and wonderful costumes. I'm sure I spot a genie or two and a mermaid here and there. The guests have come out in their finery for what must be matinee performances of shows going on.

"Just wait until the spring gala; this is practically empty compared to the big events. I've seen the guest list; it's certainly going to stretch my security skills to the limit. Stella has gone all out on everything."

"Blimey! I'm still reeling from New Year's Eve. It's a shame I didn't get to mingle with the crowd afterwards with the, err..."

"Bathroom *incident*," Max finishes, grinning playfully at me. We both laugh at the memory of that crazy night.

"The gala is to be my biggest security job experience. Now that Mimi Glass has been revealed to be alive and well, it will be absolute pandemonium."

"How come it's not more chaotic now then? Everyone knows Mimi is alive, like you said, and I agree it's busy but not over the top busy."

"The general public, paps, Pink Club's members and guests have been led to believe that the Glass twins have flown back to Tuscany with their parents, Pandora and James. I managed to grab a Joshua and Mimi look-a-like to accompany Pandora and James to their secret location."

"That is insanely cloak and dagger," I mumble, unbelieving of the lengths Max has had to go through to protect the family's privacy and keep them out of harm's way.

"Pretty standard procedure. We're always throwing red herrings out there for the press and paparazzi."

"Yes, I used to read in *Dance Now Magazine* how when photographs would surface of Joshua or Mimi before her *non-murder* event, there was always speculation as to whether it was them or not being seen out and about."

"I do my best, but it's not always the case to keep the paps hot off their heels—and it won't be for you, either, which is why I must schedule in some personal safety training for you once your identity has been revealed."

Sighing, I take a moment to reflect on the crazy world of glitz, glam and celebrity I now find myself in, wondering if it will ever fully sink in that this is my life for the foreseeable future. A waitress and pole-dancer-now-proud-lead-dance-act for one of the best kept secrets in London? Probably not, but this is what I wanted, and just knowing how proud my gran and grampy would be of me is the fuel that keeps me going through my occasional fears and reservations.

We arrive at my dressing room door and find that Penny is already there waiting for me. Max and Penny exchange further security details with code names, and to be honest, it's all over my head. Once Max has departed, Penny smiles and informs me we will be taking a service lift down to the car park.

Great! Another lift. It's all I seem to have done today. At least my lift ride with Joshua was worth it.

Remembering Joshua's body being so close to mine, and knowing I was his only source of warmth and comfort while we had remained stuck, made me silently wish we had been locked inside the lift longer.

Shaking my head, I am trying but failing to force the lusty thoughts about my boss out.

Professional, Darla, let's keep it professional, shall we!

"Everything ok, Darla?" Penny asks. She is watching me as a brief shiver shoots throughout my body after thoughts of what Joshua said to me about Mimi's kidnapping resurface, fully dowsing my previous lustful thoughts.

"Yeah, I just got that weird feeling. You know, when it feels like someone's just walked over your grave."

"Once I drop you home, I need to pop back here for a few hours, but if you need me for anything, here's my mobile number." Penny hands me her business card. "Don't pocket the number. Save it to your mobile now and then hand it back to me."

"Oh, my mobile. I left it on the floor in the other lift. It got damaged when the lift stopped."

"Ah, ok, no worries. Let me just sort that for you now." Penny pauses to ring through a number. "Hello, is this engineering? Yes, I'm calling about the mobile phone that was left on the floor of the lift that is currently being serviced at the moment...that's right, the one that had Mr. Glass and another member of staff inside...it's been handed into lost property? Great, thanks. Bye."

"Thank goodness it hasn't fallen into the wrong hands," I say, relieved to know it's safe and well in lost property.

"I will collect it for you on my return here. For now, here is a spare mobile phone; I always carry two. Sorry, it's an old standard model—no smart phone—and there are no contacts saved to the phone book, but I'll put my phone number in for you...one sec. There you go. I'll bring your phone back this evening if there's time."

"Thanks," is all I say as I hand Penny back her card and take the fully charged mobile she handed me.

"Don't worry about battery life. That thing lasts forever," Penny assures me, as if reading my mind on what I'm meant to do should it run out of juice.

On the ride home, Penny asks me if I need anything from the shops, but I tell her I'm good on the food and drinks front. By the time we do arrive back to my apartment, it's already 4 p.m.

~ Chapter 7 ~

Having had time to cool off while Max parks the car outside Stella's London apartment, Joshua makes the better, much wiser decision, having asked Max to go and fetch Mimi from the demon queen's clutches instead of marching inside himself, all guns blazing. Mimi's mental state is still incredibly fragile, and for most parts of the day she remains silent. It has been hard to get any sort of conversation out of her. So, to be fair to his sister, Joshua sits silently, stewing in the car while waiting for Max to return with Mimi in tow.

It is during the time that he is sitting in the car alone that Joshua's mind floats back to having been stuck in the lift with Darla earlier on. He marvels at how well she carried the conversation with him—boldly asking the more probing questions and not once flinching when he asked if they could share body heat between them. His growing opinion of Darla was that she was one tough cookie, and he wanted to find out how she ticked all the more. The thought jolts him back to reality. It had been a long time since he'd felt any sort of *attraction* to anyone of the opposite sex, and being a straight heterosexual man, Joshua had probably experienced one of the longest dry spells in the sex life of a man his age—or what felt like it. The fact his primal driving buttons were now being switched on wasn't what the issue was; it was that it was Pink Club's leading dance lady—meaning she was one-hundred and ten percent hands off!

Then Joshua remembers that the no staff relationship rule was a 'Stella' rule, and after what she did today with Mimi, Joshua wasn't just feeling murderous towards her but also rebellious. His inner devilish side surfaces and wants to come out to play. Joshua can think of no better way to get revenge on his demon queen boss than to break one of the biggest rules in place by pursuing one Miss Darla Pebble. The very idea of imagined disgust and rage omitted from Stella at Joshua's insubordination feels too tempting now to resist. His relationship to Stella is now no longer just about business. No, Stella Almasi had seen to it that things were now very personal indeed. How dare she go anywhere near his sister after having stolen Pink Club directly from under them both?

A knock at my door signals the arrival of Penny. Hopefully, she has my phone with her, but undoubtedly I'll need to get it sorted with phone repairs.

"Hi…Midnight? Medley? Digit? Siren? And Mixer? This is very unexpected," I say, red-faced at being caught out with my pale blue pyjamas, which are covered in different types of fruit designs. (I have an affinity for funky pyjamas—always have.)

Opening the door, I step aside to let them across the threshold.

"Whoa, cool jammies," Digit comments, making me blush a deeper shade of rouge.

"Come on, get dressed—we're taking you out-out," Midnight orders, as the guys start to make themselves comfortable. Mixer is raiding my mini-bar, and Medley starts flicking through my various thousands of TV channels. It's now 8:15 p.m. and I'd just been getting comfy for the night before bed. Thoughts of going '*out-out*' now seem painful.

Another knock at the door elicits an eye roll and sigh out of me as I now wonder who this could be.

"Well, hubba-hubba—somebody call the doctor, because it's hot in here!" a man dressed in what I can only describe to be 80's punk-rock style clothing says, as he strides inside my apartment.

Oh, yes, do come on into the madhouse, I think, unbelieving of what is now happening in front of my very eyes. *Hello, fate? I'm totally spent on unsuspecting surprises after my earlier lift ride!*

The mystery man is tall and drop-dead gorgeous—

another one for my inner sex-goddess to drool over but no complaints here! He's wearing pale blue jeans with designer holes, black boots, a white T-shirt and black leather jacket. A small silver hoop earring hangs from one of his earlobes, and his hair is slicked back with what looks to be just the right amount of hair product.

"Ok, tutti-fruity—you best get your butt into gear, because *tonight* is gonna be wild!" the man proclaims, walking right up to my personal space to play with the collar of my pyjamas. This makes me go all giddy and silly inside.

"Here, take this and get it down you," Mixer orders, handing me a feisty looking purple and luminous yellow concoction he's made up from what I can now see is a sort of homemade cocktail bar in my kitchen.

Midnight and the guys soon fill up the space on my huge sofas, and I now get the relevance of why they are so big. With their drinks in hand they chill out, watching TV. I walk off half-dazed to my bedroom, willing myself into party mode and swearing under my breath. I simply pinch the bridge of my nose and down the drink Mixer handed me.

Holy shit balls! I think, as the strong moonshine type of drink whacks me hard in the chest—warmth now blooming forth along all my limbs from its utter atomic strength.

Hit hard and fast, the booze makes me instantly feel woozy. Binks is hiding under my bed. I catch his eyes' reflection in one of my floor-length mirrors. Seeing as it's now a party atmosphere, I head straight for my 'glam rail', picking up my new luminous, turquoise-sequinned dress, which is extremely bright with bling all over.

Fixing my hair and make-up, I then don my mega sparkly pink strappy heels, which are gladiatorial in design, taking a moment here to absorb how good I think I look in the mirror. I give myself a cheeky little high-five before heading on out to join my dance team.

"Hey, guys! Where are we going tonight?" I yell back to them, having popped my head out of the door.

"Luci's!" Midnight shouts back.

Whoop! Whoop! Lucifer's Haven! I'll get to see all my old gal pals!

I do a little happy dance, now knowing I can glam up even more by adding some pale turquoise fairy wings to my pink glittery mask to finish my look. When doing my online shopping, I'd discovered somewhere local that stocks up on fancy dress items, and they just so happened to have a special offer sale, so I may have gotten every pair of fairy wings in every rainbow colour, along with some very nice—and quite pricey—masks. I've always been surrounded by costumes at *Lucifer's Haven,* so perhaps it's become a bit of an addiction. But knowing I now have a perfect reason to break into my fun box of fantasy items, I can't help but grin like the Cheshire cat.

Music starts playing from the lounge, and it sounds quite busy through there. I'm sure I even hear women's voices now!

That must be Eva and Octavia.

Just as I'm spraying some hair and body glitter all over myself, the worrying thought comes: *Oh, shit! Are we even authorised to go out?* But I can't dwell on this for long before Midnight is knocking on my bedroom door, hurrying me up.

Throwing caution to the wind with some much-needed help from the drink given to me by Mixer, I step outside amazed to be confronted by a beautiful dark-skinned woman, who sidles up to Midnight before kissing him on the cheek. She is criminally good looking and has a serene look on her face. I'm guessing she's also sampled Mixer's '*blow your head off*' moonshine.

"Darla, Moesha; Moesha, Darla, our new leading dance lady for Pink Club," Midnight introduces.

My jaw near on hits the floor. He's just announced to this woman who I am. Is he *nuts?!*

"Errrm…"

"Don't worry; we all invited our officiated partners to come with. They all signed the ND, so no worries," Midnight assures me tipsily, as he and Moesha head on back down the corridor to my living area with me following closely behind.

Has everyone had head transplants? Where's Penny? Can I risk going out? I'll look like such a prude if I don't go. I can't not go now.

~ Chapter 8 ~

"Ok, ok, now that we're all here, present and correct, it's time for some introductions. Psyche here is our *new* dance safety man, so we are back to being an even six. The ladies here are Moesha, who you've briefly met, who is a PA for a top high-end designer, Bea Siren's partner in crime. Medley's other half, Craig; Lucy, Mixer's recently betrothed; and Trinity, Digit's geeky sidekick. Bea is a fiery redhead from Cork in Ireland. Craig's a carpenter from Wolverhampton. Lucy works the back staging lighting rigs at the national theatre here in London, and Trinity is, as you've guessed it, a computer whizz."

"It's l-lovely to meet you all," I stammer, ever so slightly, at the sheer awesomeness of this very situation. Here I am with Pink Club's senior dancing staff in my living room again—this time, however, with their PARTNERS! It's a shame Psyche is single and working for Pink Club, as I wouldn't say no.

"Listen up! Tonight is about us having fun. No Pink Club dramas, no work stress—just good old-fashioned letting-our-hair-down fun," Midnight announces, as if he's re-enacting the *SPARTA* scene from the Roman film.

Everyone cheers before downing the remainder of the contents in their glasses. The gang then link arms with their prospective partners, leaving Psyche and me to bring up the rear. As a gentleman, he holds out his arm for me, and it is then I realise the man is stone cold sober.

Just before stepping outside my apartment, I re-fill Binks' food and water bowls, slipping my small pink sequinned bag over my shoulder, which contains my purse, some blister plasters, a plastic bag for any alcohol-induced vomiting incidents, and the small Nokia phone Penny had given to me.

Once we are all down in the car park, I see that there's a party bus waiting to set off. I'm informed by Psyche that it has disco lights inside, as well as comfortable plush deep purple seats, tables affixed to the floor and—of course—a mini-bar and in-built sound system.

We're dead; we are soooooo dead! Bye-bye, Pink Club—it was nice knowing you! My thoughts race with how wrong this all feels. *Oh my God—what if we are papped?!* Fear courses through my alcohol laden sense of self, because since I started at Pink Club, the constant theme has always been *to 'keep a low profile'* and to not tell *anyone* we work for Pink Club. Yet here we are on full display, EXPOSED to all and sundry.

Oh well, can't chicken out now, I think while walking

towards our doomed ride with shaky legs. My common sense continues to scream aloud inside my head of just how bad an idea this is. Having little choice in the matter now, and against my better judgement, I step onto the party bus. My sense of doom abates as soon as I'm handed a glass of bubbly from a hyperactive Bea, downing it in one go before indicating for her to fill me up again. This elicits cheers from everyone, and I start to truly unwind then and feel that whatever happens now, we're well and truly all in it together.

We arrive at our destination, music still blaring loudly out of speakers with disco lights spinning (along with my head), causing people queuing outside *Lucifer's Haven* to watch on bemused as the bus comes to a halt. My very loud almost shouty conversation with the other ladies is abruptly cut short when the driver enters the body of the bus and shouts, "IIIIIIIT'S PARTY TIIIIII-IIIME!" Then he sprays us all with a glitter confetti cannon. Everybody erupts into whoops and cheers, steadying themselves before making a grand exit. I wait to be the last to leave, convinced we've all committed career suicide but oddly now not really caring. This is the most fun I've had in a long time. Psyche again offers his arm and helps to steady me as we move on towards *Lucifer's Haven*.

Why is he not drinking?

"Stay close to me tonight, ok? I don't mean that in a creepy weirdo sort of way, but the other women each have a person, and you don't."

Psyche's words cut through me deeply, hitting me

squarely in the chest. A sudden anger now bubbles under the surface, driving me forward, wanting to gain entry to *Lucifer's Haven* more so than ever before while possibly also losing Psyche. I need to grab something stronger than party bus champagne.

I deliberately manage to lose Mr. '*Debbie Downer*' Psyche in the queue as I make my way to the front. There are tuts and mentions of unfairness hurled at me, as well as the occasional catcall and wolf whistle, by people queuing. Thankfully, I'm granted immediate entry after revealing myself briefly to one of my old pals on the door by lifting my mask and winking. My plan works; he recognises me instantly. Handing him a £50 note, swearing him to not let anyone know I'm here, to which he agrees, I walk on inside.

The lyrics to "Base in Your Face, LONDON!" are blasting through the speakers, while special strobe lights flash over everybody, rapidly making my head spin. Bonnie and Co., I spot, are up on their podiums, having a blast and unaware I'm even here. The realisation of this makes me feel saddened again as I glimpse my old life.

Managing to find a free barstool (which, believe me, is a miracle in itself), I sit down and begin to ponder more on this crazy evening. *I'm going to sit here, keep myself to myself and NOT get into any trouble!* I think through my drunken haze.

"Hey, pretty lady; what can I get you?" the barmaid asks. She finally gets to me once she's finished serving a very inebriated gentleman, who is practically drooling on the bar in a drunken stupor, although still aware enough to order more beer—or in his case, "bweeeeearr." I'm guessing it was due to a broken heart, poor sod—yet a regular occurrence at Luci's.

"I'll have a diet Vanilla Coke, please."

"Rough night, or are you one of our T-totals?" she asks.

"I'm just trying to...*pace* myself." *No point getting plastered all by myself,* I think, remembering the image of my mother on the bride and groom's table splashed all over the next day's newspapers as the wedding crasher from hell. My stomach swirls at the memory.

"Fair enough." The barmaid goes to the small fridge and pours my drink in a glass with ice and two thin red straws, adding a mini golden umbrella to at least make it look a bit more festive.

"Diet Vanilla Coke?! Oh, I'm sure you can do better than that, *pretty lady,*" a man sitting to my left says.

"Excuse me?" I say, turning to my left and almost choking on my diet Vanilla Coke.

Holy shit! Joshua Glass, what are you doing here?!?

My heart begins hammering a million miles an hour; perspiration breaks out all over my body, and I feel as if I've been caught red-handed doing something I really shouldn't be doing—because I have!

"Nice outfit, by the way. The name's Joshua...Joshua Glass," he says, as I take in what he is wearing. Dark blue denim jeans and a crisp white shirt open at the collar. Oh, and he smells just yummy too. The scent makes my head swim with lust.

Thank fuck for that! He doesn't recognise me! Now for a quick exit. Come on, Darla, you can drool at home.

"Cool...well, I'm actually here with some friends of mine, so..."

"Yet you're sitting here all by your lonesome," he smirks, interrupting me.

I begin to make a slurping sound as my glass empties, noticing I've suddenly drunk my diet Vanilla Coke very quickly.

"N–no, my friends...they're just over – *buuurp!*"

It's my worst nightmare. This is officially my worst nightmare coming true right here right now.

"Whoa, easy there, gassy lassie," Joshua jests, making us both fall about laughing.

As the ice is officially broken between us, I feel myself beginning to loosen up. As long as I can keep my identity hidden, all will be well.

"Ok, you got me. I'm alone," I admit once I am recovered from my fit of the giggles, choosing to not chuck Midnight and Co. under the bus, as they are well out of sight up on the balcony part of the nightclub.

"No...*special* someone?"

Is this really how he picks up women in bars? Yowzers, it's so cheesy it's painful.

"Please excuse me. I need to go to the ladies room."

"No worries. Nice chat, *pretty lady*." Joshua grins at me with those fierce *'come to bed'* eyes.

Quickly manoeuvring myself away from Joshua and the bar, I squeeze through the crowd on the dance floor and I finally make it to the toilets where the queue is, thankfully, short. A female member of staff sits on a stool outside with some basic sundries. There are lollipops, pocket mirrors, mini body sprays, and breath mints on sale to the ladies coming and going from the toilets. I decide to get some breath mints, but on reaching for my purse, I realise I have left my bag back at the bar.

Shit! Where the fuck is everyone?! Nice how no one's come to see if I'm alright. I should've stayed with Psyche. Bloody pride!

~ Chapter 9 ~

Eventually, I get to use a toilet cubicle and I take a moment to collect my thoughts and think of a solution to my current predicament. My head is still spinning though, from the remnants of my earlier drinking, so this poses quite the challenge.

Leaving the ladies' and feeling quite despondent by now that my so-called work friends have abandoned me —and now without any means to pay for a taxi home or mobile phone to call Penny—I start to think more on how to get myself out of this mess.

"Ah, there you are," Joshua says, leaning against the wall adjacent to the toilets while holding my bag out towards me, dangling it on one finger.

"Th-thanks!" I stammer, taking my bag from my boss, relieved to see everything is still contained within.

"You're welcome. Right, come on."

"I beg your pardon?"

"Let's dance. After all, what else is there to do in a

club such as this—apart from drinking, and you're clearly not doing that."

"You want to dance...with me?"

Gulp!

Joshua nods and bows Prince Charming style, before asking me for a dance.

Be still my beating heart.

"Ok, but just one dance."

"We'll see," Joshua winks. He places my hand in his, pulling me closer and weaving our fingers together before leading the way towards the main throng of club revellers.

Joshua and I move effortlessly on the dance floor together. Our bodies are way too up close and personal to one another than would be deemed appropriate for boss and employee. The sheer awkwardness of this entire situation is unbearable, and I can't wait to get away from him.

A crowd gathers, forming a ring around us, and cheers and whoops begin to erupt as we dance in time with each other, reflecting both our dance skills. A spotlight comes down, and suddenly all eyes are on us. I'm lost in Joshua's eyes, though, and as flashes, cheers and music carry on around us, for a moment I forget where I am and who I'm with. By the time we stop dancing, I momentarily stand back and place a hand to my mouth before turning to make a beeline for the exit. Joshua, however, must have pre-emptied my intention, because he grabs my hand firmly to pull me back towards him. The crowd is now breaking up and they go back to dancing by themselves.

"You got some nice moves there, *pretty lady*. Any chance of a quick peak under the mask?" Joshua demurs, raising his hand, which triggers me to slap him.

Joshua fast puts his hand to his cheek, now glowing red with a look of astonishment that gets replaced by a big goofy grin. "Ah, my bodyguard is here. That's my cue to leave," is all that Joshua says before wandering away post-haste back through the crowd, leaving me standing in stunned silence and wondering what just happened.

I just dirty danced and slapped my very good-looking boss on the face. Fuck!

Beginning to feel tired and washed out, as the alcohol has fully worn off, along with any adrenaline, I decide to make my own way home, feeling completely abandoned by my dancing crew.

Turning to head for the exit doors, Psyche manages to accost me—probably having seen the dance between Joshua and myself—and he offers to share a ride home with me. It would be safer to travel with a companion this late, so I agree.

"Well, that was spectacular," Psyche says, indicating the dance with Joshua.

"Thankfully, Joshua didn't recognise me."

"You guys have some serious chemistry. Your dancing certainly got me all hot under the collar," Psyche states, seemingly unphased by my antics at *Lucifer's Haven*.

A line of taxis is ready to collect the punters that will soon be leaving the club. Psyche pings a message to

Midnight to let him know we're heading home as we clamber into the back of one of the taxis.

"Sorry about losing you in the queue earlier. I realise now how irresponsible this was."

"Oh, Darla, you are a *DAME!* Honestly, think nothing of it. I got to chat with some nice women this evening and exchange a few numbers. I've never been a 'groupie' type of guy; always like to fly solo."

"Well, I'm glad you're accompanying me home all the same."

I give the taxi driver the name of a road near my apartment complex as we head off in relative silence.

Thankful to not see anyone loitering about in the road or on the pavement—given the fact it's 2 a.m. as I exit the taxi—I thank Psyche again for accompanying me home and wait for the taxi to drive away before walking the rest of the way to my apartment.

Getting through reception wasn't a big issue—even if I am dressed as a masked pink and turquoise glitter ball, and a cold one at that—but forgetting a coat was a big error, as I'm now quite literally freezing my boobs off.

Once I'm safely back inside my nice warm apartment, I make myself a nice cup of tea before heading to bed. My repaired mobile phone sits on my kitchen countertop, and I suddenly feel bad for not being here when Penny went through the trouble to have my mobile fixed and brought back here. I then feel a sense of dread that she will undoubtedly have told Joshua and Eva I was not at home this evening.

~ Chapter 10 ~

Awakening the next morning with a sore head and mildly upset stomach—which I'm guessing is due to mixing my drinks—I stretch and wait a moment before becoming fully alert. A sudden memory of dancing with Joshua flashes through my mind, and within mere moments, I'm jumping out of bed. That was a mistake, as my head swims, forcing me to lean against the wall to steady myself as nausea threatens with my head now spinning. Picking up my mobile from my bedside table, I can see a message from Eva that alerts me to the fact that Penny will be here to pick me up for rehearsals in no less than…TEN MINUTES!

With little time to get ready, I rush for a quick shower—the hot pulsating jets helping to calm some of my earlier nausea. The swimmy feeling in my head is still strong, and I know I must get a grip if I'm to make it through rehearsals today.

I am rapidly drying myself just as there is a knock at

the door, and I manage to hurry to the front door to let Penny in. I quickly turn once she enters my apartment and head back to my bedroom. Now flying across to my walk-in wardrobe, I go for a very classic and basic dance outfit of black leggings, a loose-fitting pale pink T-shirt with matching leg warmers and pack a pair of my ballet pumps along with a pair of pole shoes. I don high tops on my feet for the journey into Pink Club, remembering this time to wear a jumper and to take a coat.

"I've made you some Alka-Seltzer and toast. I'm good on breakfast this morning. My husband made me bagels before work and I've got my coffee ready to go in my flask," Penny tells me cheerfully.

I wish I had her head on my shoulders this morning. "Thank you. Sorry about not being here when you returned my phone."

"Don't worry about it this time. In the future, please give me a heads up if you and the guys go out again."

I almost choke on my drink. Penny knows about our wild night out, which means Eva and—oh no!!—Joshua will too!

"How did you find out we went out last night?"

"You'd best take a look for yourself. Just count your lucky stars you were masked," Penny responds, showing me her phone where a video of Joshua dancing with a 'mysterious masked dance partner' has gone viral. The internet has erupted into all kinds of theories, but the strongest one coming through is the question: "Is this the new leading dance lady for Pink Club? Is this blonde bombshell Bella Fitzroy's replacement?"

"Oh, crap!"

"Indeed. Are you ready? We need to get a move on."

It is now that I notice Penny is not dressed in her usual business attire but instead wearing a very dressed-down pair of denim jeans, pale blue T-shirt, walking boots and a duffle coat.

"Yes, all set and ready to go."

As we head on down to the reception area of the apartment block, Penny quickly pulls me back inside the lift as I'm about to step outside. Just as the door closes again, I notice a man with a long lens camera hanging around his neck, loitering right outside the entrance and exit doors.

"Don't worry, it's all in hand. The press is desperate to catch a glimpse of Pink Club's new leading lady after this recent speculation, so they will be going anywhere and everywhere they know who has links to Pink Club, Mimi and Joshua. I've just texted Max to let him know we may be late and also that we need assistance."

My heart rate quickens as we climb back up to the thirteenth floor and make the short walk from the lift back towards my apartment. Once inside, I make a pot of tea while we wait to hear what the next move is to be.

"You look so worried, Darla. Honestly, this is all fine. And believe me, it will become more frequent once your identity is revealed. We just have to keep a lid on who you are the best we can for now, ok?" Penny is sitting next to me on one of my kitchen bar stools, placing a reassuring hand over mine.

Joshua Glass sits in his office with legs stretched out in front of him, his hands placed behind his back. Across his face is the smuggest of grins as his ex and bitch of a boss yells down the phone to him. Little does Stella know that Joshua has put her on loudspeaker and placed the phone volume to barely noticeable. A knock at the door gives Joshua the excuse he needs to interrupt and hang up on Stella by simply saying, "Sorry, can we finish this later? Mimi's psychologist has arrived for her session." He doesn't wait for Stella to answer, as the mere mention of Mimi stops her dead in her tracks, unable to think fast enough for a response.

"Come in," Joshua calls, shuffling papers on his desk as a very frazzled Eva enters.

"I take it you've seen the papers?"

"Actually, I just had the pleasure of Stella filling me in about everything."

"Oh, right. Well, Max has just informed me that Darla and Penny are presently stuck outside with a slight 'press' issue."

"Ah, fuck! Ok, what do you need from me?"

"Max suggested putting one of the 'plants' to be seen with you quite publicly...as in right now?"

"Alright, alright. Mimi, do you need anything? I'll be gone just a few hours. Eva will look after you."

"No, thank you. I don't need a babysitter," Mimi snips, looking up from her new mobile phone where she was playing Sudoku to try and keep her mind occupied.

Joshua exits his office feeling annoyed and frustrated at the Mimi he doesn't recognise anymore. Whereas they were once so close as his twin, she is now so distant from him. This recognition gains him a sympathetic look from Eva, as he makes his way to see Max to orchestrate the rouse so that Darla and Penny can get over to Pink Club.

"I can take you home if you like, back to Joshua's apartment?" Eva suggests gingerly, while wringing her hands.

"Actually, you know what? I think I'd like to go and stretch my legs...alone!" Mimi says, placing her phone in her trouser pocket while standing up to make an exit out of Joshua's office.

"Mimi, would you mind waiting just until I —"

"Confirm with my brother? He's my twin—my equal. I'll call you if I get into any bother, ok?" Mimi snaps as she leaves Joshua's office, leaving Eva in stunned silence.

Heading out to follow Mimi, Eva is glad when she catches Midnight's eye in the corridor, rounding the corner having just come from the dance studio.

"Midnight, you wouldn't mind keeping an eye on Mimi, would you? Just don't let on that I've asked you to do this. She seems a bit...tetchy today."

"Sure, no worries. By the way, where is Darla? Octavia is doing her nut waiting for her to arrive."

"I'll explain later. Now go—watch!" Eva commands, making moving motions with her hands just as Mimi heads towards the Juliette staircase to begin her descent down.

~ Chapter 11 ~

Before long, there is a knock at the door and it is indeed Max with another security gentleman, both dressed down in casual clothes just as Penny is.

"Ok, are you ready to leave now, Darla?" Max asks, sounding confident, which helps me to relax.

"Certainly am."

"Good, right. So here is the plan. You and Jamie will be partnered up to look like a couple. You just have to link arms and pretend you're together until you get to the car. Penny and I will follow down after you, ok?"

"Err...yeah, ok, cool," I say, taken aback at the absurdity of my life.

Jamie holds his arm out for me and smiles gently, holding my hand and assuring me everything will be fine. I find myself blushing slightly and smile at him, feeling some more of the earlier anxiety now melting away. Jamie is strong and good looking with lovely big and strong hands that positively dwarf mine.

As we exit the lift and walk through reception, my heart quickens, Jamie cracks a joke and I genuinely laugh out loud. He leans down to whisper in my ear that I'm doing very well and that the car is right there in front of us. The woman on reception momentarily acknowledges us before getting back to typing. Thankfully, not a cameraman or woman is in sight now. Once in the car—which is a basic estate vehicle, nothing flashy—we head on out and onward to Pink Club. I cannot see and am not aware if Penny or Max are in fact right behind us, but I feel safe to be on the move now and ready to get stuck back into dance rehearsals with the spring gala just weeks away.

Eventually, I'm back at Pink Club and reunited with everyone in the dance studio. Octavia seems stressed because we already lost a few hours but understands my predicament and softens once she knows what I'd been through.

My earlier brief hangover has abated, and it looks as if everyone else is on top form as well.

"Ok, let's take it from the top," Octavia says, starting up the music.

On the night of the spring gala, I will be doing three main performances in between singers and other performance acts. I'm to open the show, perform a dance midway through, and then close the show with the final dance performance of the evening. It is just myself and my dance crew that perform on the raised stage at any and all times; all other performers will be on a stage attached to the floor.

Having a run through the dances until we move with nothing but fluid motion and in great timing to one another—satisfied we are on top form—Octavia dismisses Midnight and Co. so that she and I may get in some more practice with my aerial dance skills.

"How are you feeling?" Octavia asks, checking in with me.

"I'm good, but nervous about the gala. Excited as well."

"Good. It's going to be an awesome night, even more so with Mimi alive and well. How are your feet doing?"

"Achy, but nothing unusual."

"Here—call this woman. She's a magician with sports physio and she will do wonders for your feet." Octavia hands me a small white card with the physio's details on it.

"I will. Thank you very much."

Placing the card in a small compartment in my phone case, I prepare to work with the silk ropes. My body feels warm and loose; it will be nice to do dancing off the floor for a while, but it won't be any easier, as I'll be requiring the use of all of my muscles to practice all the moves I'm learning.

"Ok, so for the first move, let's get you flipping into the hammock. Stand right below the rope; that's good. Remember, you need to help your hands into your chest, then lift your knees up to your chest and flip back. Good, now just hang off the hammock and come back to standing," Octavia instructs, guiding me through the first manoeuvre.

I feel so free using the rigging, and it's nice to learn these new skills. I'm really living my dream, and this knowledge sends a buzz throughout my body.

"So the next move...excellent, now straighten your legs while squeezing your glutes together to help support your back and balance. Ok, so now let's come back to standing and put you in a simple swing pose."

We work on my aerial skills for another solid hour before deciding it would be a good idea to break for something to eat.

"Well done today, Darla. You're doing amazingly well."

I feel myself blushing slightly at Octavia's compliment.

"Man, I'm so hungry I could eat a hippo," I joke, rubbing my tummy.

Laughing, we head out of the dance studio and make our way over to the Fairy Forest room. The dim lighting is soothing, and it's nice and quiet in here today since there are no bands playing or shows being put on. Plinky plonky magical-styled music floats around the space of grass, trees and forestry plants, which—along with the purple glow from the lights—makes you really believe you're in another world.

"Good afternoon, Octavia...Darla. What can I get you?" A smartly dressed barman, wearing a tight dark purple waistcoat with shiny golden buttons down the front over a crisp white shirt with black trousers on with dark purple pinstripes approaches us.

"Good afternoon, Marcus. Darla and I will have two wild wizards, but make mine blueberry flavoured, please. Darla?"

"Oh, um...I've never had one before, so..."

"In that case, make hers a raspberry. Trust me, you won't be disappointed. You can sample mine as well for next time," Octavia says, interjecting and making the choice for me.

"Might I suggest the lady have a menu to take with her for next time?" the barman, Marcus, suggests. He hands me a small fancy laminated drink menu and winks at me before busying himself with making our drinks.

"Should we be drinking now? Is it allowed?"

"Relax—we're off the clock. Here, check out their food menu. It's scrumptious," Octavia insists, handing me a very fancy looking menu with purple and golden accents throughout.

"Err...I feel I may need to study this as well," I confess, confused with all the fancy names and in want of something simple like a burger and chips.

"What do you fancy?"

"A burger and chips," I answer sheepishly, thinking how common I must sound.

"Have you ladies decided what you'd like to eat?" Marcus asks, placing our rather large ornate-looking cocktail glasses of luminous blue and pink in front of us.

"Yes. Can we please have two firecracker grills—beef, please—and seasoned Fairy Fancies?"

"Would either of you like cheese on those?" Marcus asks, to which I respond with a vague expression.

"Do you want to make it a cheeseburger? They originally come with bacon and cheese," Octavia explains, her face lighting up having already taken a big slurp of her... what was it again? Wet wizard or something?

"Sure....I mean, yes, thank you." I take a big draw of my own wet or wild wizarding drink and am amazed at how sour and raspberry tasting it actually is. "Woo! That sure is —"

"Ha, ha, strong. Yeah, I know. We'd better pace ourselves before our food arrives."

"The food will take about twenty-five minutes. There's time for a reading if you'd like. Madame Scarlet is in her gypsy caravan. Might you both prefer a table closer to the forest queen?" Marcus says, winking at Octavia.

Move over Hogwarts—where the heck am I?

"Wonderful idea. Come on, let's go see Madame Scarlet. She really is very good." Octavia sounds giddier by the second as the wizard whatchamacallit seems to be hitting the spot, and I must admit to feeing rather giddy myself.

~ CHAPTER 12 ~

We make our way over to the faux—but very realistic—fairy forest where, off to the left, sits Madame Scarlet's gypsy caravan. The smell and feel of real grass and flowers fill my senses. We sit down at a table made of wood to look very wilderness-like indeed alongside backless tree stump stools. Plinky plonky music continues to float around us from various speakers dotted about the space. A few more people enter and begin to take up seats as they make themselves comfortable. A band starts setting up on stage in front of us; they look to be about college student age.

Octavia ushers me to go and knock on Madame Scarlet's door before I lose my chance. Apprehension courses through me. Do I really want to know what the stars say so close to the gala? Swallowing my nerves, I knock and head inside.

"Hello, my child. Lock the door, won't you? We don't want any interruptions." A woman dressed all in red, in a style I'm guessing is from the 1800's, with a fiery red wig in an ornate up-do atop her head and long dark red talons adorning her hands beckons me forward to sit at the small table opposite her.

There are big red curtains hanging from the small space around us and it feels very comfortable and cosy—not claustrophobic at all.

"It's a pleasure to meet you, Darla, our new leading lady for Pink Club. Don't worry, I can't read minds. I saw you briefly from your tour of our establishment the last time."

The band begins to warm up outside as Madame Scarlet takes my hands and looks over my palms thoroughly.

"I see you have a long lifeline—some trouble in your past, a dream unfulfilled. There is pain here...a recent loss but then also a repair of a relationship. Your mother?"

I can only nod in stunned silence as my reading gets underway.

Once my palm reading is over, Madame Scarlet breaks out a big deck of fantastical looking tarot cards consisting of swords, unicorns, fairies, dragons and angels among the designs.

"Ok, Darla, I want you to hold the deck to your heart and ask in your mind an answer to any question you may have, but do not tell me anything. The answers within are for you only in meaning. Do not even let me know if I am correct or not. This is all down to fate."

I breathe deeply and ask the questions to myself.

Will I be a success at the spring gala? Will it all go

well? What else...what else...oh heck, will I find true love someday?

At a loss for anything else to think or ask, I place the deck of cards back onto the small table covered with thick dark purple velvet cloth.

Madame Scarlet splits the deck into three stacks and takes the top card of each one before beginning my reading. "I see the eagle. You are set to soar high and have great success and wealth in your life. Now we have the family of unicorns. Some unrest will befall you or those close to you, but this will be short-lived. A burst of energy here from the dragon suggests you keep your own cards close to your chest and...here...oh, my..."

Alarmed, I look at Madame Scarlet with the look of concern now etched across her face. She clears her throat and rapidly collects the cards.

"What is it? What's the matter?"

"I feel that card was not meant for you. Do not fear; all will be well. I see only great things for your future, Darla," Madame Scarlet says, trying and failing to steel my nerves.

A knock at the door indicates our time is up, and I thank Madame Scarlet. But as I turn to leave, she grabs my right wrist, looking me squarely in the face while stating, "Hold on tight!" She then shakes her head as if to wonder what just happened and let's go of my wrist.

Feeling shaken up as we say goodbye to one another, I head on back to the table were Octavia is now sitting with our lunch, convincing myself the whole thing is just a bunch of hocus pocus nonsense, but unable to shift that uneasy feeling completely.

"So, how was the reading? No wait, don't tell me anything. If you do, your dreams are sure to not come true," Octavia chuckles, taking a bite out of her beef firecracker grill.

My stomach reminds me of how hungry I am, so I begin tucking into the food, which explodes in flavour into my mouth. This must be the very best burger I've had to date.

The conversation then turns to how good the food is here, which helps ease my mind over my earlier reading with Madame Scarlet, and I begin to swiftly forget the perfect nonsense she's relayed to me.

"Man, I am absolutely stuffed now, but this definitely hit the spot. Right. Best we start heading home. You need to rest your feet and call the physio. Seriously, she's a magician for feet," Octavia says, as we stand to make our exit out of the Fairy Fantasy room.

"Thank you for lunch today. Can it be my shout next time?"

"Absolutely. As I chose where to eat today, you get dibs next time, ok?"

"Cool, thanks, that would be great. I think I might quite like to experience the 90s Area 51-themed room."

"YES! One of my favourite places. They do a spectacular American diner menu. Maybe for Halloween this year we can put on an UFO themed show. I'll put this by Eva."

"Wow, that would be amazing! I was a huge fan of *The Files* growing up."

"Get out of town—me too!"

Octavia and I continue our conversation as we thank Marcus and head back out into the main body of Pink Club. It takes a while for my eyes to adjust to the pink hue of lights throughout the club, having been in the dimly lit Fairy Forest room.

"It's getting busy now; I'll walk you the back way to your dressing room."

"Thank you. Yes, I don't want to get lost again."

"When I began working here it took me quite a while to learn the layout of the place. I'm still not convinced I've seen all the nooks and crannies," Octavia admits, which gives me hope that I'll eventually get my full bearings of this place.

Back at my dressing room, relieved to be in a quieter space of Pink Club, Octavia excuses herself to head home, and I take a moment to relax before messaging Penny to ask her to take me home.

A message pings back almost immediately as Penny heads on down to collect me.

~ Chapter 13 ~

At home, I ponder on messaging or calling my mother. It's been a few weeks since her move up to Scotland, and I still don't know how to explain my job to her—well, fictional job that is. A pang hits me in the chest as I realise how much I'm missing her, and so biting the bullet, I pick up my phone and call her.

"Hi, this is Rumer. Wait for the beep. You know what to do." I hear her cheery voice coming through her answering machine.

"Hey, Mum, it's Darla. Just calling to let you know I have a new number now. Love you lots and miss you."

Hanging up the call, happy that I've now dodged a bullet having more time to think on what to say to Mum, I call the physio Octavia recommended. She has a space free this evening, so I book the appointment.

Changing into the recommended attire of loose-fitting shorts and T-shirt before my sport physio session,

I turn up the heating slightly. Though we are in spring in England, it is still jolly cold, as is usual for our seasonal change from winter to spring.

Sitting on the sofa alone with my thoughts, I replay in my mind the dance with Joshua. We were hip grinding together, for goodness sake! Mortification and lust don't mix well in my mind, so to distract myself, I put on a free thirty-minute yoga video on the TV to watch before the physio arrives.

———

8:25 p.m.

An unusual sound emanates for the first time around my living room space, and it is the sound of my *doorbell!* I never knew I had one until someone rang it, as everyone seems to insist on knocking. It's quite a pleasant and gentle *bing bong*.

"Hi, I'm Amanda. Are you Darla? I hope I have the right place." A broad shouldered, stocky woman with shoulder-length blonde hair stands before me wearing loose-fitting sports trousers and a green fleece with her name and job title sewn in to identify herself. At her feet lies a huge folded up massage table.

"Yes, please, come in. You can set up over there by the windows," I tell her. I let Amanda inside and notice she smells of sweet almond oil and lavender.

"Thank you. You have a beautiful place here, Darla," Amanda says, taking in my lavish surroundings with a look of awe that I'm guessing almost matched my own when I first saw this apartment.

"Would you like a drink?"

"A tea would be *lovely,* thank you. I've just been massaging for a local rugby team and I'm feeling rather parched. May I please use a bathroom to wash my hands?"

"Sure, just down the hall and off to the left."

As Amanda goes to wash her hands, thoughts once more of Joshua penetrate my mind, and this time it's recounting our lift venture. I'd successfully managed to get him to open up to me about Mimi, but now, after our dirty dancing at *Lucifer's Haven,* I wonder if I'd manage to be able to stand being so close to him again without my resolve completely crumbling—sort of how Cinderella must have felt when she had to dash away from Prince Charming so her identity wasn't revealed.

Needing a quick wee, I dash off to my room, and when I return, I can see Amanda with a mug in her hand, giving Binks a lot of love and fuss on her now erect massage couch.

"Come on puss, I've got to see to your mummy now," she says gingerly, picking him up and placing him on the floor. He flicks his tail in disdain at having his pampering interrupted and saunters off to his cat tower to climb inside, I imagine with the equivalent of a cat sulk.

Amanda and I run through a series of health and wellness questions before I'm invited to hop up onto the couch face down.

"So how long have you been a physio?"

"Gosh, it must be fifteen years now. My actual title is Sports Massage Therapist. Physio is a more broad-spectrum term."

I grunt in discomfort as Amanda locates a nice bundle of knots in my shoulders.

"Ooh, you're a bit tight in here. Let me loosen that for you."

By the end of my physio—correction, *sports massage* session—I feel a bit fuzzy headed but also as light as a feather. Amanda told me how sorry a state my feet were in but not to worry; she would have them in the best condition they'd ever been in, in no time, so we arrange a massage session for once a week.

"Thanks, Amanda. I feel amazing."

"Great. Now don't worry if you get any bruising or feel tightness tomorrow. It's all normal but shouldn't affect your regular dancing activities."

"Fab! How much do I owe you?"

"That will be thirty-five pounds, please. You can do pay as you go or up front if you like."

I pay Amanda for a month's worth of sessions since we have already booked in another three for this month. She thanks me before saying a cheery goodbye to myself and Binks.

Alone again, I pour myself a glass of water, which Amanda recommended having explained she's cleared a lot of toxins out of my lymphatic system through the massage. I cannot shake thoughts of Joshua out of my mind, so I try to distract myself by watching TV, but the first thing to pop up is the news, and the woman on the screen is, of course, talking about the scandal surrounding Mimi's kidnapping. Next, a photo pops up on the screen of me dancing with Joshua in all my glittery turquoise garb. Perspiration breaks out all over my body and my heart begins to pound away while my cheeks pink up with the all too powerful memory of our dance together overwhelming me.

My phone rings making me jump. It is my mother.

~ Chapter 14 ~

"Hello, my beautiful girl. How are you?" my mum says quite cheerily to which I am unaccustomed. It immediately puts me on edge.

"I'm...ok. How are you? How's Scotland?" I want to quickly put the focus to my mum and her new life up north and as far off topic about my own as I can possibly get.

"It's simply *wonderful!* You must come and visit me soon. Oh, and what's your new address, sweetheart? New friends keep asking me where you live and work, and it's a bit awkward when I don't actually know."

Shit!

"Err...good point. I don't yet know it by heart, but once I do I'll be sure to message you ASAP."

"Be sure that you do, as I will also be coming to visit from time to time to see you and my London friends, and I don't expect to pay out for a hotel. You wouldn't mind putting up your old mum, would you?"

"Sorry, Mum, I have to go. My boss is trying to call. Talk later. Love you loads...bye."

I hang up and switch my mobile to airplane mode. I don't want Mum calling back until I've had a chance to speak to Eva or Joshua.

Chewing my lip, I lean against the kitchen counter, pondering what to do. I decide to sleep on it before speaking to Eva in the morning and wearily head to my bed.

---

3 a.m.

I awaken with a start, after just having the most erotic dream of Joshua. My heart is racing and perspiration has broken out all over my body. Heading to the bathroom, I splash some cold water over my face to awaken myself fully and try to shake the raunchy images from my mind but fail to do so. Feeling annoyed that my mind insists on torturing me like this, knowing full well any kind of relationship between us would be impossible, I take off my slightly damp pyjamas and throw on some loose-fitting jogging bottoms and a fresh T-shirt before making my way to the lounge, moving the sofas to the side so I have room to dance.

It begins to rain heavily outside from an ensuing thunderstorm, and before long the lightning flashes, illuminating the floor space I have created. Thunder crashes, shaking the building, and the rain pounds at my windows as I spin and twirl, jump and go and go until my lungs burn and perspiration pours from me. I want to force these thoughts and images from my mind, hoping to physically dance this newfound energy out of my system. It is not until my feet begin to burn that I realise now may be a good time to stop, and just as this occurs to me, there is a massive boom of thunder. Suddenly, all the lights go out, leaving me alone, standing in the dark and panting—my wanton lust for Joshua no less than before.

---

3 a.m.

Joshua wakens with a start. Mimi's screams can be heard along his long corridor. He leaps from his bed and sprints down to her room, roughly opens the door, and bursts inside to awaken her and make her realise she is only dreaming. Mimi hits at Joshua and struggles in his arms until fully awake, shaking and crying. Max, having heard all the commotion and presently living with the Glass twins, follows shortly after. Joshua instructs him to call for the doctor at once, to which he does.

"Shhh, it's ok—you're safe," Joshua says gently, holding Mimi to his bare chest. He is wearing loose-fitting pyjama trousers. Stroking her hair, Mimi's shivering abates a little.

She cries into her brother's chest, clinging weakly to him and unable to muster even the strength to sit for a moment.

"Here, lie back. The doctor will be here soon."

Mimi grabs for Joshua's hand as she lies back on her pillows, feeling afraid he may be about to leave her. The look of terror on her face cuts deeply in his heart, as he can only wonder what sort of hell his twin sister had been subjected to the past five years. He wants to murder those responsible.

"Dr. Jameson will be here promptly. She is just dealing with an asthma case and then is coming right over," Max says, giving a reassuring smile to Mimi, to which she responds.

"Thank you, Max," Joshua says to his long-time friend and bodyguard.

"Can I get you a drink? Tea or coffee?"

"I'll have a hot chocolate, please," Mimi says, her voice hoarse.

"Tea for me," Joshua answers, still holding his sister's hand.

Once Max has left them in peace until the doctor arrives, Joshua announces to Mimi that Milagros Morena's family wishes to meet with him and their parents and so will be arranging something for a few days' time. Mimi also says she would like very much to meet them, but Joshua doesn't feel she will be strong enough to cope with the fallout of their grief. Mimi turns away from her brother, pulling her hand away and turning her back on him, feeling frustrated.

Joshua takes this as a sign his sister needs some space and heads out of her bedroom as Max hands him his tea and goes into Mimi's room to place her drink on her bedside table. Then he joins Joshua in the lounge as they wait for Dr. Jameson.

"Thank you for the tea. I'll be down in the gym while Dr. Jameson is here. See to it my sister is looked after, please."

"Don't you think you should be here while she is assessed?" Max interjects. But a look from Joshua tells him he may be overstepping his boundaries here, so he puts his hands up to indicate he's backing off.

Nothing more is said between them, and Joshua heads down to blow off his anger and frustration in the gym at what those animals have done to his beautiful twin sister's spirit. Mimi no longer smiles or laughs; she is a shadow of her former self—frail, malnourished and frightened all the goddamn time. The murderous thoughts begin to return as Joshua places his tea on a small table out of the way before laying into his punching bag. He hits and hits and hits at it until sweat pours off him and he has to hold onto the bag for balance, breathless and spent of energy. Once his breath is collected, he drinks his tea, which—although lukewarm—now hits the spot.

Max alerts Joshua that Dr. Jameson has been and gone and that she's given Mimi a sedative to help her sleep. He hands Joshua a small orange tube with a white lid and little white pills inside. Max explains that Mimi is to only be given one of these tablets if she should have another nightmare episode and to book her in for an appointment with her psychotherapist as soon as possible.

Joshua thanks Max for all his help this evening and they say goodnight. Joshua heads upstairs to grab a shower before going back to bed. The lights flicker in his apartment, and then everywhere is plunged into darkness from a power cut, eliciting a chill racing across Joshua's sweat-soaked body. It instantly reminds him of the cold lift he and Darla were trapped in just a day ago.

Darla in mind, Joshua's thoughts now turn very much to something else entirely, giving him need of a very cold shower.

Max, while illuminating the space with two torches of which he hands one to Joshua, alerts him to know that before he heads off to shower that the power cut has hit big areas of London and that also there is an issue with the water—as in it's turned off. Huffing loudly, Joshua heads on towards the kitchen (having thanked Max for the update before dismissing him for the rest of the early morning hours), where he grabs two small white pillar candles, a box of matches and a big litre bottle of icy cold water from his fridge. There is nothing for it but for him to douse himself in icy cold water from the bottle of drinking water he now holds in his hand—the feel of coolness a sure promise of what's to come.

Joshua heads off to the bathroom and, using the torch light, strikes a match to ignite both the candles. Once lit, he places the candles onto a shelf, giving the bathroom a nice amber glow and relaxing hue to the environment. Joshua, now naked, steps into his shower, his nicely toned body still wet with sweat illuminated from the eerie glow of the candlelight. He prepares himself mentally with a few deep centring breaths for the icy cold blast of water that is about to hit him. Bracing himself by putting his left hand up against the cream tiled shower wall while raising the bottle above his head, Joshua begins to dribble the water gradually over himself, which gives way to his breath catching in his throat and an eruption of goosebumps to scream in protest all over his body (in all areas) with previous thoughts of Darla having abandoned him as the sting of cold water jolts him to the very present moment.

Mission accomplished, he thinks regarding the extinguishment of fiery sexual thoughts of one Miss Darla Pebble.

~ CHAPTER 15 ~

"Darla, what on earth is the matter with you? Your turns are sloppy and your balance is terrible. Have you been drinking?!" an annoyed Octavia says, as we stop once again where I've faltered with my footwork. She comes close to smell my breath.

"Ok, guys, let's break for lunch. Not you, Darla. You stay. I think we need to have a chat about your sudden decline in performance in my rehearsals."

Once everyone has left, giving me quizzical concerned looks over their shoulders, I breathe a sigh of relief. The tension in the dance studio could have been cut with a knife.

"I'm so sorry, Octavia —"

"Darla, please call me V."

"Sorry —"

"And stop apologising. Now what on earth is the matter with you?" Octavia and I sit on the floor together.

"I didn't sleep well at all. I rarely suffer from dreams this intense, but after a massage session with Amanda—"

"You saw her? Good! Sorry, go on."

"Well, I had a very restless night. I awoke at 3 a.m. and the only way to clear my head was to…dance."

"Ah, I see. Bless you, you must be shattered. Listen, if anything in the future happens like this, you *must* tell me. We can't afford to have you injured so close to the gala."

"To be honest, I could use all the distraction I can get right now, but I will rein in my dancing when on my own time."

"That sounds like a very wise decision indeed. How did you find Amanda?"

You mean by her being a bit to over familiar and nosy?

"The session was good. I've decided to see her once a week for continual maintenance of my body and feet."

"Excellent. She really is the best in my opinion. Did wonders for a lordosis of my back."

Meeting concluded, Octavia and I head toward the Pelican Brief bar where we indeed find Midnight and Co. sitting around a large round table, eating and drinking. Sitting down to join them, I'm given what I can only depict are *strange* glances. Octavia whispers to me to go and sit alone to not pull suspicion from members of Pink Club that I'm attached to anyone here.

"So lovely to see you again. We must catch up soon," Octavia says loud enough for surrounding visitors to hear before going to sit with Midnight and Co., leaving me standing like a spare prick at a wedding, no longer acknowledging me.

"Table for one?" Eric the bartender asks, coming to my rescue.

"Yes, thank you."

"Right this way."

Eric seats me at a table in a dimly lit corner where there is a wall between me on the right-hand side that now shields my presence from anyone else in the bar. If anything, I must admit to feeling relief that I am no longer being scrutinised by Midnight and Co.'s disapproving looks. Fatigue washes through me, so I decide to head home. I'm hungry and don't want to sit here a moment longer feeling like '*Billy no mates*'.

Standing up, I make my way out of the bar and head to my dressing room. No one so much as bats an eyelid at my presence on exiting, be they staff or Pink Club members.

Oooof! The wind gets knocked out of me as I round a corner and bump hard into someone else.

"So sorry," a man's voice says, as he steadies me with what feels to be big strong hands.

Looking up, my voice catches with my breath in my throat. "Josh—erm—Mr. Glass, so sorry," I stammer, feeling myself blush.

"It is my fault. I'm just heading for some lunch if you'd care to join me."

"Err...that would be, actually I was just going to request a ride home. I'm really tired."

"I hope Octavia isn't working you too hard. Perhaps I should have words?"

"No, I had an...unsettling night."

"Me too. Come on, we can have lunch back at my place."

Suddenly, I'm feeling very alert and wide awake. Did he just invite me around to *his* place for lunch?!

"That would be —"

"It's not a request; I insist. Go and get your belongings. I'll wait here. Max is already preparing the car for Mimi and I to travel home in."

Gulp

"Okay."

"See you soon, *pretty lady.*" As Joshua says this, an instant memory of us talking at the bar at *Lucifer's Haven* flashes through my mind, making me go all weak in the knees. But without turning round to acknowledge him, I carry on towards my dressing room.

Once inside, I breathe a huge sigh of relief, which is short-lived, as I know there's no escape from this situation now. Feeling still sticky from dance rehearsals, I dash into the shower room and quickly wet and wash just my body, leaving my hair dry in its messy bun. Towelling off at breakneck speed, adrenaline now coursing through my body, I struggle to get dressed into my jeans, a pale pink T-shirt and matching thick polar neck jumper. Once dressed and ready to head out, I see Joshua is indeed exactly where I left him standing.

We walk through all the back ways and use a service lift to get down to the car park.

Max greets Joshua and I with just a slightly puzzled expression on his face. Once inside the very swish-looking car, I come face-to-face with Mimi Glass, and my heart skips a beat as I sit next to her, Joshua taking up the seat on the other side of me.

This is surely a nightmare! How can I be sandwiched between the Glass twins?! All I wanted was cheese on toast, a nice warm bath, and my bed. Is that too much to ask, universe?

"Hi...Mimi. Lovely to meet you."

She says nothing but rolls her eyes and turns to look out of the window, balancing her chin on her hand.

My hands are placed on my lap, as are Joshua's on his, and they feel so close yet so far away as if to torture me further since our outrageously inappropriate dance at *Lucifer's Haven*.

'Pretty lady' dances through my mind and I cough at realising Joshua may know it was me that night. Why else would he be mimicking the bar staff's sentiment to me?

"Really, it is such a lovely offer to have lunch with you and your sister, but I'm truly very tired and — "

"Do not worry so much, Darla. I'll have Fiona, my housekeeper, make up the spare guest bedroom. You are my guest of honour now, our leading dance lady, and we are going to be seeing much more of each other as we learn to work together to get Pink Club back on its feet after the tarnishing of its reputation from Bella's death and drug taking scandal."

"Who can be surprised she turned to drugs after the

pressure you put on all of us after your breakup with Stella and having her steal everything away from us?" Mimi shouts venomously.

I wish to suddenly be anywhere then here. It's hell!

~ Chapter 16 ~

Mimi storms off to, I'm guessing, her room once we arrive at Joshua's apartment, the slamming of a door possibly confirming my suspicions. I see a moment of fleeting angst cross Joshua's face and feel bad for him.

"Fiona, can you prepare my other guest bedroom for Miss Pebble?"

"Certainly, sir," says a woman with fiery red hair pulled back into a plait, wearing black trousers and a long-sleeved white shirt with a charcoal grey waistcoat over the top.

"May I also take your bag from you, miss?" the woman called Fiona asks as she reaches her hand out.

Giving Fiona my bag, I wait until she heads off to my room for the night.

"Come—let me show you around," Joshua says excitedly, holding out his arm. He smells divine and looks so gorgeous in tight denim jeans and a crisp white shirt open at the collar. As we link arms, my heart does a grand national all of its own.

The space is huge *(naturally)*, with photographs adorning the walls of Joshua, his parents and Mimi during what I'm considering were happier times, as the twins in many of the photographs are children. Joshua was such a good-looking little boy. I imagine what children he might make and what would they be like if they were to be made with me but hurriedly scramble to get that idea out of my mind.

We enter a room with exotic artwork, an easel, fireplace, and many bookshelves. An antique desk sits over in one corner. The space brings a 'ye olde England' vibe to the room, which I find rather comforting.

Stepping away from Joshua to fully take in the room's allure, I walk over and brush my hand gingerly across the smooth wooden desk, fully taking in the vibe. I look at Joshua, who now stands with arms folded across his chest. He leans against the doorframe, his big frame and *'come to bed eyes'* giving me flutters in all sorts of unmentionable places. I snatch my hand away from the desk, determined to break my reverie of continual *naughty thoughts* about him. As we exit the library, Joshua this time does not offer me his arm or a hand, and it is a bitter relief.

"Your place is beautiful; I can't wait to see the rest of it."

Joshua smiles at me as we head towards the rest of his apartment. I'm shown Mimi's closed bedroom door, gym, lounge, kitchen and dining area, and also where

Joshua's closed bedroom door is (which makes me feel instantly more curious to know what's behind there).

Once the tour is concluded, I'm feeling quite famished, which is announced by the loud grumbling of my tummy. Joshua grins and walks to the kitchen. I take up a pew on a plush cream bar stool before he hands me some take-away menus, instructing me to choose whatever I want. He heads to ask Mimi if she would like to join us for lunch and confirm what she would like to eat. While he is out of the room, I peruse the lavish menus from local top-class restaurants offering their finest food for take-away, finally settling on Chinese.

Joshua returns a short while later with a very sad and drawn looking Mimi.

"Hi," she says timidly, lifting a hand to me. She is wearing an oversized dark blue jumper over a pair of pale blue jeans, the sleeves pulled down over her hands. It positively drowns her, and I wonder if this is not a jumper of Joshua's.

"Hi. Joshua just gave me the grand tour; it's really beautiful."

Joshua busies himself making the food order. It appears we are all having Chinese.

"Yes, it feels nice to be around familiar surroundings again," Mimi admits, slightly brightening with a small smile.

"Oh, before I forget...here, I kept this safe for you," I say, reaching around my neck to return the gold ballet slipper necklace to Mimi. It's not right I should hold onto it with her safe return.

Mimi raises a hand to her mouth, and a look crosses Joshua's face that I am unable to distinguish. Is he angry or shocked?

Shit! I hope I am not wrong about this.

"Thank you," Mimi says, tearing up and enveloping me in a big bear hug. Over her shoulder, Joshua mouths *'thank you'* as relief floods me to know he is not pissed off.

"Would you mind...?" she asks, indicating for me to put it on for her which I oblige.

Joshua pours us all a glass of red wine and we "cheers" before heading to the dining room. A large round glass table sits atop a white fluffy rug, and windows surround us with floor-length white drapes. The space is quite airy and bright. Cream leather highback chairs surround the table, and covering the walls is beautiful floral wallpaper, duck egg blue with silvery lilies all over it.

"Joshy, I wonder if I can speak to you in private for a moment," Mimi says timidly, placing her wine down and heading out of the dining room.

As I sit down in one of the dining chairs sipping my wine, my awareness fixates on the classical music playing from a wall speaker. My eyelids feel heavy as my earlier fatigue comes back with a vengeance. Fiona enters the dining room brusquely, which awakens me with a jolt. She's announcing that she has come to set the table.

"Can I get you another drink, miss? A top up of wine, or perhaps a tea or coffee?"

"Please call me, Darla, Fiona. I'd love a coffee please."

"Very well. How would you like your coffee, Darla?"

"Is it possible to have a latte?"

"Certainly. Is that with sugar or sweetener? I also have an array of syrups. Vanilla, toffee nut, crème Brulé, caramel, cinnamon, gingerbread -"

"The crème Brulé sounds exotic; I'd like to try one of those please."

"Coming right up."

Fiona leaves and I stand to stretch and wake myself up, deciding a splash of cold water will help. I head on out to find the bathroom. En route, however, I catch what sounds like a heated discussion coming from the library between Joshua and Mimi.

"What are you doing bringing her here? If Stella finds out—well, what on earth do you think she is going to say?"

"Stella will not find out. My business at home is my own. Outside of Pink Club she has no say as to who and who I do not invite round to my place of residence."

"Just be careful. That afternoon, she made me go to her place. She's still in the belief she is the top dog, and I feel she just wanted to ensure I was going to keep my mouth shut about her scandalous theft of Pink Club from both of us. We have a noose around our necks; the fraud is too perfect. All our solicitors have said just as such. So please don't rock the boat."

I hear a sound as if someone kicks something and decide now is my cue to duck into the bathroom.

What are you doing here, Darla? You're playing with fire; you must insist to go home.

~ Chapter 17 ~

"Gosh, I am full to bursting. Great choice, Darla. Right, I'm heading back to my room, bro. I'll see you in the morning. Lovely to meet you *properly* again, Darla. Thank you for taking such good care of my necklace. I'm very grateful to have it returned to me."

"You're more than welcome. I believe it brought me good luck on stage at the New Year's Eve bash."

Mimi grins while fingering the golden ballet slippers before heading off, leaving Joshua and I to rest and digest while still sitting at the glass dining table.

"Would you care to join me in the lounge?"

"Actually, I'm feeling rather bushed myself. Would you mind if I get a ride home? My cat, Binks, will require feeding."

"Don't worry about it; I can get Penny to —"

"Look, Joshua—please, I really just want to go home

and get a good night's sleep. This all feels, well, inappropriate somehow—me staying the night here."

"I have made you feel uncomfortable. I apologise. Max will take you home." Joshua sombrely heads out to rouse Max from wherever it is that he is residing in the apartment, and before too long, I'm saying a hasty goodbye and hitting the road back home with Max at the wheel. The rhythmic hum of the engine and smoothness of the ride lulls me to sleep in the passenger seat.

"Darla…Miss Pebble."

"Mmmm, yes Joshua, I would love a cuddle," I murmur, while slowly awakening from the dream I was having of Joshua asking me if he could hold me.

"Miss Pebble, we're back at your apartment," Max says, awakening me fully.

I now panic, wondering if I just vocalised what I was saying in my dream. "Sorry, Max."

"It's no trouble at all. Let me see you up."

Once back in my apartment, the time reads 10:30 p.m., so there is plenty of time to get my head down and catch up on sleep. Relief washes over me in my own surroundings again. Thankfully, I'm feeling too exhausted to even contemplate on the strangest of afternoons I've just been subjected to with Joshua and Mimi. I feed and water Binks then head off to my luscious fluffy cloud bed, letting the world fall away as I enter the land of nod, leaving my troubles behind me for at least the next several hours.

I awaken to see that it is before my alarm is due to go off. I stretch and lie still a moment to fully come to my senses. Memories of Joshua's hand in mine, his warmth and kindness extended to me at wanting to both introduce me to his sister and show me his wonderful home soon come flooding back to me, and I cringe at how fast I shut him down, having heard Mimi's warning to her brother before making my excuse to leave. Worrying what today may bring, I throw back the covers and head to get ready before Penny arrives to pick me up.

"Good morning, Darla. You're up and ready, I see," Penny greets cheerfully on entering my apartment.

"Yes, thankfully I caught up on sleep and arose early refreshed."

"Shall we go then?"

"Sure, have you eaten?"

"Ever since I told my husband Jack of your kindness bestowed on me on my first day on the job when you made us both omelettes—at having missed breakfast that day—Jack's ensured every morning to make sure I'm fed before leaving the house."

"That's very kind of him. Maybe one day when I meet my own true love they'll be just as kind."

"I've no doubt that when your identity is finally revealed you'll have complete pick of the field from all of Pink Club's famous eligible bachelors."

I blush as Penny says this to me. I had not given a single thought as to the possibility that my identity being revealed at the spring gala could potentially line me up with the perfect man of my dreams. The memory of dancing with Joshua flashes across my mind, disrupting any such thoughts, and I shake my head as Penny and I make our way onto Pink Club.

"Ok, everyone, listen up. There are only two weeks until the gala. Darla, you look to be in better shape today. I'm taking it you caught up on your sleep?" Octavia commands the dance studio space. I simply nod, which elicits a smile from her.

Just then, the doors to the studio open, and Eva walks in with a woman I've never seen before. She is a sight to behold! I'm guessing 5'2 in height, wearing a denim skirt on the knee, bright pink shirt with ruffles at the front, and over the top luminous yellow leather zip-up jacket. Her hair is an array of pink and yellow dyed hair done up in fancy curls atop her head. On her feet are striking pink stiletto shoes with matching ruffles to that of her shirt on the front. On her face are severe-looking, sharp angle framed pink glasses. Big hoop earrings hang from her lobes, and a very fancy sparkly expensive-looking necklace hangs around her neck.

"Everyone, meet Polly. Polly, this is...well, everyone. Now I know it's the start of rehearsals for you all, but could Polly please watch you run through your performance on the stage—just at floor level? She needs to see where to place the florals for the spring gala, as the stage is to be fully dressed up per Stella's request."

We all momentarily glance around at each other before filing back out of the dance studio. On passing Joshua's office, my heart momentarily skips a beat as I wonder if he will be here today but remind myself just as fast that this is of no concern to me.

"Sheesh, talk about a Battenberg on legs," Psyche says, jesting with me as we walk. I playfully bat him on the arm but cannot help to break out in a smile and small giggle.

Octavia and the guys glance back at us misbehaving, and I make a quick zip-locking motion.

"Right, you guys prepare down at basement level, and we shall see you in the main performing area shortly," Eva orders before walking away with Polly. Psyche does a mock salute while no one is watching and again I giggle.

Octavia comes over to speak to me just before we take our positions on the stage ready for it to be raised up. "Are you sure you're ok today? How is your balance?" she asks me, a worried expression covering her face.

"Honestly, I'm good today. Look, see?" I assure her, going up onto toes in my ballet Pointe shoes and doing a perfect twirl, which gains me a whistle from one of the guys but don't know which one.

"Ok—just be careful, all of you," Octavia says, pointing a wary finger at everyone before allowing us to prepare.

~ CHAPTER 18 ~

The stage is lifted to marry with the main performance arena floor. Octavia starts the music, and we begin to go through the motions but have to pause momentarily to let Polly see the positioning of our feet and how far away from the edge we are.

"There will also be some aerial dancing as well, so Darla will be exiting on and off the stage mid-air," Octavia explains to Polly, who is now feverishly making notes while in-between biting the end of her biro.

"Can you point out which areas she is to leave and land back on the stage please?" Polly requests, walking to where Octavia points. "Right, I have everything I need now. None of this is likely to change, is it? The choreography will remain the same? It's just once everything is affixed to the stage, I won't be able to change or move things around."

"Yes, everything is indeed going to stay the same—no

last-minute adjustments or changes. The guys work like a well-oiled machine and that is not going to be changed now."

"Great, well–it's been a pleasure," Polly says. She looks down her severe angled glasses at us before heading off to re-join Eva, who is sitting in one of the audience seats.

"Seeing as you're all here, let's do a complete run-through on the stage before we break. Then, Darla, I want you to begin your aerial skills with me up there this afternoon to get you used to the hoops and the rigging," Octavia says authoritatively, as my stomach now becomes knotted.

"I would like to join Darla for the aerial rehearsals. Having two of us up there with her will be safer and also give Darla more confidence, I feel," Midnight says, grabbing Octavia's attention.

"If Midnight's going to support Darla, then I want to be up there with her." "...and me..." "...me too," the guys start to chime in. Having earned their approval literally feels as if it lights me up inside.

They really do like me!

"Very well; I know there is no point in arguing with any of you. Let's just keep it a short rehearsal for today, ok?" Octavia resigns, coming around to where I'm standing and placing a reassuring hand on my shoulder.

We run through the dance up high on the stage, which feels much less scary now, as I have full trust and faith in my dance crew. However, once we break and then come back to the stage ready to go through my aerial skills, I begin to feel a bit unnerved and sick.

"Ok, Darla, just like we practiced. You're to run through the middle of the cross and off the end to the hoop. You can do this; just don't overthink it," Octavia says from the ground, as the guys stand around me to help give me courage.

Midnight comes close, his body heat and presence instantly relaxing me. "Just breathe with me in 2...3...4... out, 2...3...4...you got this, now go— fly," he whispers in my ear.

Steeling myself, I begin my short jog to the edge, and just as I'm about to leap, I make the fatal error to look down, making my feet slam on the brakes as my brain screams in terror at the sheer drop ahead, which makes me overbalanced and fall forward.

Strong arms envelop me and pull me back from the edge. Turning, I can see it is Siren.

"What happened? Darla, you ok?" Octavia shouts from the ground.

"Yeah—just need a moment."

"Ok, take your time, you can do this," she says, which does nothing to abate the fear running through me now.

"Right, plan B. Here, sway with me. Ok, now go forward then backwards...forwards...backwards. Get used to the motion at the edge. Ok, now we are going to walk back, back, back...a bit more; now let's jog. Ok, don't think, and—JUMP!" Siren shouts the last word as he runs with me to the edge. The sharpness of his tone shocks me into obeying, bypassing my fear mechanism in my mind as I leap and effortlessly grab the hoop, settling into the first position.

"Well done, Darla. Fantastic effort. Now let's go through positions one to five and then you can go back onto the stage."

I complete all the poses with ease, my fear now melted away with the guys cheering and whooping for me once I'm reunited with them on the stage. I get hugs from all the guys and really begin to get a sense of... family. Never really having had a sense of a family, though—apart from my hair-brained mother and having lost my grandparents to whom I was so close—I tread carefully to opening my heart fully.

The stage lowers to floor level and we all step off before it carries on down to the basement. Octavia gives me a big hug, telling me how proud she is of me, but also informs me that we will now also be practicing my aerial skills on the stage, as the spring gala is just over a week away. This makes my stomach do little flip-flop motions.

One of the main doors to the arena closes loudly, and I can see Joshua has entered the space. Now my heart feels as if it's doing flip-flops, as I'm sure I feel it skip a beat or two with excitement and trepidation.

"V, I wonder if I might steal Darla away for a while."

"Actually, we've just finished for the day; you missed a terrific rehearsal from our main star of the show here," Octavia proclaims proudly.

"I'm afraid I'll be missing a lot more. Mimi and I are

to fly to meet our parents in Tuscany for a few weeks to help with her recovery."

"Oh, that's a shame. Great work today, Darla. See you and the guys here tomorrow morning promptly instead of the studio. From now on rehearsals are to be in here."

Gulp!

"Well done today, Darla." Midnight says, leading my dance crew out of the performing arena.

"Superb job today," Psyche adds.

"You got this; you were on fire today," Siren tells me, passing me after Psyche.

"Really impressed with your balls," Mixer also adds cheekily, winking before leaving the space.

Then Medley says to me with his deep London cockney accent, "Looking forward to watching you fly tomorrow, pigeon," followed by Digit's final comment of, "Bro? Pigeon? Darla is a Phoenix up there," to which Medley argues with "No, pigeon...what's wrong with pigeon? I like the name; it's endearing."

They carry on their bickering until everyone has exited, leaving just me and Joshua here a moment. Our eyes lock and I find myself unable to look away, as his smouldering *'come to bed eyes'* bore deep into mine.

"Shall we?" he suggests. I notice how clipped his tone is.

My reverie of wanton lust bubble pops and I find myself simply nodding as I follow Joshua with a sense of a naughty schoolgirl whose about to get a dressing down by her teacher.

As we walk side by side towards the Juliette staircase that will undoubtedly take us to Joshua's office, I feel the heat rolling off him, along with some tension. Looking down and seeing how close our hands are to one another instantly makes me flush a deep red.

There is a hub of staff and members milling about, but no one so much as bats an eyelid at me. Perhaps it's because I'm dressed in just a plain pair of dark blue leggings and pale grey T-shirt today. The fact of how invisible I appear to everyone oddly comforts me.

A man stops Joshua as we reach the bottom of the stairs, and I'm instructed by Joshua to go ahead that he will be along in a moment.

Entering his office, I sit in the pink and black chair opposite his desk and wait...and wait...and wait. An hour goes before the door to his office opens. Turning to see who it is, I'm surprised that it's not Joshua but Penny.

"Hi. Joshua said he is sorry but had some unexpected business to attend to and that I am to take you home."

"Oh...ok, sure," I say to Penny, gingerly standing with a feeling of confusion now as to what is going on with Joshua.

Once back at home among my belongings and surroundings, I remember I need to speak to Eva about my mother after her probing questions as to where I'm now living and working. My mobile rings, as if on cue, showing Eva's number. I discover upon answering that she is calling to inform me that we are all being given a long weekend break while the performing arena is decorated for the spring gala.

"Oh, Eva, before you go, my mother...she's been asking again where I'm living and working; she wants to know the *truth,*" I explain.

Eva tells me that I can tell my mother where I'm now living and working (which in all honesty feels like a load off) but to be extremely discreet about it and to fax or scan in an email her the NDA to sign. Seeing as I now have three days off, I'm contemplating flying to Edinburgh to visit my mum. Talking this through with Eva on the phone, we agree to kill two birds with one stone. I'll go and visit Mum, get her to sign the NDA, and then fly back ready to crack on with rehearsals until the gala. Eva says she will arrange my flights there and back.

Once our call has ended, I flop down on the sofa and Binks jumps up to give me a friendly cat hello. My phone has no other messages or missed calls, so I resign myself to the fact that I won't be hearing from Joshua anytime soon.

I decide to start packing a bag for my visit to Mum's, which reminds me that I'd better phone ahead and alert her to my visitation in case she cannot have me at the house and I need to book a hotel.

~ Chapter 19 ~

Within the hour, Eva sends me all the relevant info for my travel plans tomorrow. Mum has confided to me that she has a live-in lodger, so I will, in fact, need to make my own arrangements of where to stay. She recommended the Bruntsfield Hotel near her house, and Penny—having checked it out online—said it's actually very nice but more importantly safe and secure. I haven't been on a plane by myself before—I'd always travelled on holidays with my grandparents and Mum—and the feeling of anxious excitement that now pools in my stomach at the realisation I'll be travelling alone tells me that sleeping will be a challenge. Popping two herbal sleeping tablets with a glass of milk, I head to bed to try my best to at least get a few hours' sleep before my early start in the morning.

As predicted, sleep didn't really happen for me. My nerves were completely shot to pieces at the prospect of having to travel all by myself. *Wimp!* I think, inwardly scolding my cowardice.

"Hey, Darla, only me," Penny greets cheerfully, walking into my place at the crack of dawn.

"Eurgh! It's 5 a.m. How can you possibly have so much get-up-and-go?"

"Rough night?"

"Yes…err, what's with the suitcase?" I say, suddenly noticing Penny's very casual attire with a small black pull along case at her feet.

"I'm coming with you, silly! You didn't think you'd be allowed to travel on your own to Scotland, did you? Darla, you are funny at times."

"Oh—of course not. I'm actually quite relieved, to be honest. Eva didn't mention I'd be having a plus one."

"Time for coffee! I'm excited to be going back to Scotland. I went on a holiday with an ex to the Isle of Skye. We saw dolphins, and the stars were so bright at night; it was truly romantic."

Penny carries on speaking, but my mind wanders off to thoughts of Joshua, Tuscany, heat and love-making among the vines of his family's vineyard—which had been mentioned numerous times in numerous highly esteemed magazines.

"Here we are; that'll perk you right up," Penny says, handing me one of my China mugs filled with the caffeine buzz I shall surely need for the journey ahead.

We land at Edinburgh airport in good time. I managed a sleep on the short 90-minute flight. We flew coach—which was fine by me—as Penny explained it would help with keeping a low profile. This way, we just looked like two friends taking a trip to Scotland. I honestly wasn't fussed, as this was the same way I'd travelled with my family back when Mum and I could enjoy holidays with Nana and Grampy.

"I'll go grab our luggage. Wait here with the trolley," Penny instructs as she trots off, still very much in high spirits. She is donning dark denim jeans, denim heels, a plain white T-shirt and black duffle coat. I'm wearing a pair of comfy Blueberry jogging bottoms, a T-shirt and hoodie. On my feet is a pair of black and white converse. I decided to travel in comfort. Both of us have baseball caps on, which helps hide our identities.

All of a sudden, I realize I forgot about Binks. Turning suddenly, while exclaiming, *"Oh shit"* loudly, I bash into some poor unsuspecting traveller, who already had their luggage atop of their trolley that was now brakes off and is sent hurtling towards a poor unsuspecting Japanese traveller, who looks up just in time to see this trolley full of luggage careening towards him. I am hoping the man will bring the trolley to a halt, but to my horror, the man somehow becomes attached to the speeding mass, his weight undoubtedly adding to the speed at which it now travels. It is here I see where this now oriental trolley express is going: straight towards a restaurant packed with people sitting both inside and outside of it. I stand and raise my hands to my face as the owner of the trolley continues running after it.

CRASH!!!

"There you are. What on earth?" Penny exclaims, catching up to me with our luggage and the trolley I'd abandoned.

The owner of the trolley apologises profusely as a very angry Japanese man shakily gets helped up off the lap of some poor unsuspecting, rather large, woman in floral dress. I think I hear she is busily yelling something about hot prawns and burnt breasts. The man with the trolley tries to back out of the restaurant, but I see he knocks into a waiter dishing up food that requires a flame to a table directly behind him. The waiter falters and ends up setting fire to a customer's shirt sleeve; a woman adjacent to the table yells and grabs a jug of iced lemon water which she proceeds to throw over the man.

"Oh, my God! Maybe I should go and offer some first aid!" Penny cries with the look of shock still clearly across her face.

"I'm sure they'll be fine. Look, they have people attending to them," I say, seeing two people in airport ground staff uniforms running to the scene—a great big green bag with a white cross on it between them.

Thankfully, it's so busy we can lose ourselves in the crowd as we head to meet our driver.

"Man, I'm *starrrving!* I checked out the menu at the hotel and the food looks yummy!" Penny says, as we arrive at the Bruntsfield Hotel.

Once the car has stopped, I'm helped out by the driver as Penny whips around to the boot, beating the bellhop to it. She assures him it's fine, she can take the luggage. The smartly dressed gentleman looks a bit miffed at probably missing out on the chance for a tip.

Where does she get her energy from, and can I have some? I think as we head into reception to check in.

The inside of the building is *really* fancy and boasts at just having had a bit refurbishment. I've never seen or even stayed in somewhere as posh as this. Don't get me wrong, Pink Club is beyond posh, but this is...so captivating and I'm getting to stay here. I can AFFORD to stay in nice hotels like this. Oh, I want to soak up this moment and never let it go. Nana and Grampy would be so proud of me!

"I'll take the bags up with Rose here, who is kindly going to show us the room we will be sleeping in. Don't look so worried; I got us two singles, ok?" Penny says, winking at me, which earns us both a quizzical look from Rose. "Go and relax in the bar; we'll order lunch shortly."

I head off in search of the bar, which doesn't take me long to locate as it's where most of the hub of activity is now happening with it being lunchtime.

"What about Binks?" I call out, feeling bad for having forgotten my furry compadre a second time today.

"Max is cat-sitting. Don't worry; all is in hand. Now go—behave and relax."

Yeah, right—relax! Fat chance after the episode with

the hot prawns and burnt breasts episode!

Upon entering the bar, a few people glance up at my presence before a smartly-dressed man indicates to me that I should have waited by the stand at the door to be seated.

"I'm ever so sorry!" I exclaim, feeling dead embarrassed at my clumsiness once again.

"Not to worry. Table for one or two?"

"Two please; my friend will be along any minute."

I'm seated next to a lovely window where I can see people and traffic going by. The furniture is dark wood and amber tones.

"Would you like to order a drink while you wait for your friend?"

"Here she is now," I say, indicating to Penny with a slight wave of where I am. She bounds over happily with a big smile on her face. "Do you have Vanilla Diet Coke by any chance?" I ask the waiter on the off chance.

"Afraid not, but I can recommend a Diet Coke float if you'd like."

"Yes, lovely—thank you."

"It is no trouble. And for you, miss?"

"I'll have a beer, thanks."

Just then, my mobile rings, and I notice it's my mum's number. Looking up, I can also visually see my mum standing in the doorway to the bar, waving animatedly. I had texted her to let her know where I'd be staying, but her unannounced presence has definitely set my heart racing.

Shit!

~ Chapter 20 ~

"Hi, Mum," I greet, standing and walking over to her.

She envelopes me into a big hug, and it feels so good to be in her arms again. I hadn't realised until this very moment just how much I'd missed cuddles with my mum.

"Darla, I'm going to sit at the bar to give you and your mum time to catch up," Penny says, beating a hasty retreat.

"Who's your friend?" my mum asks, looking curiously at me as we head back to the table. Mum is now sitting in place of where Penny was.

"Mum, I —"

"Oh, hello madam. I see your friend is now at the bar. Everything ok?" the waiter asks.

"Yes, thank you. Lunch is on me today, Mum, so please pick anything you want."

"How very gallant of you. You haven't won the

lottery, have you?" Mum jokes, an excited gleam crossing her gaze as she picks up the menu.

You could say that! I think, cringing inwardly about how once the cat is out of the bag, this could turn disaster out.

"Mum...I have to talk to you about something. It's my new job."

"Is everything ok, sweetheart? You've gone deathly pale," my mum says, and I admit my head begins to feel a bit woolly.

"I'm good. Here. I need you to read over this and sign it please. It's an NDA, and I won't be allowed to discuss anything further until you do."

Mum gingerly takes the form from me and begins to scan it. "Err, waiter, yes...sorry, can you hurry up with that wine, please?" she mumbles, clicking her fingers and looking very flustered indeed.

Penny, having noticed my outward discomfort, indicates to me that she's heading over with her beer.

"Hi, you must be Darla's mum. I'm Penny, her chaperone while we are here; pleasure to meet you. Darla has said so much about you. If you have any questions about the NDA, please let me know. It's just a formality, but I'm sure you understand, now seeing where your daughter works, how essential this document being signed is."

Mum just gives Penny a blank expression. Penny then looks at me, indicating with her eyes and nod of her head for me to stand up so she can take over. I take the hint and walk out to locate the bathroom. By the time I return, Penny and Mum are smiling and chatting happily together.

Relief!

"My, my, look at you two becoming fast friends."

"Yes. I've explained all to your lovely mum, who's signed the papers. Actually, I'd best go and scan these to our boss. Darla, enjoy the day with your mum. I'll be in the room if you need me." With that, Penny excuses herself, and the earlier shock and confused look of my mother's has been replaced with one of pride and awe.

"My baby girl's hit the big time. Oh, Darla, I'm so proud of you," Mum says, tears lining her eyes.

I stand to give her a hug before sitting back down. The waiter is heading over ready to take our order for lunch.

"How long are you in Edinburgh?"

"Just today and tomorrow."

"Make sure you book a proper holiday to come and visit me next time, though, ok?"

"I will; I promise." I drink the last few dregs of my latte that I've enjoyed at the end of our lunch together.

"I'll wait outside while you settle the bill. Is it ok for you to do a bit of shopping with me? I thought I could show you around some of my favourite parts of this amazing city."

"I'd love that; yes, of course. Let me send a quick message to Penny and I'll be right out."

Mum half-smiles awkwardly at the seeming insaneness of this situation. I mean, I'm now needing it 'okayed' by Penny to spend time with my mum—and this is BEFORE I've been outed.

Having it deemed safe enough for me to be out with it being just Mum, I feel myself instantly start to relax. This will be my last public outing on my own before my name is out there for anyone who cares enough about Pink Club to want to know such information.

I'm taken on a tour around the 'old town' which is simply fascinating. We get a tour of the castle where we learn all about Robert Bruce and how he came to be such a legend. All I can think now when his name pops up is of naked Scotsmen on the battlefield. Who knew the sight of charging naked Scottish men could be such a great weapon? Perhaps it was the sight of their *weapons* attached to their persons that had the Brits running scared.

We finish the day with afternoon tea back at the Bruntsfield before Mum makes her excuses to leave. Roger, her lodger, will apparently be concerned about her whereabouts, which I've come to learn over the years is classic 'Mum' speak that really translates to Mum's new toy boy and she wants to go because she is missing him or wants to make sure he hasn't run away with some younger Scottish lass.

"Shall I come to yours tomorrow?"

"Yes, ok, let's meet at mine and then go for the rest of the tour and some shopping," Mum says, giving me a big hug again.

I wish we had more time together. My life's about to change irrevocably, and God knows when we will next get to share such private Mum and daughter moments like these without some pap somewhere popping up from a hedge, or a 'fan' wanting to badger me for an autograph. Yes, things were definitely going to change indeed.

I see Mum dab at her eyes just as she ducks out of the bar.

~ CHAPTER 21 ~

"Hey, Darla, how did things go with your mum?" Penny inquires, as I enter our room for the night. It's very fancy with two single beds, a TV, paintings on the walls, a desk and chair, bathroom with a decent sized bathtub and a small, terraced balcony outdoor area for smokers.

"It's been a really lovely day. My mum seems... different somehow; calmer."

"Glad to hear today went well. Have you made plans for tomorrow?"

"I'm going to see the new house and the lodger, Roger."

"My, you're a poet and you didn't know it." We fall about laughing at Penny's sentiment.

"What have you been up to today?" I ask, hoping Penny hadn't spent the hours stuck in here.

"I went for a walk around the old town and checked

out the new town, but it's the old part of Edinburgh that's my favourite. Look, I bought my hubby a kilt key ring." Penny proudly holds out a red kilt key ring that says, 'I love Edinburgh' on it.

"What else did you do?"

"Walked up Arthur's seat. It's a very steep hill. I didn't climb the whole way up, but boy it's a good workout for the lungs and legs."

"I'm glad you were on your own then. That definitely does not sound like my cup of tea."

"Speaking of which, can we go down to dinner now? I'm famished," Penny says, rubbing her tummy, which appears to growl in agreement.

A mobile phone rings, making Penny roll her eyes. She checks to see who it is, and groans, mentioning something like 'so hungry.' "Hey, Max, how's tricks?" I notice that Penny's face, although answering the phone in good spirits, has suddenly dropped and she has a look of shock across it.

"Oh my God, what's happened?" I mouth to her.

"You want me to...to turn on the TV? Ok, sure, the news...one sec...there we go." Penny drops her mobile, which bounces along the floor before she scrambles for it.

I sink onto the bed, for there in front of us is one Stella Almasi in HANDCUFFS being carted out of her London home by police, who appear to be carrying boxes of what I'm guessing may be incriminating evidence of some description. The sound is down, so there are only the subtitles available. Reaching for the remote, I turn it up so we can hear it. Penny's voice, whom I'm no longer focusing on, carries on speaking to Max in the distance.

Yes, Stella Almasi, who you can see behind me here being escorted away by police, is believed to have been embezzling money from charity events held at her notorious nightclub PINK CLUB.

"Right, bit of a FUBAR situation going on as you can see. Max said there is no worry for us to rush back, which is a relief, but it means our position here is precarious, because if Stella reveals your identity, it could easily be leaked to the press, and then...well, prematurely, your life will change."

I let what Penny says to me try to sink in, but I can't think straight. I've potentially been working for a company who steals money from charity—charity aimed at helping raise money for the poor and underprivileged...people like my mum and me.

Marie Adams appears on screen and my head snaps up to see what and why the bitch is being given airtime. "It's dreadful, absolutely scandalous what's happened. Stella and I were, of course, great friends. It's with thanks to Stella that I have such an amazing client base at my dance school, *Busy Bee's*. Never in my wildest dreams would I imagine she'd be capable of such a crime. Those poor families and the children!"

EURGH! LYING BITCH! I think, unable to hear her drawl on any longer, switching the TV off.

"Darla, do you understand what this means?"

My mobile rings and I see it's Eva. "Hey, Eva. Yeah, we have just seen the news. What happened?"

Eva explains how she'd been called to Stella's apartment to get someone into fix a leak in her lounge, which was dropping water onto a very expensive bureau. As it was lifted by two male staff members, one of the legs gave way and a whole ream of papers, files and USB sticks came sprawling out across the floor. Thankfully, Stella hadn't been home at this precise moment in time, so on picking everything up, Eva said it became apparent very quickly what everything was. She had no choice but to call Joshua, who immediately instructed her to call the police. By the time Stella did return, police were all over her London apartment, helping themselves to reams of evidence.

"Now, I don't want you to worry about your job or role within Pink Club. Joshua and Mimi's lawyers are in conversations with Stella's legal team as we speak. They're confident that with everything that's recently come to light, a resolution shall be reached very soon."

"Right...sure, ok. I guess I'll just wait to hear from you then?"

"Keep your mobile close by."

The conversation ends and I take a moment to sit and let everything soak in.

"Come on; let's get a nice bottle of wine and a steak!" Penny says, breaking my reverie, helping my mind to switch from FUBAR to food.

Walking into the restaurant of the hotel, I take in how beautiful the space is. There are pillars that have been decorated with mirrors on all sides, and large round tables adorned with crisp white tablecloths fill the space, which is a hub of activity. A smartly-dressed waitress greets us and shows us to a quieter area tucked away among other smaller tables. Great displays of flowers make up table centres, and the ambience of the room helps to take the edge off my earlier anxiety about this latest drama with Pink Club.

~ Chapter 22 ~

Having stuffed ourselves on steak and chips, followed shortly after by a very gluttonous chocolate-orange fudge cake alongside copious amounts of wine—more than satiated and merry now—Penny and I decide it's time to get our heads down for the night.

I fall into yet a more restless slumber. Dreams of Joshua and dancing plague my subconscious as I'm jettisoned back to that night—our bodies so close, making my heart race with wanton lust—yet him un-knowing of who I really am. I want to pull away from him on the dance floor, but it appears we are tethered together at the wrist. I struggle to pull free, but he pulls me close, trying to lift my mask up which will reveal my identity. With my free hand, I go to slap him hard, which is when I am rudely awoken by Penny, who has just as rudely been slapped by me!

I feel 'mortification' would be an understatement

here to describe how embarrassed I feel at having just slapped my friendly bodyguard around the face. Penny said I'd been yelling and thrashing about in a nightmare.

"Honestly, I'm fine; please don't worry about it," Penny assures me, icing a big welt on her face where my handprint is currently showing itself in its entire ugly five-digit imprint on her swollen cheek.

Mum is calling me, so I tentatively answer while still looking at Penny through my very sorry eyes.

"Hi, darling. I've booked us tickets to see *Mary Kings Close,* and for tonight I thought we could all go for a ghost tour through Greyfriars cemetery."

"Err—great, yes, we would love to go on those tours with you."

Penny's eyes become wide as I say this, as she points to her cheek before holding a hand up, shrugging.

"What's that, Penny? You're still feeling sick? Oh, that's no good. You stay here and I'll go with Mum. Sorry, Mum, looks like Penny is out for this one."

"That's ok. I'll bring Roger along. Right, I'd best finish getting ready. See you soon, my little starlet."

So it begins! I think while inwardly groaning to my mother's *'little starlet'* comment.

"You'll be fine without me today; no one knows who you are for now. It's better I'm not seen with this great big welt for now. It will go down in a few hours, but you need to spend time with your mum," Penny says. I feel she is trying to reassure me that everything about the slap is fine, but I still feel tremendously guilty.

Once freshened up and indeed glad to see that a lot

of the redness has gone down on Penny's face, we synchronise our watches and arrange two other rendezvous points in case there are any FUBAR situations. Phone fully charged, I pop it in my handbag before heading out to meet Mum, who's already eagerly texted me to say she is now down in reception waiting for me... with Roger.

"Are you sure you'll be ok by yourself? I still feel bad."

"Don't be silly! The hotel has Webclix (a very popular TV streaming service), so with that and room service, I am all good," Penny says, grinning snugly while taking up a relaxed position on her bed.

I exit the room feeling marginally better at seeing Penny looking relaxed and quite happy with her decision to stay behind.

Entering reception, I see Mum and Roger with arms linked, but as Mum turns to see me, she quickly snatches her hand away from him.

A-ha! I knew it! Toy boy! I think, while grinning smugly to myself.

Roger has the physique of a builder and practically dwarfs Mum. His tight white shirt and denim jeans shout at his very tango orange face, and atop his head is a mop of dirty blonde hair and very expensive-looking sunglasses.

"Hey, you must be Darla. It's lovely to meet you," Roger—of about my own age—says. He shakes my hand and gives me a small kiss on the cheek, which I notice makes my mother squirm a little.

Mum comes up to give me a hug and a kiss to which she whispers into my ear, *"Don't worry. I haven't told Roger anything about your new job."* Before she pulls away, she gives me a little wink, which makes my stomach lurch. My mother being in possession of such delicate information makes me realise the spring gala and revealing of my true identity really can't come soon enough.

Before we set off, I notice Roger and Mum giving each other odd glances, so sighing and raising my eyes to Heaven, I simply re-link their arms while exclaiming, "Come on, you two. Honestly, Mum, lodger? Really?" Both get a look of relief across their face as we step out of the hotel.

"I never could keep anything from you, my little star —"

The look I give Mum tells her mid-sentence to kindly rein the new turn of phrase in immediately, to which she obliges.

Feeling like a third wheel, as Mum and Roger coo all over one another, gaining ominous glances from the general public, I'm very thankful that come night-time, Mum's too scared to go through to Greyfriars cemetery, so the pair of them are left behind while I sally forth with the tour group.

I've linked up with a very nice young woman named Kate, whose friend is also too scared to come through this part of the tour. To help distract ourselves from all the scary open tombs and terrible ghastly tales of grave robbers the guide is filling us with, we chat about mundane everyday things. It is when we get to the McKenzie poltergeist mausoleum that the fear really sets in.

We all squash inside the pitch-black space where you can smell the fear rolling off everyone in waves. All of a sudden, a man unseen before jumps out in horrific mask, making a scary sound at the entrance and eliciting screams from everyone, and then laughter. Kate and I had been holding onto one another for grim death before this and I think we may have bruised each other's ribs.

On exiting the cemetery, I see that Mum, Roger and Kate's friend have pale scared looks about them, as they want to know what made everyone scream so loudly. Kate and I had plotted already to tell them there were scenes of people being thrown about and choked by this infamous McKenzie poltergeist, until we can hold the straight faces no more and spill the beans of what actually happened.

Parting ways with Kate and her friend at the entrance to the cemetery, Mum, Roger and I begin the walk back to the hotel. It's late, and as much as I'd love to go for a coffee at Mum's house, I know I need to catch up on sleep. Penny and I have a very early start tomorrow.

Reaching the entrance of the hotel, Roger says goodbye, opting, it seems, to stay outside, giving Mum and I a bit of privacy.

"It's a shame you couldn't see my house this time. Goodness knows when we will next see each other like this with you being all famous now," Mum says, fidgeting with the collar of my coat.

"You will be coming to see me next time. Now you have *clearance* to know more, which means you can stay with my anytime."

My mum's face instantly brightens on hearing this before she holds onto me in a vice-like grip and whispers, *"I'm so proud of you, Darla. Your nana and grampy would be too. Very well-done, sweetie. I love you!'*

Struggling to remain composed, I hug Mum back just as tightly, also reflecting how proud I am of her for getting her life together and how well she's doing here in Scotland. We make a pact to remain in regular contact before parting ways. I begin what feels like the longest walk of my life back to mine and Penny's room.

~ Chapter 23~

Joshua shakes hands with his solicitors once all the paperwork has been organised and documents signed, meaning he and Mimi now have full rights to ownership of Pink Club and all of its assets. Joshua and Mimi decided not to press charges over the theft of Pink Club's true ownership; they were just relieved to have everything the way it was always meant to be.

Stella is to face a lengthy suspended prison sentence (undoubtedly squared away by her extremely wealthy husband), and all the monies stolen were immediately paid to the charities. An anonymous donor had come forward, but everyone knows this was more than likely Stella's husband. The next news story would be of Stella's very public and humiliating divorce from the billionaire yacht salesman.

"It's been a pleasure working with you and Mimi, Mr. Glass. We wish you every success for the future, moving forward with Pink Club," the head of their legal team says as everyone shakes hands. Then they are shown out by members of Max's security team.

Once alone, Joshua, Mimi and Eva come together for a big group hug, and there are many tears of happiness shed here this afternoon.

"I will see to it that an email goes out, informing everyone of an update. Are we still running the meeting tomorrow with Darla and Co.? Her return from Scotland with Penny will be early, so I can set something up around lunch time," Eva says fashionably, reverting back to business in her unique professional way.

"That would be great; thank you for everything, Eva," Mimi replies, confirming everything and giving her another hug.

"Come on now, this is too much. You'll crinkle my designer suit!"

Eva leaves Joshua's office and he and Mimi hug once more before making arrangements to go home. Both their phones have been blowing up with calls and texts from their parents. It appears much explaining needs doing.

"Mum's so going to lose her shit when we tell her about you and Stella and how she stole Pink Club from us," Mimi says, jesting with her brother.

"As I imagine so will Dad. Shall we pick out plots now?"

"I'll get the chalk for our body outlines," Mimi laughs. Then she realises this actually happened for her.

The moment passes quickly and then an awkward atmosphere returns between the twins.

Having just collected our luggage from the carousel (without incident this time) at Gatwick airport on our return to London, we head to meet Max at arrivals, ready to head straight to Pink Club for a big meeting. During the previous night, there were no more steamy dreams of Joshua, and I'm relieved to see there isn't even the smidgen of a bruise on Penny's face after my face slapping faux pas.

"Darla, Penny," Max greets as we approach him.

Suitcases away, and with both of us safely in the car, Max sets off towards Pink Club. I'm in the back by myself, and from a standpoint of professionalism, it's better that Penny is in the front with Max. Her earlier and more lighthearted and friendlier approach to bodyguarding evaporates, as she's now all brusque and business like again. Oddly, I find the switch in her demeanour comforting. I hear Penny and Max catching up, and Max is giving Penny security updates —but again, this kind of jargon is all over my head.

Flicking open my phone, I go to busy myself with an online game but see I have a new email from the address I set up for Vera. It reads:

Dear Darla,

I hope you are well. Sorry I haven't emailed yet—we've had so much business it's been great! Let me know when you're next thinking of coming to Angel Cake so I can make sure I have the time off for a proper catch up.

Lots of love, your faithful friend always,
Vera.

Relaxing in the back of the car, smiling that my friend has been in touch and remembering that she already knows my *big secret,* I wonder how, in the near future, I will ever be allowed or able to just *'meet for coffee'* with my friends—Dante and Sarah included.

My thoughts begin to run away with me, but fortunately it's not long until we turn into Pink Club's underground car park. Press is absolutely everywhere; it's complete and utter chaos.

"Damion, get Brad to come down here and cordon off the press, NOW!" Max yells into a radio, making me jump at having never seen this usually calm and well put together man get authoritatively angry.

Note to self: don't piss Max off—ever!

A short while later, some men and a woman, wearing security business attire, burst out of the doors of the underground lift to help ferry press, who have bled onto the property and sauntered to the underground car park. Within moments, the press—realising they have been rumbled—leave. A huge shutter comes down, officially closing off the car park from anyone else including guests, members and staff until police and extra security can get a better handle of the situation.

"Darla, you okay?" a concerned Penny asks, turning in her seat to look at me.

"Yeah, I think so."

"It's only going to get worse from here on out—especially when your identity is revealed. We'd best sort out some personal safety training for you as soon as possible," Max states, which makes my heart race.

Only going to get worse?! Max's sentiments make me worry...a lot.

"Come on, we had best get you inside," Penny says, ushering me into the lift after we've exited the car, our luggage left in the boot.

Realising I'm about to see Joshua again makes butterflies go mad in my stomach. We've had such awkward chemistry between us—especially on the dance floor at *Lucifer's Haven*—but...he still doesn't know that was me. Rejecting his offer for an overnight stay at his apartment I saw wounded him, but that was back when Stella was still head honcho here. What does this mean for any type of relationship moving forward? No—I must keep my head on straight. The chemistry could all be one-sided and in my head. Maybe I'm still grieving the loss of my former crush, Dante?

My thoughts continue to plague me until I reach the conference room. Eva, Octavia, Midnight, Medley, Digit, Psyche, Mixer and Siren are inside, but no Joshua or Mimi. My earlier trepidation at getting to see him again bursts as I go to take a seat at the big black glass table.

Phew! At least not having Joshua here will make things less complicated for now. Oh, shut up, woman; stop lying to yourself! My rational and irrational minds argue before the meeting commences.

"Good morning, everyone. Darla, I hope you're

feeling refreshed after your short break in Scotland," Eva says, opening up the meeting.

"Yes, thank you."

"Glad to hear it. I know you all have busy schedules with dance rehearsals, so I won't take up too much of your time. As you've undoubtedly seen on the news, Stella is now no longer a part of Pink Club's family —"

"Ding dong, the bitch is gone!" Digit cries, interrupting, which earns a stern look from Eva.

"I am very well aware of the fact Mrs. Almasi has gone, Digit; as are we all. Now please—no more interruptions. The spring gala WILL still be going ahead, thanks to Mohammad Almasi putting things right with the charities and paying them the monies owed, as well as several other *debts* belonging to Stella being paid off. Pink Club's record has now been cleared, and all illegal activity and blame for this lie squarely with Stella, so we needn't worry moving forward."

There is a brief pause before Eva continues. "Now... Joshua and Mimi are not here, as I'm sure you can all see, which is because there was a bit of an *incident* that thankfully we've kept away from the press. I can't say anything further on this at the moment, but they are both fine. For the foreseeable future, however, they will be residing in Tuscany with their parents, Pandora and James, until they deem it safe and appropriate to return."

It feel as if all the air has been sucked out of the room and someone has just poured concrete inside.

"Does this mean they will both miss the spring gala?"

Octavia asks with the same shocked expression across her face we are all sharing now.

"Joshua will be coming to make an 'appearance' but won't be staying long. There is much healing to be done with the Glass family, so it's only right we respect their privacy for the time being," Eva answers.

"Now Darla, your identity is still going to be revealed on the night of the spring gala. How are you feeling about everything? We can get an in-house counsellor to help with your adjustment into the world of celebrity."

"I–err...can I just let you know on that one?" I respond, shrinking into the chair, feeling suddenly self-conscious of the fact that everyone is now glancing my way.

"Certainly. I have already taken the liberty to email you all the counsellor's details; it's up to you if you wish to arrange any appointments."

Once everyone's on the same page that it's to be business as usual, we are dismissed, but Eva asks me to stay a while before going to join my dance crew in the studio. "Now Darla, tell me something: are you really ok with everything? All focus will be on you a week from now and your old life. Your private life will never be the same again. Are you sure you feel ready for that?"

"About as ready as I'll ever be. Thanks for the counsellor's details. I'll keep them in mind."

"Make sure that you do. There is one other thing I wanted to discuss with you. Do you have any photographs of you when you were a child? Joshua and Mimi want to do a timeline of your life pre and present

Pink Club. We have a professional photographer from *Hello!* magazine coming to take special stills of you and your crew before the gala. They have agreed to a special deal with us to help make Pink Club's reputation shine amongst so much controversy with Stella's exit."

"I'm...to be in *Hello!* magazine?!" The last part of my sentence comes out sounding strangled as I struggle to contemplate this latest bombshell.

"Yes; they are going to release the article to tie in nicely with your unveiling. Do you have any questions for me before you go for rehearsals?"

"No, I think I'm all up to speed with everything."

"Good, right. You'd best get moving. The clock's ticking and it's just six days now until you become a star."

Hearing the last words Eva has just said injects their significance as if I've just slammed into a brick wall at high speed.

I'm going to be a star! A dancing star! Am I dreaming? Is this even real?!

~ Chapter 24 ~

The days blur together as they fill with continual dance rehearsals and costume fittings. The designer for Pink Club's costumes is a very talented tailor named Marcus O'Neill, a cross-dressing father of two girls and married to the love of his life, Marcella.

I've been banned from seeing my dress at every fitting, needing to be blindfolded as I'm measured and fitted into my performance dress. Marcus prefers to be called by his cross-dressing name while at work, which is Marsha-mellow, so I, of course, oblige him. The preferred shortened version of his name is Marsha.

"Hi Marsha, how goes the dress making?" I say upon entering his magical space full to the brim of weird and wonderful costumes, masks and other disguises.

"Ah, ah, ah! No, it is not time for you to see your dress yet. That was a close call. Had you not alerted me to your presence, it would have spoiled the surprise for you."

"This evening we have the dress rehearsal. Surely I should be getting to grips with my dress up on stage tonight, no?"

"A clever ploy you use there, Miss Pebble, but no—you will wait for the grand unveiling for your big debut tomorrow. It is one, if not *the* best, piece of tailoring I have ever done."

"Ok, ok. Fair enough. I'll wait," I resign, feigning huffiness in my tone, which makes Marsha beam with pride and excitement.

"Now, how have you been getting on with dancing on the stage?" Marsha asks, helping place my blindfold over my face and then giving me his hand to help me step up onto the platform where I'm to be measured yet again for this mystery dress.

"I feel I could literally do the performances with my eyes closed; we have practiced so much."

"This is very good to hear. Ok, hold still. I don't want to stick you with a pin, my dear. Just like before, relax your stomach, breathe out, stand in your natural relaxed pose...and now breathe in and stretch your arms above your head in a ballerina pose. Beautiful. Ok, the last adjustment is done; let me just remove your dress carefully. Ok, you're good to get dressed," Marsha says, whisking my dress away before I have a chance to peek under my blindfold.

The main performing arena has been completely transformed into a forest wonderland. Enormous arrangements of flowers adorn the walls, the stage, tables, chandeliers and practically any and every surface you can imagine to be decorated with floral designs; there are even rented real trees and grass! Eva was not kidding when she said they were going all out this year for a Midsummer Night's themed event. I'm very thankful here that I don't have hay fever or pollen allergies. At least two staff members have had to go off sick due to suffering from it.

"You'd best be off. Octavia has pinged me a few messages asking how much longer you're likely to be, but I've just let her know you'll be back to rehearsals promptly. Honestly, we weren't even fifteen minutes today!" Marsha tells me, throwing his hands above his head before making wafting motions at me to hurry out of the door.

"See you tomorrow for the great unveiling!" I say in a sing-song voice as I exit out of the costume department.

Taking all the back passages that I've fast become accustomed to now to stay out of sight of everyone, I take one of the lifts to the floor where the dance studio is situated. While inside, my mind flits for a moment back to the time when I was stuck in the lift with Joshua, his body so close to mine, his scent...

The lift doors open, and as I step out, music can be clearly heard blasting from the dance studio just up ahead.

"There she is, our star of the show," Octavia calls out, beaming at me. "It's our very last day to practice before the big night. How are you feeling?" Octavia walks over to me and rests her hands on my shoulders, looking me squarely in the eyes.

"I'm ok. Anxious, but in a good way, you know?"

"It's good to be nervous; it means your ego will not be clouding your judgement tomorrow night," Midnight says in his rich buttery Caribbean accent.

Yeah, not like Bella's used to. Man, the woman was such a pain in the ass," Siren adds. I can't help but notice a bitter tone to his voice.

"Lest we all forget what happened to our friend Fixer," Medley reminds us sorrowfully.

"Ok, ok, everyone, settle down. I appreciate everyone is still raw about Fixer, but let's not spoil the festivities to come by harbouring grudges. Bella is dead. She paid the ultimate price for her bad choices."

"Yeah, just soon enough after she destroyed a man's life," Mixer grumbles, interrupting Octavia, which earns him a death stare.

"Come on guys, V is right; let's not spoil the festivities with bad tempers and frayed nerves. We need to shine and give our best performances up there tomorrow night. We need to do it for Mimi more so than Joshua with everything the poor woman's been through, so please, let's calm the heat and have a great night."

My dance crew make nodding motions with their heads and silent murmurs beneath their breath as we all get in position for the rest of the day's rehearsals.

By the time I get home, I'm completely shattered. Rehearsals were massively intense and held all throughout the day, but as a reward, we have all been given the day off tomorrow and only need to go into Pink Club two hours before we go on stage. We've been given strict instructions to hunker down and rest. Amanda is coming over to give me a full body 'm.o.t' in the morning, so with this in mind, I decide to just soak my feet, feed Binks and head to bed.

~ Chapter 25 ~

"Ohh...ahhh, too hard! Too hard!" I yelp as Amanda uses her elbow to help release one of the many knots she's discovered in my back and shoulders today.

"Sorry, Darla. There, has that eased off now?"

"Yeah, phew, that hurt loads."

"I think I've managed to iron out as many of the knots that I can. You've been overworked with your dance rehearsals. I shall be having words with Octavia later." As Amanda says this, I notice a twinge of almost 'motherly sarcasm' to her voice.

There is no disagreement from me over Amanda's observations while doing my sports massage today. Octavia was so hard on all of us yesterday, it's a wonder no one ended up injured. I can only wonder that she isn't just as nervous making everything 'perfect' for tonight's big show. Marie Adams used to get just as tense pre-competition time, but Octavia at least was kinder with her request for us to dance for all those hours. At least when I practiced my aerial skills it gave my feet chance to rest but not my arms, upper body and leg muscles. Amanda is a godsend in that respect; she really is.

"I'd best be heading to my next appointment now. Bye-bye, Binksy Winksy. See you next week, Darla," Amanda says, while packing up before I show her out. The woman is good for sure, but man if she isn't damned nosy!

Once I'm alone with Binks, I decide to order pizza for lunch and veg out watching my favourite TV shows, catch an afternoon nap and then prepare to perform the biggest event in my entire dancing life.

For once, my day seems to pan out the way I'd expected it to. The time is 12:30 p.m., so I head off to my room to get my head down for a power nap before all the mayhem that will surely be ensuing over the next part of the day. By the time I come home again, I will be known (to everyone who cares to know anything about Pink Club) as the woman who is now Bella Fitzroy's replacement, and my identity will be known among high society types and celebrities; heck, even some royalty. The whole concept seems mad to me how quickly my life has changed in such a short time.

*Hey, pretty lady...*Joshua's voice flits through my mind as I jolt awake just forty-five minutes after having fallen into a comfortable slumber. Remnants of a dream forgotten soon fade, and I stretch as I prepare to mentally get ready for tonight. Penny is coming here to pick me up soon, but I still have time to bathe and meditate beforehand.

Running a nice warm bath with sounds of soothing jazz playing through my bathroom light speakers, I climb inside, waiting patiently for the bath to fill so I might relax a while.

The warm water does wonders for all my previous aches and pains. Amanda—having done her best with the short timeframe she had to sort out all my tension spots and knots—had also given me a few sachets of special Epsom bath salts to use, and if nothing else they certainly helped me to relax.

By the time I exit the bath, time is already getting on. The water has cooled quite considerably as I pull myself up and out of the tub. Wrapping a fluffy towel around my body and one atop my head to help dry my hair, I head to my walk-in wardrobe where I pick out jogging bottoms, a T-shirt, hoodie and pair of loose-fitting trainers to wear both there and back.

Once dressed, I look at myself in the mirror one last time as a 100% anonymous free soul, ready as I'll ever be to face what may come with being a celebrity performance artist. Someone knocks on my door and, checking the time, I see it's a bit too early for Penny so I'm wondering who on earth it could be.

A delivery man with a large bouquet of flowers in his hands stands on the other side.

What the —

"Hi there, are you Miss Pebble?"

I nod while opening the door to relieve the man of

the huge bouquet of bright pink roses, who also hands me a small bag—much like the ones you would have a jewellery box placed into.

Tipping the delivery man, I find myself standing in stunned and confused silence as to who this delivery could be from. Just then, the idea occurs to me it may be Joshua, but that wouldn't make any sense.

I see a card attached to the bouquet, which came already set up in beautiful ornate vase. Pulling the card off the top of the holder, I carefully open it to where it says:

Darla,

The very best of luck tonight. We hope you enjoy the flowers. We wanted to get the first bouquet in before any of the guests. Enjoy them and the bling. May it bring you good luck on stage tonight. Sorry we can't be there.

J & M xx

Upon opening the small bag, I see that it is indeed a jewellery box. Opening the very expensive-looking dark blue velvet box, I place a hand to my mouth at the sight in front of me. A gorgeous pink sapphire star pendant hangs off a silver chain, and noticing the jeweller's identity, I have to hold onto the sideboard unbelieving of just how expensive this 'bling' most likely is. Another immediate reminder that I am entering a whole new world of glitz and glam.

Holy guacamole!

~ Chapter 26 ~

My heart pounds away and a small buzzing emanates from inside my ears. I feel shaken all over as my breath comes in brief shallow gasps.

No, not now; not now! I think as panic races like a lit match along every fibre of my being. I call my mum, but the call goes straight to voice mail. I try Sarah next, but again am unable to get through.

Shit!

Binks, noticing something is wrong with me, comes bounding over, meowing before rubbing his body by weaving himself between my feet; the feel of his soft fur against my shins takes only a smidgen off fear's vice-like grip of me.

My body begins to contort and spasm with the lack of oxygen; everything around me becoming blurry. Steadily, I begin to hobble my way to my bedroom, leaning against the wall for support, Binks in hot pursuit.

My head is in an inner battle where I'm being made to feel like a lion is about to eat me, but even knowing this is not true cannot shake the overwhelming sense of fear. Tears run down my face, and as I reach the bathroom and continue onto the shower where—with great difficulty— I manage to finally press the shower on, a blast of freezing cold icy water hits me, literally taking my breath away. But it is as if the intense squeezing pressure of fear suddenly retreats, its fire firmly doused to leave me instead now shivering from the cold, fully clothed and in need of a complete wardrobe change.

Once changed into dry clothes and feeling better composed, I go into the kitchen to make myself a nice mug of relaxing camomile tea. Penny knocks on my door just as I'm downing the last mouthful of tea. While in Scotland, Mum bought me some herbal spray called *saviour salve*—which is especially for anxiety—so I do as instructed on the bottle and spritz two lots of the potent, very floral-flavoured ingredients into my mouth. Can't say whether or not it worked, but time will surely tell. I pop it in my bag as a friendly companion to me for the night ahead.

"Hi, Darla. Are you all set to go?" Penny greets, glancing momentarily at my huge vase of pink roses sitting on my kitchen side.

"About as ready as I'll ever be."

"Nice flowers," she comments with what I sense is an ominous tinge to her voice.

Relax, Nancy Drew. I don't have some unaccounted-for boyfriend!

"They are from Mimi and Joshua. Here, they also bought me this for good luck," I say, proudly showing off my new pink star necklace. On revealing these details, I notice Penny relaxes.

"Wow! That's very generous of them," she says, undoubtedly having noticed the small silver tag that states just what type of a necklace this is.

"Yes, I don't feel I'll ever be taking it off."

"I'd say that would be a very wise move indeed."

Once we enter the car park of my apartment building, I pause a moment to take in the sheer stillness, knowing full well that when my identity is revealed, luxuries like this are more than likely going to become few and far between.

"Is everything ok?" Penny asks, looking at me quizzically.

"Yeah, just—you know—enjoying the peace."

Penny just gives me a knowing look before getting in and starting the car before I go to join her.

Once inside the car, I decide to tell Penny about my most recent panic attack. "Penny, there is something I'd like to talk to you about."

"Sure, go ahead. Oh, wait one sec. Hey, Max," she says, answering her mobile hands-free. "Yes, I have the precious cargo on board. Ah, ok, yes—we shall indeed divert to the Mimi Glass Hotel."

Penny ends the call, and another bout of anxiety rises within my body. Scrambling about in my bag, I eventually clutch my *saviour salve* and spray yet a further two doses into my mouth. I hadn't fully read the instructions but figure it must be a 'use as needed' remedy; after all, it is only herbal. This time, I feel the calming effects almost immediately, and the knot in my stomach begins to loosen.

"Sorry, Darla, you wanted to tell me something?" This is the last thing I hear from Penny before I'm out for the count.

"Darla, can you hear me? SHIT!" Penny exclaims as she parks the car.

"Hi, Max—I need help. I'm at the Mimi Glass Hotel...we're in the car park...Darla has just passed out and I can't rouse her. She sprayed something in her mouth; hang on a moment...ok, I got it. It's called *saviour salve?* The first aid kit from the boot, yes... smelling salts? Ok hang fire." Penny races to the boot and all but rips open the emergency first aid kit bag. Locating the smelling salts, she runs back around to where Darla is slumped in the seat before holding it under her nose.

"Thank fuck for that; she's coming to," Penny says to Max as they end the call after Max tells Penny to expect a first aider to check Darla over at the hotel before he can make his way to collect them.

Holy hell, what the heck is that! I think, jolting awake to see a very scared and also relieved Penny looking at me with some weird bottle of pong in her hand. "You fainted, I think, after taking that *saviour salve*. What on earth is it?"

"It's an herbal remedy for stwess." Oh boy; I can't form words properly.

"Stwess?"

"I mean stwess...you know, narves!"

"*Ohhhh,* stress and nerves, got it. Well, I don't think it entirely agrees with you, so how about I hold onto this for now?"

I simply just give Penny a thumbs up in response as I'm helped out of the car, still feeling super chilled out. We head on into the Mimi Glass Hotel and my it is glam-o-rous! Yes, siry-bob!

~ Chapter 27 ~

Penny takes me to sit in a quiet dimly lit bar area of the hotel not too far from the entrance. "Here is the plan. As predicted, it's pandemonium at Pink Club, so Max is coming with a team to collect us from here. I'd offer you a tipple of Dutch courage, but I think you've had more than enough of that for one night. Here, drink this coffee. Max assures it will help reverse the effects of the herbal spray."

I take my very strong black-looking coffee off Penny and, realising there isn't really a choice, begin to sip the intense dark, bitter caffeinated drink. "God, that's awful!" I exclaim, struggling to knock it back. But Max was not wrong; I'm soon back with all my faculties in working order—cognition fully switched back on.

"No, what was awful was the terrible scare you gave me back in the car park. Promise me to always read labels of things now—including homeopathic remedies. *Saviour salve* states this is a tincture for insomnia and doses should be spaced out eight hours apart. So, what was it you wanted to speak to me about?" Penny says, reminding me that I'd just been about to confide in her of my earlier panic attack.

"I don't remember, so it can't have been that important."

"You sure? It seemed pretty urgent."

"I need the toilet, so perhaps that was it...excuse me," I say, standing to locate a bathroom.

"Down there on the right," Penny tells me, as if reading my mind.

On entering the bathroom, which is indeed super lavish—there is even a baby pink chaise long in here for crying out loud, a chaise!—I splash some cool water onto my face and collect my thoughts. A few women come and go during this time, giving me wary glances. Once I've relieved myself, I head out to re-join Penny.

Max is with Penny and two other gentlemen. Apart from Max, who's dressed in a suit, the two men and Penny are in smart casual relaxed attire; they could pass for tourists.

"Darla, how are you feeling now?" Max asks, walking up to me to shine a pencil light in each of my eyes, making me squint.

"Much better, thank you."

"Good. I think in the future it's better if —"

"I know, I know—read labels properly. Honestly, I was not prepared for how potent an herbal mouth spray could be."

"I've confiscated it for now," Penny interjects assuredly to Max, whose face now softens to me.

"Right, well seeing as all is ok here now, let's head on into Pink Club. But before we do, you two will need to get dressed into these," Max says, holding out two bags of neatly folded uniforms inside.

We are to dress the same as catering staff—genius!

"This is certainly a first for me," Penny says, helping me to zip up the back of my neat little black waistcoat.

"I think we both look rather fetching," I comment, as Penny and I take in our costumes in the mirror. Penny had locked the main bathroom door to which there was now a very angry person banging on the opposite side.

As we exit, Penny makes an apology to a very red-faced, alcohol-inebriated woman on the other side, whose only concern seems to be heading to a cubicle to throw up into. Making our way back to the bar, I giggle slightly to see now Max, as well as the other two men with him, have also dressed as catering staff. This feels beyond bonkers!

The car of choice to head over to Pink Club is a little yellow five-seater run-around. I find myself well and truly squashed between two brutish security guys. Penny sits up front with Max and at least has her own foot space and elbow room. My knees may as well be up around my ears. The guys hold onto the loops up on the roof of the car (yes that's how old this rickety thing is; not even proper handles) to at least try to move away from me so I can breathe, but my hips and shoulders are well and truly wedged between them.

"Where are we going?" I ask Penny, realising we have diverted away from the normal route to Pink Club's underground car park.

"As we are posing as kitchen staff, we get the luxury of using the far less busy staff entrance and exit!" she shouts above the sound of the noisy engine and cranky gears that Max is presently battling with.

"Bloody decrepit piece of junk," Max grumbles, effing and blinding about the sheer state of this low-key form of transport that was meant to detract from gaining any attention.

We zoom loudly past press, police, stars and celebrities in all their finery just as the exhaust backfires with a gunshot sound making people duck down, shout and yell with surprise.

So much for not drawing attention.

Turning into a side road a considerable distance away from the massive hoard of people now outside Pink Club, it is here that Max announces we are to head on to the side entrance on foot, which is apparently only a ten-minute walk away. He brings the car to a stop, as it is now squealing and smoking. As we exit, I feel as If I'm a cork popping off a champagne bottle when the man on my left leaves first giving me space to breathe and move as I wiggle on out of the car myself.

Walking a quick pace, it actually only takes five minutes for us to reach the side entrance to Pink Club. It's so well hidden out of sight you'd never know it was here.

"Penny, take Darla straight down to costume. I've got

to catch up with my team," Max orders, rushing away with the two men as Penny and me hot foot it to Marshamellow's costume department.

"Knock-knock, here she is, the star of the show," Penny calls out, knocking on Marsha's door before poking her head around announcing my presence.

"Good Lord, Darla...what is with the outfits?"

"Don't ask. So, can I see my dress now?"

"All in good time, of which we don't have much. Penny, you may leave us now please."

"Oh sure. I'll let Eva know Darla is here," Penny says, leaving Marsha to help me get ready.

~ Chapter 28 ~

"Ok young lady, now last blindfold, I promise, and then your big reveal, ok?" Marsha is wearing a pair of smart black trousers today and a long-sleeved white shirt with ruffles on the front.

I smile, indulging Marsha with his request. He has such a lovely fatherly manner about him, and briefly I'm reminded of the hole in my heart at never getting the chance to know my own father. But it's easy to squash, as what I don't know can't hurt me…right?

As my dress is put on the last time before I see it myself for the first time, it sort of feels different, slightly heavier, and…is it damp?! There's a very strong floral scent that fills my nostrils, and once Marsha announces the dress is on successfully, he removes my blindfold and walks me off the dress fitting platform to a curtain that I'm sure wasn't here before. As he pulls on a rope to open the curtain, I'm blown away to see in front of me is Joshua, Mimi, my entire dance crew, Octavia, Eva, and my MUM and Roger all here, clapping and cheering as I step forward.

A floor-length mirror is off to one side covered with a draped piece of material. Marsha whips this off, and it is here I take in the full extent of my dress.

It is beautiful. The bodice is full of real life rose blossoms. Marsha informs me that there is an organic skin friendly panel at the front which will keep all the flowers in place while I'm dancing; the skirt is a real fairy styled design that gives me a really impish look.

"Oh, my God, guys, what are you all doing here?" I say as my hands go to my mouth with utter shock and amazement.

"I'm so proud of you, darling," Mum says, giving me a sort of sideways hug as to not squish any of the flowers.

"Mimi and I were not meant to be here, but we decided as you've done such a great job with helping to save Pink Club's reputation—first with the New Year's Eve Bash and now the spring gala—we just wanted to make tonight very special, as it's not only your unveiling but also Mimi's first big appearance since she went missing."

"Thank you so much, Joshua. I don't know what else to say. I'm speechless!"

Midnight begins to sing, "For she's a jolly good fellow," to which everyone follows suit.

By the time the singing and merriment have calmed, focus pours back to the space, as it's time for Mum and Roger to take their seats with Joshua and Mimi, and for me and the guys to get ready before we take up our places on the stage.

"Best of luck, sweetheart; you go knock 'em dead," Mum says, her face practically beaming with pride while toy-boy Roger is trailing fast behind her.

That explains why Mum wasn't answering my calls earlier, mid-panic attack.

Joshua gives me a lustful glance as he looks me up and down, a smile creeping across his ruggedly handsome face before exiting the costume room after Mimi, which makes my heart definitely do flip-flops.

Oh, boy; I'm in trouble!

From here on out everything moves with lighting speed giving me no time to dwell on my nerves. My hair is whipped up into a fantastical shape by the hair and make-up artist on duty, who's come to sort this all out for me. She adds flowers and even twigs to the design, and by the time she's finished spraying my hair art with spray, I'm sure I've consumed half a bottle of the stuff. I'm then blitzed to within an inch of my life with body glitter spray, facial glitter and sparkly eye shadow and lipstick. Memories of *Lucifer's Haven* 'toxic box' as I used to call it, where we'd all prepare to dance, float to my mind as false eyelashes are attached to my already long ones as I'll be wearing a fairy mask until my unveiling. Me and the make-up artist double check to make sure the lashes are not going to end up all wonky. A special facial glue is put on to keep my mask in place, but when I pull it off my face, it won't do any skin damage or hurt, I'm assured. The guys wear an array of sequin loose-fitting trousers and not much else—just matching top hats atop their heads.

Once fully dressed and ready to perform, we make our way through the hidden channels down to the main performing area. No one speaks; there is just the hint of excitable buzzing energy between us all.

The stage cannot go all the way down to basement level, as it will squash all the heavy blooms attached to it, so the lights are to be dimmed upon our arrival while we set up inside the main staging area until we take up our positions and the platform can be raised to its usual height of forty feet.

Everyone in the audience is now seated inside; outside, all is still. Staff open the heavy doors, and we are guided by an usher to the stage with a small torch. It's so quiet you can hear a pin drop, which enables goosebumps to erupt all over my body. Even though I can hardly see in front of me, I feel the many pairs of eyes focusing on us.

"Ok, Darla, someone is going to introduce your act, then the lights will come up and you can begin your first dance act," the usher says, their voice barely above a whisper but so only I can hear them.

It's challenging to navigate onto the platform. I'm being careful not to squash or damage any of the massive blooms now surrounding and hanging off the stage. Midnight keeps me close to him, which helps as the others find their way. Once we are in place, he speaks into his mic that we are ready.

The stage is then silently raised, and I begin to clearly

hear excited murmurs from the audience around us. My eyes have adjusted ever so slightly to the darkness, and I can see it's certainly sold out. My heart quickens its pace, so I focus in on my breathing using pre-performance skills that I used when dancing for *Busy Bee's*. In the back of my mind I'm praying that I don't have a panic attack, so I take my thoughts to being at home relaxing on the sofa, Binks happily purring away in my lap. Joshua then invades my thoughts, and as my eyes snap open, the lights come up and the music starts.

Shit! I must have completely missed the introduction!

We begin our routine without a hitch. Midnight maintains eye contact to help keep me focused, and throughout all my twists and turns, the guys are right where I need them when I need them. Feeling myself relax, I start to look out and take in the sight around me. Everyone's come out in their finery and not a camera flash in sight (as, of course, no one is allowed any recording equipment of any kind inside). My heart leaps into my mouth as I do my first lift of the evening with Midnight, but we pull it off in true professional style. Marsha left two panels down the side of my dress so that none of my real flower bodice would get squished.

As I land from the first lift, I feel an odd vibration throughout the stage and I'm not sure if this has happened before but shrug it off—it must be the added weight from all the flowers, nothing to worry about.

Finishing the dance, eruptions of applause and feet stamping ensue. The crowd begins to chant one word: *Reveal, reveal, reveal, reveal!*

Joshua's voice comes through the speakers at this moment, stilling the crowd. I can't see below the stage where he may be, so I turn to look at the big projection screen that I see the guys are now watching.

Be still my beating heart...

~ Chapter 29 ~

"Ladies and gentleman, it gives me great pleasure to introduce you all to our brand-new star performer here at Pink Club..."—*Oh, my God, here we go!*—"...Our very own...Cosmic Storm!"

What?!

"Cosmic, will you please reveal your face for everyone?" Joshua says, winking into the camera.

My hands are now shaking uncontrollably, which Siren has spotted, so he comes to help me with the ribbon at the back, which is also clipped to my hair to hold my mask in place.

Thoughts of *'blow job girl'* flit through my mind, and I'm suddenly terrified everyone will recognise me and remember this tabloid story—perhaps begin to chant it —but it's too late to stop it now.

My mask is off; cooler air reaches my face as I feel perspiration start to evaporate. The crowd starts cheering and applauding, giving me a standing ovation. It's hard to try to recognise any of the faces, but I'm sure I see Angelina and Madonna somewhere in the mix.

"As you all know, my sister Mimi's now *non-murder* event has been revealed, as has her safe return for which me, our parents and family are all truly thankful for. But sadly, this cannot be said for Milagros Morena's family. Her parents are here with us tonight, but I shan't point them out, as they requested we respect their privacy this evening. Mimi and I would both like to invite you now to all join us for a minute silence for a poor innocent life taken far too soon."

Everyone falls silent, and tears threaten to spill over from my eyes, but I know this will destroy my make-up, making me look more corpse bride than Midsummer Night's dream, so I hold them in the best I can.

The microphone is now passed to Mimi once our minute silence has passed. She looks done up to the nines but still so frail behind the make-up and all the glam. "Hi, everyone. I would just like to say thank you for all the support over the years for my brother and our parents, family and friends. To lose a child, I can only imagine, is one of—if not the worst—things that can happen to a person in life. But to lose five years believing your child, sister, cousin, niece etc, is dead and then to realise this is not true, but rather have been held captive all of this time...well, I assure you that as much as it was a relief for our parents and my twin brother Joshua; it was also a big shock. Our hearts are with Milagros's parents and family. And in light of everything that's happened, Joshua and I have helped her parents to set up a charity in honour of Milagros's memory called the *The Brave Dove Foundation*. This is a charity that will help give the best resources available to anyone anywhere in the world who has lost someone unexpectedly who goes missing. The charity will use the best and most up-to-date and cutting-edge technologies, skills, manpower and resources available, whose contacts have been helped by our chief of security. The charity also pledges to help rehabilitate anyone unlawfully imprisoned, as I was, back into society, getting them the best doctors and mental health care professionals available.

"I'd just like to give a shout out to Mark, my own psychotherapist, who again is here this evening but who wishes to remain anonymous. Without further ado, I'd just like to thank everyone here tonight for giving us another chance after the controversy with Stella Almasi. To find out more, please read the *Hello!* magazine article that will be coming out this week. Thank you." Mimi hands the microphone back to Joshua as the audience goes mad with applause.

"Thanks, sis. Yes, unfortunately, who you believed to be the true owner of Pink Club was in fact a fraud. Pink Club has always been an idea of mine and Mimi's. We were way too green to recognise a smooth-talking con-woman when they came along, and all too quickly she got control of everything. This latest revelation about her embezzlement of money from our faithful charities was to be her undoing but fortunately not ours. Mohammad Almasi has kindly paid the charities everything they should have received from the five years of fundraising events here—while also making grand donations himself—and we heard on the grapevine that Mrs.—soon to be Miss—Almasi is to evade prison life for 800 hours community service and a suspended prison sentence for drugs. Tonight, though, is not about a con artist. Tonight is about family reunions and raising money for worthwhile causes—also revealing our newest biggest star, Cosmic Storm!"

Applause erupts again as all focus surely comes back to me.

"Enjoy the night!" he shouts, finishing off his speech.

The stage begins to lower, and once it's down to floor level, I'm helped off by staff alongside Midnight, Mixer, Digit, Medley, Psyche and Siren. I've lost sight of Joshua and Mimi as they seem to have left already. People are now engrossing themselves in conversations and eating their oh-so-fancy-looking food for those who are seated at dinner tables. The next act, a very popular singer, begins setting up on stage with their band.

As me and the guys make our way to exiting the main performance arena, the people closest to us shake our hands and congratulate me, especially on an amazing performance. Some of the stars and celebrities I recognise straight away are making me feel if this is a dream I never wish to end; others not so much, and I want to rapidly get to a nice quiet space so that I might collect my thoughts.

Once back out of the room, people turn to see us leaving and pause to begin applauding. I'm not quite sure who began the applause, but it's wonderful seeing everyone in their own finery let alone ours all celebrating this big launch of Pink Club together. I also applaud along with the guys.

Joshua appears to my left suddenly, making me jump a little, and begins rapidly whisking me away from the main hub of excited revellers until we are in one of the hidden more peaceful corridors. I didn't see where Midnight and Co. went, but I heard something from Psyche about going to grab a drink.

"That was an amazing speech, by the way," I say, not knowing what else to talk about.

Joshua says nothing but looks directly into my eyes. And as intimidating as it feels, I find I cannot break away the contact.

He moves forward and then kisses me within a nano second. I kiss him back, my primal side kicking in, over-riding my rational *'this is so wrong'* human side.

I'm gently manoeuvred backwards and feel a door open to which I'm manoeuvred through. The space is dark, but I am lip-locked with Joshua, blissfully unaware of our surroundings. The door closes and we continue to kiss until we have to break away for air.

"Oh, my God!" I simply exclaim as my hand comes up to my mouth.

I cannot see Joshua's full expression in the dark, but his smell, warmth and just feel of his intense stare make running impossible with how weak in the knees I'm feeling.

"You have no idea how long I have wanted to do that, *pretty lady.*"

~ CHAPTER 30 ~

As Joshua says those exact words *again* to me outside of *Lucifer's Haven,* I know he knows.

"You DID know it was me that night at *Lucifer's Haven?*"

A clinking sound can be heard as lights fills what I can now see is some sort of cleaning cupboard.

Well that explains the sterile bleach smell among Joshua's own overpowering masculine scent.

I pull back from Joshua but cannot go far before I'm held in place by the door. He advances forward to place both hands on either side of my head, and I feel I may very well explode in spectacular human combustion fashion at any moment.

"I'm glad you didn't slap me this time, though. Shall we practice that kiss again, Miss Pebble?"

My loins are officially on fucking fire right now, but I must desist and resist these animal urges.

Having no power of speech anymore, Joshua seems

to take my silence as a yes, and then there we go again kissing, full-on passionate snogging—in a cleaning cupboard—totally alone with no fear of interruptions. It is here when Joshua's hands start roaming that I snap back to reality, and on impulse explosively push him away from me with, perhaps, too much force than intended. He falls back, ending up sitting in an empty yellow bucket, and as his head bumps the wall, the shelf above relieves itself of various closed bottles of cleaning products that seem to hit Joshua and bounce off at odd angles.

"Sorry!" is all I can muster to say before bolting straight out of the door, practically galloping towards the safety of my dressing room.

Entering my dressing room, I yelp with surprise as everyone is inside with a glass of fizz, cheering at me upon entry.

"Ahhh!" I cry in proper Maria-Sound-of-Music style, akin to the scene where she sits on the pinecone.

"Here you go, darling. Gosh, I'm so proud of you," Mum gushes while handing me a flute of pink fizz.

Mimi, Dante, Sarah, Roger, Midnight, Octavia, Mixer, Medley, Digit, Siren and Psyche beam smiles at me and then encroach my space to give me massive congratulations.

"Joshua said he was going to find you before you're due back on stage again. Have you seen him?" Mimi asks with eyes I feel see straight through to our little rendezvous in the cleaning cupboard.

"No, I –"

"Hey, everyone. I see the star of the show is here. Sorry I'm a bit late; I got held up with a small cleaning emergency," Joshua says, cheekily grinning and winking at me.

"Here you go," Mimi says, handing her brother a flute.

Up close, I can fully appreciate everyone's outfits. Mum is in a mother-of-the-bride styled floral two-piece effort and she looks the smartest I've ever seen her. Roger dons a floral shirt and jeans with a pink tie. Poor sod looks like a spare prick at a wedding. Mimi has donned a luxurious pink gown (clearly very designer and very expensive); the train is a see-through pink veil-styled material. Joshua is in crisp white shirt open at the collar and tight dark denim blue jeans. Octavia is wearing an off-the-shoulder pink top with ruffle-styled sleeves, skinny jeans and tons of golden bling about her head and neck.

We all cheer and down our pre-celebratory drinks before it's almost time for me and the gang to set up on the stage again for the last two dances of the night.

"Where's Eva?" I ask, suddenly realising she is the only one not here.

"Up to her neck in working the room. Come on, sis, let's go take some of the pressure off her," Joshua says, holding his arm out for his sister, who rolls her eyes as they exit out of my dressing room.

"Right, come along folks; let's make this a memorable ending to a very successful night," Midnight tells everyone, as I down the rest of my very sweet-tasting pink fizz and head out with my dance crew for our second act.

As before, once everyone is seated, the lights inside are dimmed before we are literally ushered by an usher to make our entrance and way onto the stage. Eventually we are settled among the blooms once more as the stage is raised and the lights come up ready for our next two back-to-back dances that will close the show.

Everything is going really well; we're on point with our footwork and balance, all of the lifts between Midnight and I have so far landed well, my short aerial performance on the rigging with hoop goes like clockwork, and I even make my manoeuvre off the stage and back without any hitches.

The music now climbs to its crescendo for our third and final dance of the night, just as the end note plays where Midnight and I stand side by side, arms raised, ready to take a bow.

Very unexpectedly, massive firework things go off around us like huge sparklers, and the sudden unexpectedness of this makes me leap to the side, pulling away from Midnight. To his, mine and everyone else's horror, the stage then creaks and groans as I lose my balance now teetering on an edge. Midnight, along with Siren and Digit, reach to grab for me, but it's here two of the cables lose their tension and seem to come away from the roof. Instantly, the stage drops down sideways, hanging on by the other two cables that seem to be staying for now. My real floral bodice, along with my chest and ribcage, is smashed against the side of the stage, now hanging vertically instead of horizontally. I watch petals and bunches of blossoms rain down below, which is rather a long way down. I'm now hugging the stage, having somehow managed to have gripped on for grim death as the organic skin friendly bodice that had done so well to remain intact now disintegrates, leaving me left dangling—with my boobies out on full display to everyone.

Kill...me...now!

There is no chance of lowering the stage like this; the mechanism won't work. I can hear people shouting commands and then more yells from the audience, as yet another bunch of florals fall to the floor. My dance crew are above me in a better position and none can risk moving for fear of what this may do to the other two cables.

Madame Scarlet's voice haunts me here as I remember her warning of '*hold on tight!*'

"Ok, everyone, please remain seated. Cosmic, can you hear me?" Eva's voice comes out soft and smooth from a speaker. "I want you to let go of the stage; the floor will save you, trust me. It's the only way to get down safely. You can do it...let go."

"Darla, you can do this. Come on," Midnight says, looking at me and nodding his assurance.

Squeezing my eyes shut and taking in a deep breath—my dignity now in shreds—I let go and grit my teeth to prevent myself letting out the mother lode of screams. I hate roller coasters, and this is a sensation when it feels like my stomach's fallen out of me. There is a loud whooshing sound, and as I land with a feeling as if I'm on a big bouncy bed, everything bounces here...including my boobs!

Someone rushes over with a big blanket and quickly wraps it around me. Totally mortified, I burst into tears, now very conscious of the fact that everyone's just staring at me. Just as I step off the inflatable floor safety device, I see my dance crew now also ditching the stage. Petals and bits of forest blossoms fall all around them.

Once everyone's off that doomed contraption, the whole arena erupts into big cheers, applause and whistles. We all take a bow and then beat a hasty retreat with a medical team to head backstage out of sight of Pink Club members and other staff.

Joshua and Mimi, my mum and Eva come bursting through into the onsite medical room. My mum is rapidly tearing chunks off Joshua over safety issues before coming to see how I'm doing. Annoyingly, I can't stop shaking but am thankful to have been given a T-shirt and jumper by a member of staff.

"Right, well my conclusion is that apart from some thorn scrapes and shock, you're all going to be fine," the doctor says.

I'm handed a nice cup of very sweet tea from Mimi, who looks white as a sheet. "Thanks, Mimi. Well, I think we can rest assured the safety feature for the floor works. We may yet have to add stage diving to our list of dare devil manoeuvres." This comment just earns me a look of daggers from my mum and something unreadable from Joshua. Midnight shakes his head and Psyche rolls his eyes. "Come on, I was joking!"

"Hi, Darla, your presence is being requested in the foyer; a couple of fans would like to have autographs," Penny says, poking her head around the door. "They're being...persistent."

"Ok, I'll be right out."

"Darling, you must rest. We should take you straight home. You've had one hell of a shock."

"Mum, I'm fine, honest. It's only because there are such safety features that we're all ok."

"God, I was so scared I was about to lose you," Mum says, bursting into tears again, and it takes every ounce of strength for me not to join her.

"Miss Pebble, I am truly sorry about what has happened this evening to your daughter. Please let me assure you, Darla really is in safe hands," Joshua says as Mum peels away from me to now, I feel, take full advantage to cry on Joshua's shoulder.

Hand off this toy-boy, Mother! He is mine! This thought fully awakens me. I'm the last one out of the medical room to go and mingle, so I take my cue from my mind that now would be a very good time to make a hasty retreat. Joshua is dynamite and I'm the ignition. Nothing ever good comes from TNT exploding.

Mimi links arms with me as we stride out where all the stars and celebs are now congregating by the main reception. Penny is our designated security chaperone.

I'm blown away by the many more recognisable famous faces here. As much as I'm giving my autograph alongside my dance crew, I find myself asking for theirs! We even have Barri Evins in the house...THE Barri Evins.

I'm totally star-struck; so much so that my earlier naked plunge has been momentarily forgotten about, as all anyone is saying is how amazing the performances were and what a pleasure it is to meet me.

In-house professional photographers offer up the chance for celebs to have pics taken together and with other star acts. So all my photos taken with celebs are with me wearing a pale pink jumper and fairy skirt with all my glitzy make-up and hair still in place.

~ Chapter 31 ~

Once the official photos and autograph swaps have been finished, Penny helps me break away from the friendly mob to make our way towards one of the conference rooms where my presence has been requested. Mimi already found Joshua, and the two headed off a while ago.

We arrive at the conference room which has been specially decorated with balloons, banners, a buffet table, flowers, a disco ball with dim lighting and gentle music playing in the background.

"Wow, this place looks amazing!" I exclaim, entering to join with everybody.

Mum and Roger are already slow dancing; Dante and Sarah hop up as soon as they notice me—fast un-entangling themselves from one another.

"Hey, Darla, fantastic show tonight. We are so proud of you!" Dante says, coming up and giving me a bear hug. *Oh, how I have missed these.*

I hug Sarah next, glancing over at Mum, who has yet to notice I've made an appearance. Mimi and Joshua look to be having a very intense conversation with Eva, but soon one of them looks up and the trio break apart to try and make themselves look inconspicuous. Midnight, Medley, Siren, Mixer, Psyche and Digit are chilling out sitting down.

"Here she is, our very own Cosmic Storm," Joshua announces loudly enough to grab everyone's attention.

Mum awkwardly pulls away from Roger as the pair of them join in yet more applause as I take a bow, my breath silently catching in my throat with pain around my ribcage where I slammed into the stage.

"Cheers!" everyone says in unison.

Everyone goes back to relaxing and enjoying the private party vibe, and as I chat with Mum, Roger, Dante and Sarah, having a great catch up, I can't help but notice some heated discussion going on between Mimi and Joshua, ending with Mimi storming off.

Joshua comes to say a hasty goodbye to me before chasing after his sister, and a pained expression crosses his features. I feel a squeeze around my heart for him; he's hurting, and that bothers me.

Oh, boy! I'm twitterpated!

It's soon time for the evening to come to a final close. Mum and Roger have been put up at the Mimi Glass Hotel which I'm thankful for, as having to show Mum where I live now would be a whole level of excitement I couldn't handle right now.

"Right, we'd best say night-night," Mum says, giving me a big hug, congratulating me again.

"It's been lovely to see you again, Darla," Roger says, shaking my hand before kissing me on the cheek.

"Break my mother's heart and I'll break you...understand?" I whisper into his ear to which he actively nods in response.

As Mum and Roger leave the conference room, Midnight and the rest of my dance crew come to have a few words with me.

"You did great today. How are your ribs?" Midnight says, amazing me by not missing much.

"Sore," I admit.

"Next time, you're wearing a harness, young lady; no arguments," Siren says in an almost fatherly stern way. I hold my arms up as if to tell him he has no argument from me.

"Well done tonight, Darla," Psyche says, giving me a chaste kiss on the cheek.

Digit, Mixer and Medley also offer their final congratulations with Octavia before we head out. Penny opens the passenger door for me and sliding into the comfortable leather upholstery of her car, I'm not ashamed to say I fell fast asleep.

"Hey, sleeping beauty, you're home," she says, gently unbuckling my seatbelt as I sleepily yawn my apology.

Once up at my apartment, I say goodnight to Penny and thank her for getting me home safely. Crossing the threshold inside, I see that Binks is nowhere to be seen, so I figure he must have already fallen asleep somewhere.

Dropping my duffel bag on the floor next to my washing machine, and too tired to do much else, I decide to head to bed. A knock at my door makes me groan, as all I want is my bed and a nice deep sleep.

"Oh, hey, Midnight. Is everything ok?"

"I want to check your ribs if I may. Humour me."

Admittedly, they are beginning to really smart now, but I was just going to pop a few paracetamols and go to bed.

Lifting my jumper, Midnight inhales sharply, and it is then I look down myself and notice how badly bruised they actually are.

Well shit!

"You should have had them iced, but it took until now for the bruising to show itself. That's why the medic missed this damage. Go and lay on the sofa. I'll help as much as I can, but you may need an X-ray."

Doing as I'm told, I lie on one of my plush leather sofas, thankful at how comfortable they really are. Fatigue washes over me in heavy waves as Midnight approaches with a bowl of ice water and a brand-new kitchen sponge from under my sink.

He hands me a folded-up towel he fetched from the bathroom and instructs me to remove my jumper and place it over my chest under the T-shirt that was given to me by a staff member at Pink Club. Moving is agony, but my dignity this time is fully intact. Boobies well and truly covered, Midnight helps me remove the T-shirt. Gingerly, he gets to work dabbing my ribs with the sponge doused in ice water. My breath catches, which makes me moan in pain.

"You're lucky I didn't leave you like this. It hurts now, but trust me, this will really help."

Cursing at Midnight, wincing and flinching every time he has to touch my ribs with the sponge, it's not long until he announces he's done with the ice water.

"Ok, now for some warmth. Have you got a hot water bottle?"

"Err....I don't think so."

"That's ok; just relax. I have some tiger balm which is great for bruising. I need to gently massage it into the area where you're bruised and then I'll strap your ribs to give you a comfortable night."

"You appear to know what you are doing."

"My brother was a boxer for many years. I was always helping to patch him up."

"Your brother?"

"Yeah, my baby bro, Mal. He passed a few years ago —car smash."

"I'm so sorry, Midnight."

"Come on, a story for another time. Let's fix you up so you can get a good night's rest."

I must have fallen asleep, because when I next awaken, it's 5:55 a.m. and I'm in my bed wearing a set of my outrageous pyjamas. There is a note next to my bed that reads:

To the patient,
When you awaken, take both of these and rest!
M

~ Chapter 32 ~

Swallowing down the paracetamol, knowing it takes twenty minutes for them to start taking effect, I lie still in my bed running over the past twenty-four hours and that explosive kiss I had with Joshua. Groaning, wanting nothing more than to be able to erase that highly inappropriate memory, I manage to sit up and manoeuvre myself out of bed. The expertly applied bandages make me feel better put together, giving me the confidence that I can move about with ease. Everything aches from where I must have wrenched all of my upper body, clinging on for grim death. In hindsight, I could have saved myself all this pain had I just allowed myself to simply slide off the stage. Looking at my reflection in the mirror, I also see my right hip has a nice bruise on it from when I fell and landed before sliding on the flowers.

Checking my phone, I can see that it has blown up with thirteen messages and six missed calls. Scanning through, I see they are congratulation messages and a few 'boobie' jokes from my dance crew, which I do not take offence from, as it's just good humour and banter. The calls are from an unknown number, so no point guessing who that was.

Pulling up Amanda's number, I call in to have an urgent sport massage appointment after explaining that I've had a bad fall—down some stairs. (Sometimes you gotta be economical with the truth, right?) She agrees to come right away.

Waiting for Amanda, I make myself one of my frothy latte coffees from my oh-so-spectacular top-of-the-range machine. Who'd have thought I'd miss the local Greasy Spoon's coffee (a place I used to go with Mum) and many-a-happy fulfilling breakfasts we had at *The Griddle?* A small laugh suddenly escapes me while taking in the absurdity of my new life situation and looking down at my sophisticated morning coffee.

Binks trots into view to sit by my feet, reminding me it's his breakfast time. "Hey, buddy, and how was your night?" I say, picking up my furry compadre to give him a lot of fuss before freshening up his cat bowls with cat biscuits and water.

My doorbell goes, and I can tell straight away it's Amanda, as she's the only one who uses the damn thing. Plinky plonky 'high society' sounds jingle throughout the property as I go to the door, smiling and shaking my head at the sheer absurdity of having gone from street urchin to stardom quite literally overnight—super relieved to have my *real* name and identity still hidden. I think that was one of the nicest *surprises* of the entire evening. I'd clearly been stressing over nothing.

"Good morning, Amanda," I say, smiling as she enters my apartment with her hefty massage couch and gubbins.

"Hello! Ok for me to set up in the usual place?"

I nod in response.

"Right, let's have a look at you then. Nice bandages. Who did these? They have done a very good job."

"A nurse at the hospital in non-urgencies did them for me," I lie. What else can I do? I'm not about to replay events that ended up me with my boobs hanging out before a death plunge from a great height.

"I'm going to remove them if that's ok, but don't worry, I have fresh ones if needed." Once my bandages are off, Amanda's breath catches in her throat. "You really are a bit of a mess, aren't you? Any other bruising?"

"My hip," I say, pulling down my pyjama bottoms so she can see the great big purple surprise on my hip.

"Did they X-ray you at the hospital?"

"Err, no...just said deep bruising—nothing broken."
Shit! Does she think I've broken my rib?!

"Well, you can breathe ok and move about gingerly, so I'd say I concur with the hospital, but there's not really much I can do. Everything will be too painful for me to go anywhere near right now. Are you sure it was stairs you fell down? I only ask because I've dealt with a few injuries from stairs, and yours...well, it's more like you've fallen on hard ground or a hard surface."

"No-no, definitely stairs."

"Ok, right, well, all I can suggest is ice baths—one in the morning and one at night, no longer than five minutes, and anti-inflammatories. If things get worse, or you gain a fever, go straight to hospital, as it could signal sepsis. Other than that, my lovely, there's not much else I can suggest. Things should calm in about a week, so I'll re-evaluate you then, ok?"

"Thanks, Amanda. I feel it's been a wasted trip for you."

"Nonsense. I'm glad I've had the chance to at least see and assess the damage. You're going to be fine; no broken bones that I can see."

Someone knocks on the door and my blood all but freezes in my veins. *No, not while SHE'S still here!*

"Expecting company?" Amanda inquires, looking over to the front door.

Nosy bitch!

"I'll just go and wash my hands before packing up, if that's ok."

"Sure," I say while moving as fast as I can towards the door. My ribs and body cry in outrage at how fast I move. Opening the door, this rapidly developing nightmare scenario goes from bad to worse.

"Joshua! What are you doing here? You can't be here! Please leave NOW. GO!" I say anxiously before starting to shut the door.

Why won't you close, you infuriating piece of wood?! I yell inwardly at how my door is now deciding not to obey the simple order of closing. It is then I look down and see Joshua's foot in the way.

"Shall we say same time next week?" Amanda says, appearing off to my right, a confused expression flitting across her face as she looks first to Joshua and then to myself.

FAN-FUCKING-TASTIC!!!!

"Good morning, Amanda; lovely to see you," Joshua greets, giving his best charming smile towards her.

"Why, Joshua, no bodyguard today?"

"Max is in the car."

"I see. Anyone from Pink Club needing my services? Having not had any calls for some months now, one might think they had been dropped from a great height."

My stomach turns as Amanda looks pointedly at me while she says this.

"Well, I can't speak for the individual members who no longer seem to require your services, but I'm glad to see that you're taking expert care of Darla here."

"You guys are always so cagey around me. I already signed your NDA."

"Which reminds me...here, if you could just sign again on the dotted line. My sister Mimi and I have had to re-do all contracts after...well, undoubtedly you've seen the news," Joshua's says smoothly, pulling out a form from his suit jacket pocket and holding it out to Amanda.

"There you go; all signed. Don't forget to book me in *very* soon," she says, lugging her now folded massage couch through the door and past Joshua.

"Here, let me help you with this," Joshua offers,

taking the couch off Amanda and proceeding to walk with ease towards the lifts with her.

Shutting my apartment door, knowing that I absolutely cannot be alone with Joshua after the cleaning cupboard debacle, I begin hatching my escape plan.

~ Chapter 33 ~

Joshua soon returns, but I'm a lot calmer now that I have a plan in place. As he walks past me to enter my apartment, I can't help but practically ingest his scent.

Oh, my God, you smell yummy!

"Hey," he says, looking at me with his *'come to bed eyes'* and goofy sexy grin.

"Hi, can I get you a drink? Tea or coffee?" I ask, turning to head for the kitchen.

Joshua gently grabs my hand and pulls me close.

Gulp!

"Darla, let's sit down...my God, what are you wearing?"

"What? They're my so yummy jellybean pyjamas," I say quite innocently unaware of what the issue is of my bright pink pyjamas with printed photographs of different flavoured jellybeans.

"Right, cute. Umm, anyway, the reason I've come to

see you is because —"

"We kissed! Yes I know, it was wrong. We shouldn't have done it—"

"That's just it. All I want to do is kiss you—and perhaps more—which is why —"

"We absolutely cannot see each other anymore," we both say in unison instead of interrupting one another.

"I completely agree and I'm glad you said it," I say, feeling relieved but also somewhat crushed inside.

A knock at my door signals my now unnecessary escape plan's arrival.

"Sounds like you have company?" Joshua raises one of his sexy eyebrows and turns to look at the door.

"I...err, it's my mother. I've invited her for lunch."

Standing to answer the door, I'm waylaid by Joshua standing and coming round to block my way. There are no words, just more lip locking!

"This is impossible," he says, breathing heavily as we look into each other's eyes.

"Agreed."

"I should go."

"That would be a good idea."

"I..."

Joshua says nothing else to me here; he just head to open the door, saying a brief hello to my mum before stepping out of my apartment and out of my sight.

"Hello, sweetheart," Mum says, striding into my apartment. No Roger in sight. She's wearing a black leather skirt and a hot pink semi-see-through long-sleeved shirt, with a leather black jacket over the top.

"Where's Roger?"

"Wowzers! This is —"

"Huge, I know! Now, where's Roger?" I say, interrupting my mother, who now has eyeballs out on stalks.

"Relax; he's gone to meet some friends while you and I catch up. Much as I love your jammies, don't you think you should get changed?"

"Mum, these are pyjamas!"

"Excuse me for not being able to cut the outrageous *designer* outfits from the everyday."

Says she, who looks like mutton dressed as!

I'm glad I wasn't given a bear hug this time. If my mum found out about my bruised ribs being the way they are, it would have just set her going about health and safety again.

"Make yourself at home. Tea and coffee etc. is in the kitchen," I call down to hallway to Mum as I head onto get dressed for our mother daughter afternoon.

In my bedroom, I can still taste Joshua having been on and in my mouth mere moments before Mum's arrival—the feel of our tongues dancing their very own tango together setting my soul on fire. Shaking my head, I become focused on the task at hand, using Mum as a buffer between Joshua and I, but as for my thoughts, this is a battle I'm facing on my own.

"Hi, Eva. I'm going out for lunch with my mum. Do I need Penny or someone else to chaperone?" I ask Eva on the phone as I slip my feet into a pair of pale blue high tops.

"Hi, Darla. How are you feeling today?" she asks, making my mind jump back to my topless fall.

"Oh, a bit bruised but otherwise fine. So...can I go out?"

"Yes, of course—sorry, no worries. Glad you're ok. I've just messaged Max while we're on the phone and he says as long as you can keep a low profile, he doesn't see why you'd need a security chaperone."

"Great, thanks Eva."

"No worries; have a lovely time with your mum."

HELLO!

It is exactly one week since our spring gala. Nothing leaked into the press of my topless cannonball from the stage and the vibe in Pink Club in the days following the incident is as if nothing ever happened. (I really think I'm beginning to fall in love with this place even more.)

I received days of floral tributes, teddy bears, hampers, bubbly from my adoring fans—I have adoring fans, who are CELEBRITIES!! Eva had such a task on her hands trying to figure out where everything was to go, so I got her to donate all the teddies to several local hospital children's wards. We set up a table with all of my flowers and goodies and put them up for sale for the staff in the conference rooms (out of sight of the members and guests so as to not ruffle any feathers) donating all the monies to Milagros Morena's *Brave Dove Foundation* charity.

Presently, I'm en route to a secret location for our *Hello!* magazine photo shoot. Penny and I have been engaged in small talk. For me, it's been a rather relaxing start to the day. I've been instructed to wear loose-fitting clothing without any make-up, and it feels nice to be going to a job where there isn't so much stress or tension beforehand.

Eventually, we arrive at our destination. It is an old Air Force base that's been transformed into lavish studios for companies to rent out for things like photo shoots or acting scenes from movies. The aircraft hangers are massive and quite intimidating on approach.

Butterflies start to flutter about in my stomach as I walk with Penny to join my dance crew, Eva, Joshua and Mimi. Once safely delivered, Penny makes herself scarce.

"Hello, beautiful!" Marsha-mellow says off to my side. I hadn't spotted him and wonder why he's here.

"Hey, yourself, beautiful."

"Oh, stop it!" Marsha says faux blushing.

"Darla, you're to have your hair and make-up done before the photographers get here. Marsha has a special mask for you to match the colour scheme of outfits *Hello!* have picked out. You're also going to have pink strands of dye added to your hair, so we can keep your real identity hidden. You will only be known by your stage name, Cosmic Storm," Eva says. Relief floods me once more to know that I can still hold onto my true identity.

I see that Mimi and Joshua are in a hugely heated discussion. Mimi storms off with Joshua in hot pursuit, and following not far behind them is, of course, Max. They never come back.

MAY

"Pinch, punch, first of the month and no return," Psyche says actively, pinching my arms as I take a seat among my dance crew on the dance studio floor.

"OW!" I yelp in angry protest.

"Don't worry. He's done it to everyone this morning...annoyingly," Siren grumbles, rolling his eyes.

"Ok! Listen up, folks! I appreciate it's been a few weeks since the very successful gala, minus the stage diving incident, but we have a lot of *new* rehearsal work in front of us. Engineering has assured Eva, Joshua, Mimi and me that the cause of the cable breakages was down to extra weight unaccounted for from those ridiculously huge blooms hanging off the stage. Darla, with this in mind, my intention for you today is just to put you up there to get you over any literal stage fright. Our Fire Festival is coming up in just four weeks, people, so once again, there is much preparation to be done," Octavia says, expertly commanding this space. I notice today she is wearing denim shorts with a butterfly top tied at the back with strands of material. Black and electric blue braids are up in two separate buns on either side of her head.

Joshua and Mimi have been staying on a more long-term basis with their parents at their family's vineyard villa in Tuscany. I miss Joshua a lot—much more than I thought possible, considering we haven't ever really been given the chance to get to know one another. We were all given the rest of April off to recover from the events of the spring gala, but now back inside Pink Club, the lack of Joshua and Mimi's presence is being felt among everyone.

The doors to the dance studio make their familiar cracking sound as they open and in strides a very exotic-looking woman with a dark velvet cloak draped around her.

"This fire season, we're bringing a whole new level of intensity," Octavia announces, making sure we are now all looking at the woman who just entered.

Following her are another five stunningly beautiful women—dressed just as exotically. They are all clearly belly dancers and are wearing vibrant reds, oranges, yellows and pinks.

"Wait—are we all getting partners?" Digit asks animatedly.

"Indeed, you are."

"What about Darla, though?" Mixer wonders, painfully stating the obvious.

"Darla is our 'Cosmic Storm'; our stand-alone performer," Octavia says, coming to give me a comforting side hug.

The word *alone* perhaps irks me more than I'd like it to, making the ever-present lack of presence by one Mr.

Joshua Glass all the more noticeable. I'm also pissed that he just up and left with Mimi without so much a '*bye as you leave*!' No, as far as I concerned, I am done. Any foolhardy notion that we could have ever been romantically involved has been truly extinguished. Mind you, this is what I wanted, so then why am I not feeling more relieved?

'*Ho hum*' as my Nana would say.

"Gentleman, meet your new dance partners. Midnight, you're with Blaze; Siren meet Diane; Mixer, this is Viva; Psyche, say hello to Sheila; Digit, you're partnered up to Layla; and Medley, you're with Maryanne."

The guys waste no time getting better acquainted with their new partners as I now stand awkwardly alone, hugging my arms to myself.

"Right, come on you. While this lot become better... introduced, you and I have a date with a stage," Octavia says, steering me towards the dance studio doors.

Gulp!

"Just...relax...feel the weight beneath your feet holding you. Trust the equipment," Octavia whispers in my ear as we stand on the raised stage, looking out at the familiar space of their main dancing arena here at Pink Club.

Walking with Octavia around the stage one way and then the other, I do notice a much firmer sturdiness under my feet than before. There is far less vibration, and my nerves begin to settle. A flash of my topless fall floats across my mind, but this time it bothers me far less. Taking a breath, I realise I've regained my confidence back in this dance space.

"Ok, lower, please, Eva," Octavia calls out to Eva, who had been sitting patiently on an audience's seat watching us. It is here I see that she exhales a big breath of air, undoubtedly relieved I've had no lingering psychological effects from my death drop.

"Sure, everything ok up there?" she calls back.

"Amazing. Our girl here did brilliantly," Octavia says once again, giving me a side squeeze as a proud smile spreads across her face.

"Thanks, Stage Mum," I say out loud, gasping inwardly that the pet name I'd chosen to give Octavia has just slipped out.

"Aww, Stage Mum; I think I like it. You can keep that one," she says, humouring me.

Once the stage is aligned with the floor, we both step off before it continues its descent down to basement level.

"We'd best get back to the dance studio. Undoubtedly, the guys have all swapped numbers with the six 'femme fatales' by now. God, I hope they don't end up having entanglements. That's all I'd need: a fury of five jealous girlfriends to contend with."

"Do you really think there is any risk of these *entanglements* occurring?"

"Honey, these are very beautiful, unattached single women. Apart from Medley, I'd say all bets are off."

"Yeah, I agree. Best we get back."

"Mum, Dad—I've tried everything. Mimi just refuses to open up. Ever since her and Adrian called it a day and broke off their engagement upon her return...well, you've seen what she's like—impossible."

"Don't talk about your sister that way!" James snaps at his son.

"Oh, really, Dad. What do you want me to treat Mimi with? *Respect,* like the way you and Mum did for me? Just cutting me off—giving barely any notice to *my* feelings when we all thought she had been murdered?"

"Joshua, please —"

"Excuse me, Mr., and Mrs. Glass. Mimi appears to have left," Max says, interrupting Pandora's plea to her son where in the lounge the atmosphere could be cut with a knife.

"For fuck's sake! And where were you, huh? Let her slip away again like the night she was supposedly *murdered!*" Joshua spits back unfairly at Max.

While going to walk past him, Max firmly grabs Joshua's upper arm, whispering, *"Now I know you and your folks are hurting, which is why I'm prepared to let that one slide, but don't you ever for one moment blame me for anything that we thought had happened to Mimi. Are we clear?"*

"Crystal," Joshua responds boldly, holding Max's gaze to pull away from him before storming off.

~ Chapter 34 ~

Awakening to the soft sounds of jazz floating across my room from the bathroom speakers, I stretch in my bed, feeling my muscles ache after a full-on afternoon the previous day of learning new belly dancing skills. Luckily, the guys had been on their best behaviour, and no swapping of numbers had happened—yet.

On the schedule for the upcoming Fire Festival are performances by Cirque du Soleil, whose artists are coming over especially to perform here at Pink Club. All the doors to the different themed rooms will have events and functions going on inside them. The way it's been described to me is to imagine an outside festival inside. There are going to be Chinese lion dances, fire breathing acts, acrobatics and other circus performers. Our job as dancers is to open and close the show. Once we open the festival (much like a mini-Olympic opening ceremony), we will get to enjoy the festivities of the day and night until it is time to close everything down.

As there are only four weeks until the festival, I'm keen to get to the dance studio a few hours earlier so I can really get to grips with this new choreography. Presently, dance rehearsals are running from 9 a.m. to 10 p.m.

"Hi, err...you're not Penny!" I exclaim to the big brute of a man now darkening my doorstep.

"Your powers of observation, Miss Pebble, have been noted. Penny is off on sick leave. The name's Brutus. It's a pleasure to meet you, Darla," the man with a deep Scottish accent and who I now know to be called 'Brutus' says, as I step out of my apartment having just fed and watered Binks.

"I hope Penny is ok."

"That one is tough as an old boot; she'll be fine and back to work soon enough. Until then, you gotta put up with me, I'm afraid."

I just smile as we enter the lift, which indicates on a sticker that up to ten people can enter. However, I think Brutus alone fills the space for nine. He's huge both up and out.

"Thankfully there is no press here this morning. Even if they were, nothing would draw their attention with my mode of transport."

"Mode of transport," I say, quizzically echoing back Brutus's words.

"Presenting Old Bessy," Brutus announces proudly at revealing a bashed up—old indeed—decrepit-looking mustard yellow and off-white VW camper van.

"Sorry, *this* is to be my ride into work this morning?"

"Yep! And also for the foreseeable future until Penny comes back."

Oh goodie! I think sarcastically while also wondering why there may be more to Penny being 'off sick' than Brutus is letting on.

Clambering up to sit alongside Brutus, I cringe at the loud leopard print seat covers.

"Are you a...permanent fixture at Pink Club? I'm sure I've met most, if not all, of Max's onsite security teams and can't ever remember seeing you there."

"Max likes to swap staff about once in a while."

"How long exactly is Penny due to be 'off sick'?"

"For at least the next seven months. Oops; shouldn't have said that."

Seven months!!

"I see. So that must mean..."

"Yep, you are to be my security charge for the foreseeable future."

"With 'Old Bessy?'"

"It was a deal breaker for me, really. She's been everywhere I've been—on most of my security jobs. Bit of a good luck charm." I try to smile as Brutus says this but fear it may have come across more as a grimace.

We barely speak further on the way to Pink Club. Brutus squashes himself right up to the steering wheel, hunching over it while looking extremely nervous. "Got to have eyes everywhere," is all he says as we carry on our way.

We park up a half a mile away from Pink Club.

Having tried to voice my protest over being so far to Brutus meant I was met with being shot down in flames over how 'one can never be too careful on such a high-profile job.'

Gods give me the strength not to throttle this man!

"Finally! There you are! It's ok; Cherry, tell Max that Darla has arrived alive and well," Eva calls over to the receptionist.

"That'd be my fault Darla is late. Needed a safe parking spot away from the line of sight. Got any good coffee around here?" Brutus says, wandering off in his shabby chic 70's style attire: faded denim jeans and camel suede coat lined with sheepskin on the inside.

Ignoring Brutus's explanation, Eva pulls me away from earshot of anyone. "Why didn't you check your phone? So sorry about Penny's fill-in. He's a complete nightmare! I pleaded with Max to get someone else, but his staff is already stretched."

"Sorry, my phone was on silent. It's ok, really. I'm sure after a while me and Brutus will have a...good system in place."

"Don't tell me he told you about Penny's pregnancy!" Eva wails. I sense here she must have picked up on my 'after a while' comment, but at least it confirms my suspicions: Penny and her husband are going to be welcoming a new little person to their lives. How exciting!

"No...he didn't...she's pregnant?" I say, feigning surprise.

I'm a cow, making Eva squirm—I know it—a

complete bitch, but how can I throw Brutus under the bus for not actually saying anything?

"I was going to tell you today anyway, so best you know now," Eva says, looking at me with her best poker face. She's wearing her usual pale grey with pastel pink pinstriped suit, pastel pink kitten heels, a plain white blouse and a gold chain around her neck. Her pink hair is once again up in a very ornate do.

"Brutus, come with me, please. I know you've covered for us before, but all NDA's have to be re-applied after Stella's removal from Pink Club."

The pair walk away, and turning, I'm now hot footing it up to rehearsals. So much new choreography to learn; it is set to be a very long month indeed.

Arabian sounding music is already pumping out of the studio speakers. Hedging past Joshua's office door, my heart sinks just a smidgen at his absence, but I recover before rounding the corner. I then notice one of the doors to the dance studio is open, which would explain why the music appears so loud. I feel the beat pulsing beneath my feet as I go to stand at the entryway.

Watching my dance crew with their exotic female belly dancing partners is quite a hypnotic sight to behold. They are locking eyes with one another and already move in perfect synchronicity with the newly learned choreography they have been taught. Seeing how the men move with fluid motion and circle their hips is definitely something setting my pulse alight. The guys are in what I'm guessing is belly dancing pants for men with nothing on the top, which just shows off all their rippling muscular bodies in all their glory. I know they are only 'dance acting' with the women, but you'd think they were really 'together' with the magnetism they display here.

It suddenly dawns on me that I'm now feeling more alone than ever. Psyche's earlier words at *Lucifer's Haven* when he said *'everyone here has a person, and you don't'* come back to me just as the music track ends and everyone claps one another.

"Darla," Octavia says, jogging up to encourage me inside.

"Hey...sorry I'm late."

"That's ok, it gave everyone time to warm up to one another. I want them all to spend time with their dance partners to really get to know one another, so on the night of performance they relay that sense of connection between them to your audience."

Connection...something I'm finding less and less of in my life these days.

"Today, Darla, you're going to have some solo instruction with myself and Blaze. Ok, guys listen up. We need the space for the rest of the day, so you guys can practice in one of the conference rooms," Octavia says. Everyone takes their leave, excitedly chatting among themselves and barely even giving me a sideways glance.

"Here you go, my dear; this is to be your practice *uniform*," Blaze says warmly, walking over to me and placing a bundle of vibrant soft clothing into my hands.

"Shall I get dressed now?"

"You can change in the store cupboard if you like. Let me turn the light on for you," Octavia says, walking to where all the aerobic equipment is stored for the fitness aerobic dance classes she holds for Pink Club members.

Once inside the cupboard, I swiftly change from my loose-fitting clothes into a rich, dark pink belly dancing skirt and crop top.

"Wow, you look amazing!" Octavia gushes at me.

"There are five different styles of belly dancing uniform. Yours is tribal. There is also gypsy from the Roma dances that gained the notoriety from the Nordic travellers who went along the Silk Road from India to Spain. Then there is Fusion style, a combination of Spanish, Indian, Brazilian and ballroom etc. Egyptian follows next with bare midriff known as Bedlah style, which is the ultimate in elegance! Lastly, there is Cabaret style. This will be the style we shall all be donning on the night of the fire festival event and is the older style of Arabic and Turkish ways to dress as a belly dancer.

"We dance as a tribe where you are to be centre of attention at all times; you are our leader and we will worship you through the story of dance," Blaze explains, burning her gaze into mine with her partially thinly-veiled face and darkly lined eyes with use of heavy eye make-up.

"Blaze, I wonder if it might be easier for Darla to hear your instructions without the veil."

"Yes, indeed; sorry, force of habit," Blaze says, immediately removing the veil to reveal her beautiful Egyptian face that matches her just as dreamy Egyptian accent.

~ Chapter 35 ~

Two weeks into rehearsals...
"Release in, release up, release in, release up; feel the stretch where your soleus muscles are. Speed up a bit now...we're halfway...lovely. 4...3...2...1... hold—and stretch to the side—centre—nice! Now over to the other side...stretch—centre. Several more; ok great. Now moving onto hip sways, keep your chests nicely high and lifted...make sure there's a lot of room in your core areas, and let's go! 1...2...3...1...2...3...1...2...3...hopefully now you can see how your knees are also gliding across each other diagonally."

Octavia no longer oversees our choreography. Blaze has been given full rein, being the expert in her field, as head honcho for who I have learned are in fact called the Red Velvet Ladies of belly dancing. It became quickly apparent that Octavia, for all her wonderful dance experience, was out of her depth, so she bowed out gracefully.

"1...2...1...2...Egyptian with hands. Good! 1...2 and

2...3...1...2... and 1, 2, 3...step outs—push—good—all the way again from the top!"

Every day is full-on dancing. I'm now seeing Amanda twice a week to keep up with my muscle strains and sprains. Today is no different.

"Aaaaaand stop! Well done, everybody. Enjoy the weekend and remember to rest and recover. We have only two weeks of rehearsals remaining," Blaze announces, bringing our dance rehearsals for this week to a close.

"Darla, me and the lads are going to have a few chilled-out drinks at mine. Do you fancy coming along?" Midnight says, being, as always, the chivalrous gentleman that he is.

"Actually, me and the ladies were thinking we would quite like to invite Darla to a little get together of our own," Blaze says, answering for me.

I admit to feeling more than just a little relieved; the last thing I need is to see couples being all 'lovey dovey' with each other. Thinking of Moesha, Bea, Lucy and the other women partnered up to my dance crew, I'd feel like a right spare prick at a wedding, so I am happy for the other offer.

"Absolutely! Count me in!" I hear myself saying counter intuitively, though all I'd really rather do is curl up at home with a good book before catching up on some Z's. I'm totally whacked.

———

"Darling, I think you should stay here a while longer with your dad and I. What do you think?" Pandora says, smoothing the hair of her frail and stressed daughter's head.

Joshua, standing in the doorway with arms folded, finally managed to clear the air with their parents.

To everyone's relief, Mimi nods in agreement.

"What about you, Joshua? Will you stay a while longer or do you have to get back to your Pink Club?" Pandora asks nervously, looking at her son.

"Ours. It's mine and Mimi's Pink Club, Mother."

"Sorry—of course it is."

"But it's not, is it, Joshua? It's been all yours for five full years. I may as well have nothing to do with it anymore," Mimi cries while running out of the room.

Joshua starts to follow but his father gently holds him back.

"Do not touch me. I think you've done quite enough damage already, don't you?" Joshua growls, pulling away from his father.

"Enough! Either you two sort it out once and for all, or I'm going. I mean it, James; sort it now!" Pandora says, going in search of Mimi.

———

An hour later there is a knock on Mimi's bedroom door. She's sitting with her mum on her big four-poster bed. Joshua and James enter, both very red faced from crying.

"Oh, James," Pandora says, standing and hurrying

over to her husband, who holds his wife while crying. They turn to their children, who move in for a group hug.

"We're so sorry for everything," James says, holding his son and daughter in a strong group hug alongside Pandora.

"Can we at least agree on no more tears, please?" Mimi requests, as the four hold tightly to one another.

Max watches from a respectable distance, wiping at his own eyes and moving further away to give the family more privacy while they fully heal the rift between them.

Joshua exits first to find Max and ask him to bring the car around. Mimi is going to stay behind while receiving care from a top psychotherapist, helping her work through her trauma, and the peacefulness of her parents' vineyard seems a place she finds happiest to do this at. Max already has security personnel stationed at the vineyard, and although finding it difficult to leave her behind, he trusts the people in charge of looking after her —Pandora and James—implicitly.

~ Chapter 36 ~

I am driven by a Pink Club driver along with the Red Velvet Ladies to a Turkish restaurant called *La Mezze* which is owned by Blaze and her husband, Ricardo. Above the restaurant is where they live.

"Ricardo and I have decided to host a closed-door event to invite you into the fold officially as one of our belly dancing sisters, since we are going to be dancing together at Pink Club," Blaze tells me animatedly with a gleam in her eyes.

Exiting the car, a security man from Pink Club checks out the restaurant, and I'm relieved that this evening it's not Brutus in charge of mine or the women's safety. Does that make me a bit of a snobby cow? Perhaps, but nothing shouts 'notice me' louder than a man looking like a time traveller from the 1970s era with an attitude as big as an elephant's!

Once the place has been checked over with whatever Pink's security guys do on entering a property for the first time, we are left to our own devices, and the chap in question announces they are going to sit in the car until it's time for me to go home. Apparently, Blaze's husband is sorting food for him to enjoy in the car.

"Come in and make yourselves at home; no need for ceremony here," Blaze announces as we all hang our coats on the stand next to the door of the restaurant.

Ricardo, a strikingly good-looking man with Egyptian tanned skin and just the smattering of grey among his thick black hair, walks over to greet us. In Arabic, he speaks first to his wife and then to the other women before introducing himself in perfect English.

The restaurant is beautifully designed with golden tables and chairs and a black polished tiled floor. Vast red velvet drapes hang from the ceiling, and oriental flowers and large indoor plants are dotted at various corners of the restaurant. There are expensive-looking Egyptian mounted photographs and mirrors and other works of Egyptian-themed art mounted around on the wall spaces. Arabian sounding music floats across the space out of hidden speakers to give a nice, relaxed feel to the place. The smell of fragrant food and exotic flavours make my mouth water.

"It's lovely to meet you, Ricardo. Yours and Blaze's restaurant truly is beautiful."

"A-ha! No, my dear, the restaurant is *his* little venture. Mine is my belly dancing school. We have no children so can easily split our time between the guilty pleasures that are our businesses."

"Thank you, Darla. Dinner will be ready soon, so

why don't you all freshen up upstairs?" Ricardo tells me, heading back to the kitchen.

Heading up a black spiral staircase, I'm amazed at how big and spacious the second floor is. The flooring is made up of dark wood, and there is a lounge space with a difference, as a huge chaise and ottomans are dotted around with what also look to be enormous beanbag type seats. (If you can call a beanbag a seat, that is). Lavish, expensive-looking rugs cover the floor space, and the Egyptian accents follow through the upstairs, almost matching with downstairs. There are a total of four bedrooms and two bathrooms, a dining room, smaller private kitchen space, mirrored dance studio and gym.

"Blaze, may I use the bathroom?"

"Certainly. It's just down the hallway and off to the —"

"Left! Oh goodness; I left my mobile back at Pink Club!" Diane cries, as she hurriedly asks Sheila if she can borrow hers to call in and see if it was handed into lost property.

The women then suddenly become very busy chattering in Arabic about what I can only imagine is the phone drama now surrounding Diane.

Ok, just down the hall and off to the...left, I think while making my way to the bathroom.

It's dark inside and I step in, imagining the light switch must be right next to me on the wall. The door shuts and then I'm in pitch blackness. Scrambling about for the sodding light switch, I notice I begin bumping into solid objects. I hold my hands out to guide me, feeling around, and I can't seem to locate the light switch or anything that even remotely resembles the feel of a bathroom fixture or fitting.

Shit! I must be in the wrong place! Fuck! What do I do? I can't yell out, can I? Oh, my God; this is going to be so embarrassing!

Scrambling about for another few minutes, at last light fills the space which makes me blink rapidly.

Odd, I don't think I found a light switch. Must have bumped into it.

Once my eyes adjust to the light—a red light—I realise I'm definitely not in the bathroom.

"Oh, so sorry, Darla. I must have told you the wrong door. This is my...*other* business," Blaze says, indicating with her eyes the whips, chains, belts, canes, bench and other BDSM style equipment.

I realise while I'd been falling about in the darkness, I've somehow grabbed hold of something rather rude and on impulse drop it.

"Come on; bathroom's this way," Blaze grins while guiding me to the room directly opposite.

"Th-thank you."

Once safely in the bathroom, I silently burst out laughing to myself while also trying hard to keep it together so as to not have a wee-wee incident before I've had time to sit on Blaze and Ricardo's very stylish toilet. The entire bathroom, in fact, is as lavish as the rest of their house and Ricardo's restaurant downstairs; everywhere feels palatial.

Finished in the bathroom, I now head back to meet

the other women in the lounge space with the oversized beanbag seats. They have all dressed in fancy 'lounge wear' styled clothing—you know, baggy trousers, loose tops, dressing gowns—the types of clothes you wear on a day off from work or when you're home battling off a cold or a recent breakup. I'm still in the clothes I wore into Pink Club as it's all I had with me outside my now belly dancing tribal uniform.

The ladies are all reclining on a chaise or oversized 'poufy' beanbags. Sheila, Diane and Viva are enjoying the delights of a hookah. (A big glass container filled with flavoured liquid and smoking pipes coming out of the top.)

"There she is, our star performer. Would you like to try some hookah?" Blaze says, bringing me into the fold of sacred women's circle.

"No, thanks. I'm not a smoker."

"Me neither, but the ladies love it. It is a bit of home comfort for them while they come to England for our British touring events."

"Wait...so Diane, Viva and Co., they don't live here?"

"Me, Ricardo, Viva, Diane and Sheila live in the UK permanently, but Layla and Maryanne are here for six months of the year, and for the other half they live in Egypt with their own families."

"That must be hard for them—all that time away from their families."

"Yes and no. None of the women here apart from me are married yet, so the responsibilities are to their parents, siblings, cousins etc., and as the money is excellent, they have the freedom to be who they are for at least half of every year that they dance in the group."

Blaze, I notice, is the best English speaker for the group, and as the evening progresses we do determine a good way to communicate using a translator app on my phone. Also, using Ricardo and Blaze as immediate translators help much better. I've learned that Viva loves cats and has various pet cats at home; Diane is also a cat lover and she moonlights as a part-time carer for a day job, earning extra money when the women don't perform for the second half of the year. Sheila is a school cook; Layla and Maryanne just stay at home doing their duties until their parents can find them someone to marry. I shivered hearing this. For them, of course, it's culturally normal to be so under the thumb, but for me—I'm too much of a free spirit. The idea of an arranged marriage and being chained to the cots of children had out of duty and to the sink makes my blood run cold. Not all Egyptian women are treated this way, however, but many are *traditionalists* as Blaze put it.

The food has been amazing and my first real taste of Egyptian flavours. Blaze very kindly gifts me a basic cookbook of simple recipes to follow. As the evening draws to a close, I'm conscious that my driver and bodyguard are waiting in the car, and although it's his job and he may be used to sitting for long periods of time in the car, I don't want to be known as that 'celebrity bitch' who takes liberties.

"Before you leave tonight, Darla, here are some extra portions for you to take home with you. I've included the basic cooking instructions," Ricardo says, placing a Tupperware box with the freshly prepared mini ravioli I've learned is called *Manti* inside into my hands. "Also, here is the remaining half of the red velvet cake I made for dessert." He places a white cake box on top of the Tupperware box containing my Manti ravioli.

"I will walk you to your car. Maybe next time you visit I can introduce you to something in my *other* line of work." As Blaze says this, I almost drop my Manti and cake.

The driver opens the door for me, and I turn to give Blaze a big hug, which feels warm and motherly, and I thank her and Ricardo for such a lovely evening. It is here that I inform her the next outing will be *my* treat, as I plan to take all the women to *Angel Cake*.

"Goodnight, sweet girl; sleep well," Blaze says, waving me off.

~ Chapter 37 ~

I'm lying naked on a stone slab in some sort of a temple; thunder and lightning flash and crash all around me and rain soaks my naked body all over. A gong sounds, and I know I must leap up, which I do. Starting to run through a stone walled maze, I hear the sounds of the baying centaur as thunder and lightning continue to jar my senses. Trying to find my way out of the maze before the centaur sets itself upon me, I run and run. My lungs feel like they are on fire; I'm trembling from adrenaline and fear. Hooves pound away faster—faster— louder—louder, until I trip and fall face down. Turning, I see the beast bearing down on me, and a scream escapes my throat as the huge mythical beast rears up ready to crush me. As this happens, I hold my hands over my face; the rain continuously pounding all over my body. The hooves come down to strike me, and just before they do, the beast transforms into one Joshua Glass. He lies naked atop of me, holding my arms now up above my head before leaning close to my face to whisper 'got you.' Our lips lock, and I feel I may burst into flames as my body awakens with a familiar heat now travelling across every fibre of my very being.

Awakening with a start, my heart now gallops away at the sheer ferocity of my dream. I still feel Joshua's imagined naked body against my own with our lips entangled in a fierce and fiery kiss.

Holy shit! I'm in trouble!

The drive into Pink Club this morning is, for me, a silent affair. Brutus harps on about this and that, but to be perfectly honest, I'm not even paying the slightest bit of attention—my thoughts now all consumed with the beast of my dreams: one Joshua Glass.

"You ok, Darla? You look a bit out of it today."

"Sorry. Brutus. What were you saying?"

"As if to prove my point, eh?"

I can only look at the man quizzically, at a total loss.

Now used to our half a mile walk into work every day, the fresh air today gives me time to think and clear my head. With Joshua being away in Tuscany, this will give me ample time to really knuckle down and fixate only on my dancing duties for Pink Club and get to know my six new female dancing friends.

Friends...yes, I suppose that's what we are fast becoming. After all, we have shared food and cake and...secrets. Recalling Blaze's dominatrix room makes me once again giggle to myself.

"Something funny, Darla?" Brutus asks, a brusque tone to his voice.

"I just recalled a memory."

You nosy bastard! Note to self: keep emotions in check around this guy.

"Ah...thought for a moment you might be laughing at me."

"Err—nope."

"It's my own chip on the shoulder. I was bullied badly for my size and weight throughout school. Guess I'd best speak to my therapist about that."

Great! Now I feel like the biggest judgey bitch on the planet!

"Oh...sorry to hear that. Honestly, I was laughing at a memory."

"I believe you." The way Brutus says this, however, makes me think otherwise.

Rounding a corner to head on into Pink Club, I see a beige and black splodge heading towards us.

No, no, no, no! Don't tell me Bane got out AGAIN?!

Indeed, it is Bane, one of Pink Club's security dogs, hurtling towards us. Rolling my eyes at the sight of the big dopey animal, tongue lagging in the wind, saliva spraying everywhere, I just wait for him to catch up to us. I'm on my period, so I figure he must have smelled me a mile away.

"Hey, buddy, what's up? Where's your daddy?" I greet him, referring to his handler.

"Bloody animal! Why on earth Joshua allows Max to keep this soppy dog is anyone's guess. He's not fit for the job, but Max insists he 'looks' the part."

"I take it you're not an animal lover, Brutus?"

"The only animals I like are the medium rare ones on a plate with chips and peas." We laugh together, and I'm glad to see Brutus lightening up a bit again.

New note to self: big guy, big emotions—be kind!

Thankfully, as Bane wants to stay close to me, he trots along obligingly as we head inside Pink Club.

A man white as a sheet, and dressed in a classic security suit uniform, comes running over with lead in his hand.

"I think it would be better if I walk him back where he's needed. No offense, but you look a bit nervous, and dogs pick up on that sort of thing," I tell the gangly-looking, sweaty man.

"Th—thanks, but I got it from here."

"Ok, no worries." *It's your funeral!*

The man clips the lead on Bane, who makes a little growl before the guy yanks on the chain, reminding him who's boss. This simply makes Bane growl and jump up at him, which makes him elicit a squeaky yelp sound— that's the man, not Bane. Brutus and I leave him to it, as all we see is Bane now taking the man for a walk until they are both out of sight.

"Think he'll survive to the end of his shift?" Brutus jokes, looking at me.

"Nah," we both say in unison before laughing, just as one Joshua Glass walks by.

Gulp!

"Darla, I'll see you in my office please; five minutes," is all he says with his face buried in some sort of document while heading in that direction himself.

Brutus mock salutes me before walking away to busy himself with something else, leaving me standing in the now fairly empty reception area.

Fuck! Best get this over with and find out what the demon boss desires. Come on, feet.

The now familiar Arabian belly dancing music is already pumping out of the speakers, which again can be heard loud and clear given the fact one door needs to remain open to help the airflow in the studio.

Reaching Joshua's door, I apprehensively raise my hand to knock when the distinct sound of a fist hitting what sounds like a desk makes me jump back a bit. Deciding he is otherwise occupied, as I can hear Joshua yelling at someone either face-to-face or via telephone, I march onward to the dance studio.

"Hey, Octavia," I call out to my Latino friend, who's wearing a big grin on her face.

"What's up, girl? Man, these guys are on fire!"

"I'm all good. What have you been up to since we've been rehearsing under Blaze's tuition?"

"This and that. I filled in for a few classes with Dante until after the Fire Festival."

"Oh, cool. How are things with Dante?"

"The school is *buzzzzzing!* He now has a waiting list for students looking to join his dance school. I know—insane, right?"

"Sure is," I comment while watching my dance crew run through the choreography with the belly dancers until it's my turn to step in.

"Hey, listen. I just dropped by to say a quick hello,

but I have to go. As soon as I allowed my network to know I had some free time to offer for classes, boom! My schedule exploded."

I know I shouldn't envy Octavia's freedom at being her own boss, but seeing how free and happy she is, I kinda-sorta do.

~ Chapter 38 ~

"MISS PEBBLE!" a big booming male voice sounds from behind me, making myself and all the dancers in the studio freeze.

"Did I or did I not ask you to meet me in my office?"

I open my mouth to explain but think better of it. Mr. Bear-head already has his knickers in a right old knot, it would seem.

"Darla, I did not see you there. You'd best go and see what Mr. Glass wants. We'll meet you in the main performing arena ready to practice on stage, ok?" Blaze rapidly gathers everyone together to hastily retreat to the main staging area.

Digit mouths the words *'good luck'* to me on passing, to which I respond by giving him a little tricep-pinch. Waiting until everyone's out of sight, I take a deep breath and steel my nerves for whatever is to happen now between Joshua and me.

"Take a seat," he says coldly, indicating to the only

other seat in his office. The previous black and pink chair has gone and is replaced by a plain white chair with plush leather upholstery. I'm currently in my tribal belly dancing garb and suddenly feel very self-conscious being near such an irked Joshua while scantily clad.

"Is everything ok? It's just...you seem mad. Did I do something wrong?"

"No. I'd just appreciate it if in the future you could do me the common courtesy of coming to see me when I ask you to."

Starting to get a sense of how poor Bane feels now.

"Sorry about that. I don't really like confrontation. When I heard you yelling at someone —"

"Oh, an eavesdropper too!"

"No, I meant —"

"Look, all I need you to do is read the copy of your new contract with the NDA included, then sign and hand it back to me before the day is out."

"That's ok. I trust you and Mimi. Where's a pen? I'll sign right now."

Joshua hands me his personalised fountain pen, which has his initials on it and a short message "*To my baby bro, happy birthday, love M. xxx*" My heart constricts at the sentiment and immediately I forgive Joshua in my mind. I can't begin to imagine the pressure he must be under.

Standing up, I turn to head out of his office with no further words spoken between us—that is, until everything begins to slip sideways, and I completely conk out from low blood pressure due to my heavy period. As I come round from my faint, I see two people in green uniforms and Brutus but no Joshua. It probably shouldn't bother me as much as it did, but for some reason I feel I have been lanced in the heart.

"Hi, Darla. My name is Liv and this is Brian. We're paramedics. It looks like you've had a faint," the very nice paramedic called Liv states.

Sitting up slowly, my head feels a bit swimmy but not as bad as previously. The paramedics do observations on me, and I decline a trip down to the hospital. I'm not diabetic with my low blood sugar, but sometimes I can get hypoglycaemic with my periods. Explaining this to the paramedics—and once I'm offered up an array of chocolate and fruit by Brutus who, bless him, ran straight down to the Pelican Brief bar to raid their kitchens—my blood sugar is now back to normal levels which makes the paramedics accept my decision not to go into hospital.

Blaze appears and sits with me in Joshua's office. The paramedics leave after I sign paperwork stating I don't want to be taken into the hospital. Brutus shows them out.

"Oh dear, my love, this is a fine mess. How are you feeling now?"

"Still a bit wobbly but better. Where is Joshua?"

"I'm not sure, sorry. When you didn't make an appearance, I came to make sure all was ok and discovered...well, this."

"So sorry to give you a fright. I'm really ok. Haven't had a fainting episode since my school days."

"Come on, no more dance for you today."

"I'll be ok in about an hour, honestly."

"Darla, we can't have you getting injured when clearly the hours are taking their toll. Rest for the remainder of the day. We've got time to practice some more."

Just then, Joshua appears in the doorway with Max. "Thank you, Blaze. I can take over from here."

Graciously, Blaze bows out to give Joshua and I some privacy.

"Sorry I gave everyone a fright."

"Its fine. I spoke to the paramedics they explained everything."

Oh God; he knows I'm on my period! Ground, swallow me up now. Perfect ending to a shitty day!

"Blaze says I'm not to rehearse for the rest of today."

"That is certainly a good idea. I'm heading home now. I insist that we drop you home," Joshua says, meaning him and Max.

"Actually, Brutus should be back any minute. I'm more than happy to be taken back by him if you don't mind."

"No, not at all. Here—let me help you up," Joshua says. He takes my hand to help me steady as I stand from the white chair. The feeling jolts a liveliness in me again, swiftly followed by a sinking longing of what I know now can never be.

"I'm also really sorry I didn't come straight to your office earlier. I just figured whatever you were discussing was private—heated or otherwise."

"You mustn't apologise for my arrogance, Darla. Having been so angry and bitter for five long years over what I thought was Mimi's murder...well, it's an adjustment to learning how to be soft and kind again." Joshua's face brightens as he says this with that lovely warm smile of his.

"Sorry to interrupt, Joshua, but your guest has been calling to know where you are," Max interjects, his words snapping me wide awake now.

Guest?!

"Right—yes. Get lots of rest this weekend, Darla. We need you in tip top shape for commencing rehearsals on Monday."

"I shall be there with bells on."

No other words are exchanged between us before Joshua makes his leave with Max. I wait until they are well out of sight before going in search of Brutus so that I can go home and drown my sorrows in wine, chocolate and some soppy romance movies.

~ CHAPTER 39 ~

Now back at home, feeling all the stress of the day slowly melting away as tiredness begins to seep into my weary bones—actually too tired to think too heavily on an emotional scale. I head to my freezer deciding on having the left-over Manti Ricardo had made with a slice of red velvet cake. Blaze texts me to see if I'm ok, and I reply that all is well.

Once I've filled up on the leftovers, I pour myself a nice glass of house red and dilute with lemonade (I love a red wine spritzer). Binks is already curled up on the sofa, purring away happily in the land of nod. Flicking through my movies, I land on *You've got Mail*. Mum and I love this movie.

Having dozed off on the sofa, I'm jolted awake by the sound of my doorbell. *Don't tell me I've forgotten I have Amanda today; I thought she was coming on Sunday!* I think, standing to go and answer the door.

"Hi, Ama —" I stop short and then say, "You're not Amanda."

"No, I'm not," Joshua says, leaning on my doorframe with a cheeky grin on his face. Stepping into my apartment he holds my face in his hands and the next thing I know, we're kissing—mad passionate full-on snogging.

"Yaahh!" I awaken with a big start.

These crazy dreams are actually driving me...well, crazy!!

"Sod this for a game of soldiers! I'm going out!" I exclaim, seeing as the night is still young.

Heading to my room, I pick out a nice little black cocktail dress with a pink sequinned belt. I don a pair of killer designer heels and whip my hair into a simple messy bun before applying some heavy eye make-up. I then call a taxi to pick me up outside the local cinema to take me off to *Lucifer's Haven*. No one knows my real identity from Pink Club, so I feel perfectly safe in my decision to go out and actually see my old friends, Bonnie and Co. If I don't do something drastic to shake my mind off Joshua, it's going to start to impact my dance performance, and with him and his *guest* now doing god-knows-what, god-knows-where, I'm fully aware that all we shared was a bit of dirty dancing *off duty* and a few kisses. We've never been boyfriend and girlfriend—no, he's just a piece of eye candy I have to keep away from outside of professional realms.

'*Everyone has a person, and you don't.*' Psyche's words once again rattle around loudly in my head as I exit my apartment, which just fuels my desire to be 'out-out' even more.

My period has calmed down a bit now, and I'm no longer feeling faint or dizzy. The short walk to the cinema to await my taxi helps me to clear my head a bit. The evenings are beginning to warm up now, and as I look around, I notice many couples coming out to see movies with each other and spend time together. Hugging my arms around myself, I feel my taxi can't arrive soon enough.

Finally arriving at *Lucifer's Haven*, I head over to greet one of the regular doormen, who recognises me instantly.

"Darla, hey. How you been, looker?" Bill, the exotic doorman from New Orleans, says with his rich southern drawl.

"I'm very well, thank you. And yourself?"

"Same old, same old."

"Ah, bless ya. Is it ok if I go to say hi to Bonnie and the girls before their shifts start?"

"You don't know?"

"Know what?" I look at Bill quizzically.

"New owner has taken over the place and all the dancers...well, they've been let go."

The ground beneath me feels as if it will give way. "Let go?" I echo, mortified.

"Sorry, Darla."

"Yeah, me too."

"I can still let you in if you like. You can beat all the revellers to the bar."

"Thanks, but I think I'll just head home."

"Well, it was good to see you, kid. Chin up, yeah?"

―――――

"Thank you, Joshua, for taking me in like this," Stella says coolly, approaching Joshua with an outstretched hand to touch him on the shoulder.

"Let's get one thing straight right away: you are not to stay here long-term. You've got 72 hours maximum to sort your shit out, and if you attempt any physical contact of any kind, this olive branch will cease to exist immediately. Do you understand me?"

"Y-yes. Sorry. I really do feel terrible for everything."

"Good, and so you should."

"How are Mimi and your parents?"

The look Joshua gives Stella in this moment tells her enough to ensure her mouth is kept firmly shut on the subject of his family.

"Joshua, I wonder if I may have a word?" Max interrupts, indicating for Joshua to follow him down to his gym space.

Comfortable to see Stella has not followed them to earwig, Max presses the severity of danger having Stella at his place now poses.

"It is a fuck pig; I'll give you that." Joshua agrees, outwardly sighing. He leans against the wall of his gym, the cool glass of the mirrors gently pressing against the sleeve of his white shirt on his upper arm.

"I have great contacts who can see to it she's set up somewhere else," Max offers, the look of concern on his face ever clearer here.

"Let me sleep on it. I'm tired and grouchy."

"Never go to bed grouchy. Why not box for a while then head to bed? I look forward to confirming alternative arrangements with you in the morning."

Joshua just smiles at his old bodyguard and friend. Max leaves Joshua to his own devices in the gym, hoping and praying he has full permission to remove Stella from the property tomorrow. He knows all too well it would just take one paparazzi snap to set aflame controversy and conspiracies, damaging Pink Club's just renewed trust and respect.

An hour passes and Max was right: boxing and exercising before bed has helped to take the edge off Joshua's earlier anger. Walking topless to his bedroom, he hears the distinct small sound of Stella crying. Gritting his teeth and forcing himself to ignore her, he reaches his bedroom door only for his curiosity to get the better of him. *Boy, I hope I don't live to regret this,* Joshua thinks.

Suddenly, a memory of Darla dancing with him flashes across his mind, causing him to pull his hand back as if stung by a bee, giving him both a change of heart and mind. Turning around, he makes the decision to leave Stella blubbering while he grabs a shower, late night snack, and then set his head down for a good few hours.

'Ohhh, you smell so good; I want to taste you.'
'How I wish you would.'

'Come here.'

Joshua awakens from his wonderful dream with Darla abruptly when he hears Max's loud voice booming down the corridor.

"Back away from Mr. Glass's door, Stella!"

"Stella...shit!" Joshua exclaims, jumping up to find out what the hell is going on.

"Look what I found. Miss Pink Panther here thought she'd try to sabotage your honour. See the camera in her hand there? Bet she was trying to get herself some incriminating evidence," Max states, fixing Stella with a cold hard stare.

Stella appears to shrink back with the pair of them now burning her with looks of disdain. "Oh...no...I was just —"

"Pack your shit and get out of my house and my life! Take her wherever, Max. The bitch is no longer my problem."

"Joshua, wait! I was...here," Stella cries desperately, holding the camera out for Joshua.

"I'm not playing games, Stella. Just go."

"It's no game, I promise. I know my word now doesn't mean much of anything, but please...I thought you might like these or maybe Mimi would."

"Mimi! Bitch, you better never let me hear you say her name again."

Stella dissolves into tears as she half-drops, half-places the camera down. "I really...am not...not welcome here, am I? I'll go."

"Yes, that really would be best," Joshua spits back,

heading back into his room pissed that his dream of Darla was interrupted.

Now for a cold shower, he thinks.

Once Stella leaves to pack her belongings, Max picks up the camera and sees it already switched to photos of Mimi and Joshua during happier times. Seeing this as a ploy to try and wind Joshua around her little finger all the more, Max removes the SD card, his blood simmering at how she had a hold of such personal intimate images. Hatching a plan of his own, he now waits patiently for Stella to be ready to move out ASAP.

"Where will you take me?" Stella asks Max, now ready to leave. Not having many belongings to her name, packing took literally five minutes.

"You'll find out. I managed to pull a few strings. You at least will not be homeless for the next three months, but after that you're responsible for your own rent coverage," Max growls, not giving anything away. "Here," he adds, handing back her camera.

They travel to a less desirable area of London, and to Stella's horror, Max pulls into a small community of what she would deem to be *'lower class'* dwellings.

"Right, come on. The landlord is ready for us; we don't want to leave him hanging around."

Stella, finding herself speechless at just how far she has fallen from grace, proceeds onward in silence.

Max confirms that the first three months have been paid for and hands Stella the key to her new home and new life, feeling she really did just deserve to be on the streets. However, having seen her in such a sorry state did pull on the thinnest shred of empathy he had.

Happy once she is inside and has all the relevant info, Max leaves her to it, closing the door and smiling. He is quite unbelieving of the serendipity of this entire situation, for now where Stella is residing is once where two Pebble women lived.

~ Chapter 40 ~

"Good morning, my dear. How are you feeling today?" Blaze walks over to give me a hug before we commence with the day's rehearsals. My dance crew just gives me a quizzical look before we crack on.

It still feels very strange to be danced around and not to have a partner this time for the choreography. I've gotten to grips with the belly dancing quite quickly, thanks to my wide range in dance experience.

"Ok everyone, let's have a break. Darla, you are to learn yet another *new* skill today: the art of *fire dancing*," Blaze announces, as if it's the most natural thing in the world.

I full-on choke on a sip of my water as Siren comes over to pat me on the back.

"You good?" he asks. I just give a thumbs up to show that I am.

"Is this wise? It's just less than two weeks until the

Fire Festival and this feels dangerous somehow," I say in vain to try and not be made to learn how to hand fire.

"Do not worry so much; you're only going to be dealing with tiny flames that come out of two specially designed hand-held fans. Diane, if you please, demonstrate to everyone exactly what Darla will be learning."

"Of course," Diane agrees, picking up two metal fans from her bag. She pushes two buttons on both fans. I'm guessing one is to release the gas and the other to ignite it, as little flames indeed start flickering from the edges.

Diane proceeds to dance my choreography in front of all of us, proving that it does indeed actually look very safe and also quite beautiful. We all applaud Diane's efforts as we break for lunch.

"Ok, I'm sold! That is indeed *very cool*," I comment to Blaze as we exit out of the dance studio. She gives me a knowing smile in return.

I barely think of Joshua as we pass his office to go have lunch. We are to have lunch and tea in the conference room to keep contact with Pink Club members to a bare minimum in the build-up to the Fire Festival. I may not be in control of my dreams, but during my waking hours I can choose my thoughts, and I choose not to think of the miserable beast.

As we enter the conference room, which is set up with a beautiful buffet table, everyone becomes relaxed and ready to grab some lunch and chill out. Eva appears looking...constipated, I think is a good way to describe the look on her face right here.

"Here you go," Mixer says, handing me a plate of food.

"Thanks." I give him a look as if to say, *I can get my own food, you know.*

"I spotted Eva and figured you'd probably be needing to take your food with you," Mixer explains in spooky fashion, just as Eva asks me to follow her to her office.

My dance crew and the Red Velvet Ladies briefly glance my way before getting fully engrossed again in eating and conversation.

"Dare I ask what's happened now?" I ask Eva as we enter her much warmer and inviting office space that's all mocha and vanilla tones—a stark contrast to Joshua's whites, blacks and steel interior.

"You'd better have a seat."

Shit! What's going on!

"Ok, now you're scaring me." I have lost my appetite and place my paper plate of chicken wings and salad off to the side on Eva's desk.

"Well, there's no easy way to say this, but someone's leaked your identity. Not only that, but they've made sure everyone knows where you live, work, and...intimate details about who you are. Also, of course, the *'incident'* back at Chef No .9 where you were so cruelly labelled —"

"Blow job girl." My voice cuts Eva off but comes out barely above a whisper.

"Indeed."

"What happens now? Should I resign?"

"Goodness, no! Whatever gave you that idea? No,

Max is on the case to find out exactly where this 'leak' has come from, but he thinks he has a fairly good idea."

"Stella," we say in unison.

Suddenly hungry, I pick up a wing and tear into it with my teeth, offering my plate to Eva, who also takes one.

"In light of everything, we're keeping you here out of sight of anyone external to Pink Club. It's only going to be temporary, but I've managed to set your dressing room into a sort of bedroom. Also, don't worry about Binks; I'm personally going to be overseeing his feeding."

Falling back into the plush cream leather high-back swivel chair I'm sitting on, my energy drops as the sheer weight of this info begins fully sinking in.

―――

Max steps out of Stella's pokey apartment convinced of one thing: it is not her who has leaked this information. Without a single lead, this task now leaves him trying to find a needle in a stack of needles. Entering the car, Max divulges his findings to a very angry and pissed off Joshua, who proceeds to hit the dashboard in utter frustration. He had hoped to keep Darla from the limelight for as long as possible, as had always been her wishes, and he can't but help feel as if he's let her down somehow.

~ Chapter 41 ~

Standing in my dressing room, I'm amazed at what a fantastic job Eva has done to make me look as homely as possible. Marsha had popped in an hour earlier to also show me around of the bits he'd help organise, simply gushing at the bespoke French boutique-styled furniture. I have a double bed (brand-new, assembled together by my dance crew). The Red Velvet Ladies helped put calming accents around like scented candles, and pictures on the walls, to make it more homely. I have two distressed vintage bed side tables and a mini wardrobe that can hold up to a full week's worth of outfits at one time.

It's now past 10 p.m. and everyone comes in to make sure I am settling in for the night. Brutus is stationed outside on a chair and will rotate every few hours with another person from security.

"Knock, knock," Brutus calls before entering. I'm in my jammies that Eva collected from home. They are my goldfish jammies with—yep, you guessed it—blown up images of goldfish all over them.

"Come in," I call as a huge frame enters my work/home space.

"Just thought you might like a marshmallow hot chocolate. Loving the pyjamas, by the way."

"Thanks," I smile while taking the disposable cardboard cup from Brutus. The dreamy, sweet chocolate liquid within helps calm my anxieties.

"I'll be saying goodnight then. Sleep well, and don't you worry; you're safe as houses here."

Shame the same can't be said about my reputation, I think bitterly. Eva had shown me the leaked news article that broke down that awful day at Chef No. 9 with the speculation still around that I was doing some sort of lurid sex act in the middle of a fully packed restaurant. *Please!* For added measure, the arsehole that had leaked as much personal and private details about my life had also included the wedding crash disaster my mum was responsible for. As an extra damaging measure, the article was trying to intimate that Pink Club could only afford a *'has been'* as there was even mention of my terrible heartbreaking experience with *Busy Bee's*. Marie Adams thankfully had decided not to pass comment on this article, but it painted me as having been dismissed from the school—not having to leave after the promised scholarship was stripped away.

I've yet to touch base with Joshua or Max. Eva seems to be the go-between, and thinking more on this, it's probably for the best.

Lying on my newly erected bed, trying to get comfortable, a thought then suddenly occurs to me.

Arsehole!

"Brutus, is there any chance I can speak to Max? It's rather urgent."

"Err, yeah, sure. Let me go and make a quick call," Brutus says, hurrying away.

I fast change out of my jammies and throw on some loose-fitting clothing while I wait for Max by either telephone or in person. Brutus appears a short while later to say that both he and Joshua are on their way to Pink Club.

Gulp!

30 minutes later...

"Hey, Darla, Max and Joshua are here. I'll go grab a coffee and give you guys some privacy," Brutus announces and then excuses himself.

"Hi, Darla. As you know, I spoke to Stella and I'm sure it's not her that leaked your information. Brutus said you needed to speak to us urgently. Was there someone you could think of who could do this to you?"

Well, actually Max, it was just you I wanted to see, but thank you for making this one million times worse for me now.

"Yeah...sorry, I know this is late, so I'll try not to keep you long."

"Darla, please do not worry about that. Now who do you think could be doing this?" Joshua says, and I see his tone of voice is much calmer and gentler here.

"Right. Well, my last boyfriend...he had huge anger

management issues, and long story short, I ended up in the hospital over making the grave mistake of having cooked chips and eggs instead of his expected steak one evening."

Both men just look at me in what I gather must be stunned silence.

"Nope—no, this isn't going to work," Joshua says all of a sudden.

Fuck! I'm fired?!

"Sorry, you're firing me?"

"What? No! Max, I will have Darla stay with me. You're my best security guy, and if she's at mine, we can at least keep a close eye until we determine if this lunatic ex-boyfriend is, in fact, responsible for this leak."

Cannot say I saw this coming. How can I cope being under the same roof as Joshua? Tongues are already wagging. No; I must stay here for the betterment of Pink Club's reputation.

"Don't be ridiculous! How can I stay at yours without drawing more attention and controversy? No, here is the safest place for me to be, and so here is where I'll stay until we know more. Plus, I have Brutus. No one's going to mess with him."

"It's not right, Darla; you shouldn't be chased out of your home like this. I don't like it."

"What's not to like? I have a brand-new bed, comfy mattress and it's homey with an en-suite bathroom. Ok, it's nowhere near as *luxurious* as my apartment, but you forget I come from humble beginnings, Joshua. Honestly, I'm fine and happy here."

"Sir, I agree that, although it's not ideal, it's better Darla remains here where *all* my best security is. She will have round the clock safety and protection at no extra cost to you and Mimi."

I see Joshua look suddenly crestfallen and realise maybe he wanted me close by for *other reasons.*

Oops!

"Can I ask again how you know for sure this isn't Stella? It's just...well, if this isn't my ex and you guys show up, he'll undoubtedly begin snooping."

"I can assure you that Stella is clean. I put her up in that old apartment you and your mum used to live in. "

As Max says this, I spit out some of my mouthful of marshmallow hot chocolate all over Joshua's pristine white shirt and cleanly shaven face.

"You seem to have a habit of assaulting me with hot drinks, Darla," Joshua says before we all begin to crack a smile and a little giggle escapes me.

"So it's agreed—I'm going to stay here and you two are going to do your detective thingies?"

"First, we need some information," Max says.

Taking a deep breath, I begin answering all relevant information for Max, who's noting it all down, such as my ex's name, height, build, occupation, last known address etc., etc.

"Why don't you speak to Siren? I'm sure he'd be able to offer some expertise being an ex-police officer."

"That's actually not a bad idea. Are you ready to go, Joshua? The sooner I can get the ball rolling with this information the faster we can conclude whether or not Darla's ex is, in fact, our perpetrator."

"Yeah, of course. Now, are you sure you're ok here, Darla?"

"I'm fine; now come on, go!"

With no further words exchanged, once both men exit my bedroom-come-dressing-room, I find the snugness of the space oddly comforting. Slipping back into my goldfish pyjamas, I duck under my new covers where I'm asleep within minutes.

~ Chapter 42 ~

Max and Joshua have pulled up outside the last known address to where the weasel known as Darla's ex lives. Weasel is the name Joshua has given to her slimeball ex. For all his hot and cold mood swings, Joshua is completely against violence to women—especially after what he believed had happened to Mimi.

"Let me handle the pip-squeak. Stay in the car."

"I feel this is the right decision. I'm likely to pummel him soon as look at him."

"Just as well you haven't seen Darla's medical records then. Oh yes; I got everything, thanks to Siren pulling some strings with some of his old police pals on the quiet."

Joshua cracks his knuckles, imagining rearranging the douche bag's face and feels jealous Max will get the pleasure to rough him up. Having checked phone records and IP address activity remotely, it's very apparent this is indeed where their leak is from, and Max has planned the perfect punishment to ensure he will never snitch on anyone—least of all Darla—ever again.

Rain begins to fall heavily on the car's windscreen as Max exits, pulling up the collar of his coat as he heads towards the front door. The overhead grey clouds give a moodiness that Joshua feels matches his own mood. All that's missing is some thunder and lightning.

He is feeling restless in the passenger seat, wanting nothing more than to give back to this weasel wounds that would put him in the hospital and see how he likes it. All too soon, though, thoughts of Darla begin to plague his mind; memories of her body next to his in the lift, her body dancing in perfect rhythm with him at *Lucifer's Haven,* the infuriatingly hot and sexy dreams he keeps having of her.

Struggling to focus, Joshua puts his headphones on and turns the radio to a station that is discussing Pink Club and Darla Pebble. It seems to be a special call-in programme where the public can offer up their *opinions* of the infamous nightclub catering to the rich and famous. About to turn off the radio, Joshua pauses as he hears the distinct sound of a panicked man calling in to admit he's the leak and how sorry he is for just trying to cause problems for his ex-girlfriend Darla Pebble who, in fact, is *not* the new star act for Pink Club; he just spun the media a line, knowing she had been in the papers about the controversial photograph. When the radio presenter said he should hand himself into police, the man made a sort of yelping sound before saying that is exactly where he was going next. He just wanted to apologise profusely to his ex-girlfriend and set the record straight: it's not her. To clarify it was the correct individual, the caller gave up his name so the journalist he gave so-called *evidence* to would know it was him. He even requested the radio station speak to the journalist to verify everything which they said they would and be waiting to give an update soon.

Joshua laughs at the sheer absurdity of this admission and radio programme.

"Well, you heard it here first, ladies and gents. *Blow job girl,* Darla Pebble, is NOT the new dance act at Pink Club! Mind you, they'd be surely mad to employ someone after that embarrassing story broke. Ooh, Joshua Glass, you dark horse."

Joshua rips out his ear buds and—having had a pencil in his hand that he was just toying with—promptly snaps this in half, thinking how there must be a way to clear Darla's name and her honour.

"Hey, all sorted," Max announces, entering the car and starting up the engine.

"So I heard," Joshua grumbles, holding up his mobile with the radio app still switched on.

"Little shit had the radio on, and when I heard it was a phone-in opportunity, I made him call in and sing like a canary."

"Why did he yelp?"

"I broke his pinkie finger to ensure he knew in his mind if he ever pulled shit like that again he'd end up worse off."

"Shall we put him in the hospital anyway?" Joshua asks, feeling ready for the fight.

"No. Darla will not thank you or I for that. It's better this all goes away...*quietly!*

"Whatever you say, *Dad,*" Joshua says playfully, mocking Max as they head back to Pink Club to deliver the good news to Darla.

———

"Wow! Darla, you're here early!" Midnight exclaims, as I am, indeed, the first one present and correct in the studio, having already warmed up.

"Morning, lovely girl! How are you today?" Blaze greets, giving me one of her mummy hugs that I'm growing far too accustomed to.

"I'm great, thanks. Feeling refreshed and ready for the fire dancing."

"Whoop! Whoop!" Diane cheers as she hears me.

"Right, ladies and gents, you know the drill. Let's partner up. Darla, I want you to use the fans minus the flames for now, and we will switch these on later. My intention is to have all of us up on the stage for our first full run-through."

I haven't yet heard from Max or Joshua, but Brutus —having heard word—said I'm no longer to worry about my ex, as it's been '*sorted*', whatever that means. He then played me a recording of the radio show, which sounded absolutely crazy. Who in their right mind would even confess like this of their own free will? When my ex yelped, I admit it made me chuckle, but as it stands, my anonymity has been set back up—just not my honour with the old '*blow job girl*' label STILL floating around and now at the front of every listeners' minds once again. Channelling my frustration, I give my all to dancing today.

~ Chapter 43 ~

"Ok, deep breath; you okay?" Blaze makes sure I feel balanced forty feet up in the middle of the stage.

"I'm good," I manage to say, while my stomach feels in knots. *Please hold, please hold,* I think for the cables this time.

Midnight gives me a wink and a gentle reassuring squeeze of my hand before we get in position, ready for the opening ceremony run-through and then the closing choreography.

"Good luck, Darla."

"You got this, girl."

"You're so brave."

My dance crew and Red Velvet Ladies pepper me with well wishes until Mixer says the right thing that puts my unease at ease, which is "break a leg." As much as I'm all up for compliments and wishes of "good luck," I know better than most that being superstitious around the old analogy of wishing someone a broken leg is very wise, indeed. The idea is if you wish someone a broken leg then it won't happen.

There is a pause long enough for me to collect myself before the music begins. I am now twirling, hip swaying, booty shakin' and rotating my chest in all kinds of weird and wonderful ways while also making the practiced movements with the fans (not lit). The stage feels sturdier than ever before, which adds to my confidence as I see Midnight, Digit, Mixer, Psyche, Medley and Siren keeping an eye on me for a point of reference to where I am in conjunction with the stage edge. The dance moves are much more static for the belly dancing routines. It's less of a *'look at me, I'm all over this stage'* and more *'shake what ya mother gave ya!'* (as Bonnie used to say). As I think of my old group of friends from *Lucifer's Haven,* a sadness washes over me but not for too long, as I'm doing my continual flashy moves with the fans again and wobbling all of my...well, wobbly bits, I suppose.

The music stops and we end in our finishing positions with me at the top end of the stage arms and fans stretched out wide. Everyone applauds as I turn to my dance crew and the Red Velvet Ladies and take a bow before turning back to practice bowing at my imagined audience.

"Well done, Darla—you were fantastic up there today," Octavia says, walking over to give me a hug as I'm now back on terra firma.

"I didn't see you there. Do you really think I'll be ok on the day?"

"You exude confidence. Hey, Midnight, lads, ladies," Octavia says, greeting everyone else.

No one has mentioned the leak to the press or bombarded me to know how it is my ex had a sudden change of heart to reveal on one of London's most popular and listened to radio stations how he was just acting like a jealous ex trying to wreck my life. I still don't know how he came to learn I was based at Pink Club, but since he redacted his statement to the press, a new embarrassing story emerged to help take the heat of my *'blow job girl'* one. Headlines now berated the paper responsible and threw sympathy my way, as the papers now state 'Darla Pebble—just a hard-working waitress who got caught up in a compromising position after an innocent accident at work' is what set the record straight, finally, on the whole *'blow job girl'* debacle. Miraculously, internal CCTV (retrieved by Max, no doubt) from Chef No. 9 revealed—finally—from a different angle that I was indeed not giving Joshua a blow job but that I had, in fact, just fallen forward during the accident at work. I guess in a weird way I should have thanked my ex for acting as the catalyst to getting the truth of the matter exposed and my name cleared.

"You really are a star performer, Darla; so proud of you the way you handle yourself. I shall be sad when it comes time for our short contract with Pink Club for this year's fire season to end," Blaze tells me, a sombre look crossing her face.

"You forget, though, that I know where you and Ricardo live now."

Immediately on hearing me say this, Blaze's face brightens. "Indeed, and we will be periodically working on your belly and fire dancing skills, so when the next fire season is here you'll be even more spectacular."

"Come on, no more talk of non-goodbyes! Let's get some food; I'm starving!" I exclaim, linking arms with Blaze and Viva as we head on towards the Pelican Brief bar.

I'd wondered why none of Pink Club's members never recognised me, but Joshua once explained how celebrities hardly ever even read the papers these days or listen to drivel, as they call, it about bad press on anyone famous. Too busy with their own lives shooting the next big Hollywood film or getting ready for the big fashion shows across the globe etc., he and Mimi certainly were not fans of the tabloid press. So as far as anyone is concerned, my name is Cosmic Storm but Cosmic for short. No one ever called Bella by her real name, even though members knew what it was. They always called her by her stage name, Sapphire or Sapphire Blitz.

Still in our tribal belly dancing garb, we certainly do draw attention as we enter the Pelican Brief and head off to a couple of secluded booths at the back. Eva reckons seeing us mooch about in costume will be a great advert for ticket sales, and so far she has been proven right. Eva had already alerted us that the event is selling out fast. As soon as my bottom hits the plush dark brown leather upholstery, I feel I could just quite easily curl up and go to sleep.

I'm sandwiched between Midnight and Blaze as Eric the waiter comes to take our order. Orders taken down, he walks off just as the doors open and I see none other than a recognisable gaggle of hungry, jealous-looking females enter.

Oh dear! Trouble at dawn! I think as Moesha, Bea, Craig, Lucy and Trinity enter. I'd forgotten they know all about Pink Club and are also allowed to visit as guests themselves.

"I see we have company...ladies," Blaze says expertly, commanding the situation, indicating that she and the other Red Velvet Ladies were to move to another table *immediately*.

Layla, who is partnered with Digit, blushes a deep red as she scurries to keep up with the other women now taking up residence at another table away from where I'm sitting with my dance crew and four feisty females, all with glints in their eyes (minus Craig, who, with Medley, is just super chilled out). Deciding this time to sit on an end, so as not to be between any of the guys and their girlfriends, Psyche clearly thinking the same, chooses to sit on the opposite end.

"Hey, Darla, sorry...I mean Cosmic Storm. I hear you were nearly outed by your jealous ex," Moesha drawls, triggering Midnight, I notice, to fast whisper something quite animatedly into her ear.

"Don't tell me what to do!" Moesha says louder.

"Excuse me; I'll be right back," I say, getting up to

give myself some distance between the loved-up couples and domineering energy coming off Moesha in waves.

That woman is like a loaded gun with a temper like that! Her and my ex would go well together! I think angrily while checking my reflection in the bathroom mirror inside my dressing room. The bed now removed makes me realise how suddenly very tired I am.

~ Chapter 44 ~

"Well, you couldn't be good if you've never been bad; you couldn't keep cool if you've never gone mad; you couldn't be glum if you've never been glad, and lemons give you lemonade." The lyrics to one of my grandparents' favourite jazz tunes *The Lemonade Song* by Pink Martini wash over me as I re-enter the Pelican Brief bar.

Psyche holds his hand up and waves to me, indicating he is now sitting with the Red Velvet Ladies and I'm to join them. Relief floods me as I notice my dance crew very busy with their partners catching up. The thought I'd have to be the odd one out there sets my teeth on edge.

"Figured it might be easier for us to sit together *here*," Psyche says, with no other explanation required.

"Thank you," I whisper gently into his ear, squeezing his hand as I sit between him and Maryanne.

"I took the liberty and asked the waiter to set up our

meal as sharing platters so we could all enjoy a bit of everything. I hope that's ok," Blaze tells me, looking at me with her wonderful warm smile.

"Wow! Great idea...yum!"

We raise our glasses and cheer one another. I'm glad we are sitting at a large round table; it makes us appear as all equals here.

Looking around, I see familiar famous faces, making me feel star-struck once again. At a table near the doors I spot the *Impossible Mission* actor is in with us this evening with a group of friends.

"I read the papers this morning. Good to see Max and Joshua have finally sorted things for you. Bet you're glad to never being referred to anymore as '*blow job girl*,'" Psyche says unexpectedly, causing me to breathe in a piece of avocado from the spicy chilli salad I've been enjoying.

It burns! Oh dear God' it burns!

Psyche and the women do not realise I'm choking as Psyche excuses himself to go to the gents. I stand to try and get his attention, but he doesn't see me. Stumbling forward, beginning to make what feels like weird chicken bobbing motions with my head, my world starts to tip as lack of oxygen starts suffocating me. I think I hear Blaze yelling off in the distance somewhere. Things begin to get echoey and black spots start covering my line of sight. Just then, I feel a strong clamping sensation around my previously bruised ribs that are still a bit tender. Fresh pain screams out across them as this vice sensation eases and comes back, eases and comes back.

Suddenly I feel a POP as the piece of avocado lodged in the back of my throat releases and wonderful air comes rushing back to greet my parched lungs.

Rasping sounds ensue as applause then erupts all around me. Turning expecting to see Psyche there, I almost pass out for a completely different reason. It's only the actor Cam Ruise from the *Impossible Mission* movies himself!

Applause is over, with guests quickly busy themselves in their table conversations.

"Oh my God, Darla, what happened? Are you ok?" Midnight cries, racing over with my dance crew to see if I'm ok. I feel Moesha's icy stare burn into me as she and her friends stay put.

"She'll be fine. Erm…sorry, what should I call you again?" Cam says, whispering in my ear with his rich American accent.

Oh, be still my beating heart!

"Dar—err, Cosmic."

"Pleasure to meet you, Cosmic. Thank you," he says, taking a nice glass of cold water from Eric and handing it to me.

"Honestly, I'm ok now," I assure Midnight and Co. between sips of the soothing water.

"You gave everyone quite a scare," Midnight says, side hugging me, which then leads me to getting hugs from the rest of my crew. It is here I'm sure I must be on some sort of Moesha hit list.

The guys head off back to their table once sure in themselves I'm actually going to be fine.

"Would you like to join me and my friends for a drink?" Cam offers, making me buzz.

"That would be lovely. A dream come true, in fact. I'm a huge fan, but I really must return to my own table of friends."

As I say these words, my sex goddess goes to throw a right strop on in the corner of my mind.

"Maybe another time then. Lovely to meet you, Darla...sorry, Cosmic," Cam says, winking at me cheekily before heading back to his own table.

Oddly, the fact that Cam knows my identity doesn't faze me; he appears the type who can be trusted with such private information. Besides, all things inside Pink Club stay in Pink Club—clearly! Hello? Topless stage dive! The realisation my naked faux pas will never see the light of day is very comforting indeed, especially as now I will never be referred to as '*blow job girl*' ever again—or that my almost 'death by avocado' choking incident will never make the tabloids. (Man, am I a walking disaster area or what? Bloody Pebble genes. Thanks Mum!) How the tongues would wag to have seen my life saved by Mr. MI5 himself! If only the press knew of just what went on inside here and the utter gold in content they miss out on. Well, I certainly think they'd feel sad indeed.

I guess Stella did do some good after all, with Pink Club's privacy record rating still being at 100%. Who'd have thought anyone could have anything positive to say about such a demon bitch boss?!

~ Chapter 45 ~

It is now the evening before the Fire Festival, and Joshua has invited me, the dance crew and Red Velvet Ladies, Eva and Octavia over to his apartment for pre-celebratory drinks and nibbles. There was no way I could decline, and knowing how many there will be, I assure myself it will be fine to be back at his apartment since I rebuked his invitation for that overnight stay when Mimi still lived with him. Apparently, the dress code is 1940's so naturally I went straight to Marsha-mellow with this wardrobe dilemma and was swiftly clothed in no time.

"Hi Marsha, please come in, come in," I say, ushering Marsha-mellow into my apartment. In his hands is my outfit for the evening.

"Where shall I set up?"

"The lounge will be fine."

"Ok—go and get the dress on. I'll sort your make-up and hair once you're dressed."

Happily taking my dress to my room, I lay it on my bed and swiftly undress, leaving just my blue lace underwear on that I picked out to match the dress.

Unzipping the bag, I hold up my dress for the night: a vintage 1940's blue daisy chain dance dress. Suddenly imagining my grandparents perhaps enjoying a dance together with my grandmother in just such a dress brings tears to the brink of threatening to flood my face.

Dabbing at my eyes with a tissue from the pretty pink and gold tissue box on my bedside table, I steel myself to get ready for what I hope will be just a nice, relaxed evening.

"There you are, beautiful. You are done!" Marsha exclaims, holding a mirror up behind me so I can fully take in the effect of his hair styling genius skills. The curls are a typical 1940's style and the black eyeliner and bright red lipstick finish off my look aptly.

"Thank you so much, Marsha. I must say it is quite a different experience to see you dressed out of your fantastical drag get ups!"

"Outside of work, the wife doesn't think it's a good idea I draw too much attention to myself. I do see her point with it being Pink Club."

"Yes, your outfits would certainly turn heads, so I do see your wife's point. How are the children?"

"All fit and well, thank you. Come on; time for your shoes."

Having danced in bare feet all the time I've been learning belly dancing, it's nice to be able to put heels on, pain-free. Don't get me wrong, I love my Pointe shoes and ballet dancing practice, but unfortunately for many—if not all—ballet dancers do end up with battered feet.

The shoes now on my feet match the blue of my dress. I feel like a real Belle of the Ball looking in the mirror at myself here.

Brutus arrives to take me across to Joshua's, complimenting me immediately as soon as I open the door.

"Ok, I'm off. See you tomorrow, Darla."

"Goodnight, Marsha. Thanks for being my fatherly Godfather tonight."

"Anytime, sweetheart."

Brutus and I arrive fashionably late, exclaiming how he's happy to wait in 'Old Bessy' until time to drop me back. I offer to bring him some food, but he assures me the kabob shop nearby has a lamb shish kabob with his name on it, to which I'm in no doubt over.

Entering Joshua's apartment, I'm greeted by a butler, who offers to take my coat from me. Handing him my coat, I walk on into a hub of activity. Alcohol, I see, is already well and truly flowing between everyone. The sight in front of me is an array of sequinned outfits for the Red Velvet Ladies in very glam 1940's dance dresses with the hair bands and feathers to boot. Also, to my great displeasure, I see that Moesha, Bea, Lucy and Trinity are also here. The women look stunning, it has to be said, in their chosen glitzy outfits; it's just a shame the wolf pack of jealous girlfriends doesn't have the personalities to boot.

"Miss Pebble. May I say you look assuredly exquisite

this evening," a very smooth-talking Joshua says, handing me a flute of bubbly champagne.

The dance track *Bed* slows across the room from speakers dotted about, giving a real party vibe to the space.

"Thanks," I reply, feeling myself rouge up on the cheeks.

Feeling decidedly under-dressed without a sequin in sight, I can't help but feel that Joshua is just trying to make me feel better.

My dance crew are already swaying with their *women* across Joshua's lounge-turned-dance-floor space. There is a buffet table and catering staff on standby. I notice Mixer has his own little set-up with a make-shift fancy bar—Lucy at his side, also helping to hand out drinks to everyone.

Blaze comes to my rescue when she spots me with Joshua. Seeming to float over towards us, Blaze asks Joshua if we might do a single belly dance of the evening.

"Sorry, for a moment there I thought you said 'we!'" I exclaim in astonishment.

"I did, indeed," Blaze says, nodding her head to the man in charge of the music. He turns down the volume, bringing everyone's focus and attention up.

Clapping her hands to grab everyone's attention to herself, Blaze asks for my dance crew and their girlfriends to kindly move aside so that me and the Red Velvet Ladies can do an on-the-spot, un-rehearsed belly dance! Seeing Joshua's face and how the biggest grin spreads across it gives me butterflies—*everywhere*.

Music starts with a deep and heady base, and once we have found the beat, I simply follow Blaze, Viva, Diane, Sheila, Layla and Maryanne as we go through a sequence of moves and then repeat. I'm swaying my hips, shaking my ass and boobs, while also making intricate moves with my hands and arms—the champagne giving me just enough courage to carry on throughout as naughty thoughts of Joshua now surface while I'm dancing.

How I long to do a naked tango with Mr. Glass.

Joshua's eyes lock with mine, and I find myself unable to break away, the rouge of my cheeks more colourful now as a fine sheen of perspiration also breaks out across my flesh from the exertion of dancing. The track ends as does the impromptu dance where everyone —even Moesha and Co.—give a round of applause.

The vibe in the room shifts along with the next dance track; the reverie broken as everyone now gets back to enjoying the party atmosphere.

"Hey, Mixer, Lucy," I say, propping up on the bar stool, intending to never remove my bum from here until it's time to go home.

"What can I get you?" Mixer asks me. He's wearing a long-sleeved white shirt with a glitzy purple sequinned waist coat and a bright pink bow tie. Lucy, next to him, compliments his look with a just as sparkly pink dress.

"You've got to try his Pink Flamingo honeycomb sundae shots. It's like a liquid crunchie."

"Sure, hit me up!"

The Pink Flamingo honeycomb sundae shots are indeed divine. For anyone not familiar with crunchies, they are sweetened honeycomb covered in milk chocolate.

Moesha comes and sits next to me on another bar stool, and beside her now sits Bea. Both women have 'vape' pens and begin to furiously smoke the sweet-scented liquids. The smoke makes me feel positively sick, and I take this as my cue to leave my seat for the night.

Everyone looks so happy and 'connected', and as I look around me, I realise how out of place I'm really beginning to feel. Joshua is nowhere to be seen, so I take my opportunity and head for the door.

I don't belong here.

"Thank you!" I exclaim to the butler as he hands me my coat.

Stepping out, heading down to where Brutus is sitting in the camper van, I ponder on the fact that no one seemed to notice I'd left, which cements my realisation this is a world I dance in but am not a part of and perhaps never truly will be. I'm sure had I been Bella Fitzroy I wouldn't have been ignored.

Looks like I'd have been better off staying at home—ALONE! I think, angrily more upset than hurt.

~ Chapter 46 ~

The Fire Festival

Not long after Joshua had put me to bed (realising this only when I awoke an hour later) did we start texting well into the early hours of the morning. The sentiment of him carrying me to bed and taking a sweet photo of us has not been lost on me. Eventually, I must have nodded off again, because the next time I wake, it's to the sound of the music drifting in from my en-suite bathroom. Rolling over and checking my phone, I now see a flurry of un-read messages from Joshua showing in my notification feed. The last message is one of his reflections to me that I must have fallen asleep as he had no answer, so he wished me goodnight.

Knowing how busy it's going to be today, I whip up

a breakfast of scrambled eggs, toast, sausages and cooked tomatoes while dancing to music by the Ronettes. Binks harasses me for something, so I give him a piece of sausage from my plate. Before long, it's time for me to leave once Brutus comes knocking for me.

Inside Pink Club, I am now heading straight for my dressing room to dress in my official belly dancing garb for the opening and closing ceremonial dances. A beautiful huge bouquet of different pink coloured roses now sits in a big crystal vase on top of my dressing table, they smell *divine*. The message on my card simply reads,

From your secret admirer x

Realising I don't have long to fawn over the flowers, I begin to get dressed into my pink sparkly genie: Middle Eastern styled belly dancing garb. The place is a buzz with activity, which I view in increments through the two-way mirror systems as I head up to the dance studio using all the back corridors and lifts.

"Ooh, la-la! Hello, beautiful girl!" Blaze exclaims as everyone turns to look at me. "Ok, everyone—into your starting positions. We have but thirty minutes to rehearse before we're needed on stage for the opening to the Fire Festival, so come on and focus, please."

"You look stunning," Medley whispers as he joins up with Maryanne.

"Very pretty," Maryanne says.

"Thank you."

"Ok, hush now…and 1..2..3..1..2..3.."

My brilliant pink diamond star necklace from Mimi and Joshua glimmers in the lights as I twirl along with the many sequins all over my floor-length skirt and crop top, which allows for my full mid-riff to be on display (rather than my boobs!). We all flow and shimmy in unison from one move to the next.

Having heard from the horse's mouth how Joshua really feels about me—finding out how he is adamant that he wants to pursue this connection and we both have to see where it will lead—gives me a feeling of now being less alone, and this realisation lifts me up like helium inside!

"Well done, everyone. Let's give each other a round of applause then make our way down to the main staging area," Blaze announces, bringing the last of our rehearsals to a close.

As we walk en-mass past Joshua's office, it is here that he calls out to me. Now I could potentially pretend I didn't hear him and keep going, but then he all but barks my name, earning me concerned glances from my dance crew and Red Velvet Ladies.

"Its fine, I'll catch up. Don't start without me," I call to Blaze jokingly. She just rolls her eyes to Heaven, waving her hands at me and looking exasperated.

Once happy they are out of view, I push Joshua's door open, which was already slightly ajar. I am unprepared for when he gently pulls me inside, shutting the door firmly behind me and then leaning in to kiss me. I don't resist; I want this just as much as he does.

Thank goodness for smudge resistant lipstick! is all I can think as our lips get busy dancing a tango of their own.

"Am I still coming to yours tonight?"

"Yes, unless you want me at yours. Wherever you're more comfortable."

"Ok, yours it is then."

"After your first dance, I will be spending the day with you, showing you off to all our best members and guests. We need to build Pink's profile back up again now that it is mine and Mimi's brand of business."

"You sure that's not just another excuse to spend yet more time with me?"

"Why, Miss Pebble, I do believe you are a mind reader."

I simply find myself glowing from the inside out in Joshua's company.

———

Arriving just in time to the basement for the stage to be raised along with the final curtain call, I get glares and worried glances from my dance crew and the Red Velvet Ladies as I'm ushered to the centre of the stage. We are a rainbow of bright coloured delights. All the women are wearing vibrant rainbow colours, and my dance crew are topless but wearing top hats that match their black sequinned bottoms. Around each hat is a band of sequinned material that matches their dance partner's costume colour. Blaze dazzles in bright amethyst tones, Diane in lemon yellow, Viva sparkles good luck in green, Sheila is in turquoise and Maryanne finishes off our colour spectrum in orange alongside my vibrant pink outfit.

Here is some trivia for you: pink is not really my favourite colour, so to be surrounded by it and wearing it on a regular basis makes me appreciate that perhaps I should allow for some pink to eventually bleed out into my wardrobe at home. I've never been one for being a 'girly-girl' but always a tom boy. Maybe I need to femme up a bit.

"Now, remember to relax, breathe and move in time with the beat," Blaze says in a hurried whisper to everyone.

Good lucks are thrown around until, once again, someone in the darkness says a sensible 'break a leg.'"

Thoughts of Joshua and our explosive kiss we just shared in his office replay in my mind, confirming to me that *it's on now!* just as the stage reaches its highest point and the lights and music come on, signalling the start of our dance. It's nice to be dancing in bare feet again, feeling the music throughout my body, channelling the rhythm as I've been taught.

Flicking my metal fans open, I begin the intricate and ornate movements, as they are now alight. Below the stage, a circle of well-trained fire dancers start their routine just on the outskirts of where the edge of the safety floor mechanism sits (should one of us be unfortunate again to stage dive over the edge). I catch glimpses of them on the huge screen and it's hard not to get entirely captivated, but I know I must focus so as to not falter my footwork. It's always hard to spot audience members with the bright lights, but from what I can see, it is a sea of fiery-coloured costumes and outfits. People are cheering and clapping. When our segment ends, the soundtrack portrays a booming clap of thunder just as a rain machine makes it look like the heavens have opened on top of us. I was at least forewarned, this time, of the added special effect giving us all a light sprinkling of water.

Cheers, applause and feet stomping erupt around us as we take our obligatory bows before being lowered back down into the basement where we are now dried off by staff navigating us towards a temporary drying station that's been set up. Big fans blow warm air that dry off our dancing costumes within mere minutes.

~ CHAPTER 47 ~

Joshua walks back into the living room having just finished quite a long conversation with Mimi and his parents out in Tuscany. He is pleased to hear that his sister is doing better and that his parents were having *real* conversations with him again. Buzzing, he now wants to locate the object of his desire for the rest of the night: Darla.

After searching about a bit unable to locate her, the butler informs Joshua of Miss Pebble's premature exit from his party.

Thinks she can just run away from me, does she? Oh, Miss Pebble, you can run but you can't hide.

Having experienced the earlier effect on him from Darla's presence at his apartment, Joshua now realises to resist the attraction is futile; he can bear it no longer and has decided to follow his primal urges, which is where Darla now fills this space of his mind.

"Mmmmm, home sweet home! Hello, my furry little friend!" I exclaim to Binks, who comes over to dutifully greet the hand that feeds him.

Kicking off my shoes and heading to hang my dress up, ready to return to Marsha tomorrow, I carefully place the vintage piece back in its Ziploc bag and leave it in my walk-in wardrobe. Feeling relaxed in my environment, I decide just to mooch about in my blue lace knickers, bra and over-the-knee skin-coloured stockings. Around my shoulders I don a lightweight cream-coloured floor-length gown but leave it open at the waist. Feeling in the mood for something sweet now, after sampling Mixer's Pink Flamingo honeycomb sundae shots, I head for the freezer and grab a tub of Rocky Road ice cream.

Too wired for any notion of sleep yet, I let loose with a bit of improv dance of my own, starting off with the dance track *Heartbreak Anthem* and am now in my happy place, singing along quite merrily while intermittently taking a scoop of Rocky Road.

Whilst spinning and twirling and 'wailing' along to some of my favourite songs karaoke-style, I nearly trip over my shoes that I unceremoniously kicked off (that'll teach me for treating vintage footwear with little respect). I pick them up only to blanche when I look at the small TV panel, which basically tells me who is at my door. Normally, I use the peephole in the door, not really seeing the point in the tech, as it's always going to be security or Amanda coming over (minus the impromptu arrival of my dance crew that lead to me dancing with Joshua at *Lucifer's Haven*).

Moving closer to the screen, I'm relieved to see it is Joshua loitering, but...what on earth is he doing? And why is he not back at his place entertaining everyone? I notice that he is pressing his ear to my door, clearly listening in to see if I am going to sing again.

Oh Jesus! He's heard my terrible singing!

"Oh, boy. Is that the time, Binks? Looks like I'd best be getting to bed early for the Fire Festival tomorrow," I say loudly after turning off my music.

Hoping my little ruse will deter Joshua from knocking and becoming a nuisance, I'm shocked to hear that he in fact uses my doorbell! *Fuck!* Can't exactly say I hadn't heard it as the bloody thing *bing bongs* throughout my apartment.

Taking a deep breath and removing the chain to an open position, I pull the door open with a bit more venom then I'd intended. Immediately, I can see that Joshua's eyes go wide as if out on stalks as a cold blast of air from the corridor washes over me.

Of all the holy shit balls in the universe—I'm standing in front of my boss in just my UNDERWEAR!!!

Joshua says nothing, just pushes gently past me as I rapidly shut my door, hoping none of the neighbours peeked to see who was ringing at this late hour.

"Hi. Make yourself comfortable. I'll be right back," I say, now legging it to my bedroom.

Fast dressing into a pair of my funky pyjamas, and this time getting a much thicker dressing gown around me, firmly tying the waistband around me, a voice from my open bedroom door makes me jump.

"AHH!!" I scream, which also makes Joshua jump and then Binks, who shoots off my bed and out to somewhere else in my apartment.

"Hey, Darla. I have come to say—holy shit."
Holy shit? What?

I can only watch in shock horror as Joshua's feet get entangled in a pair of my stray knickers on my bedroom floor and then begins on a trajectory towards my walk-in wardrobe where his momentum is stopped by him head-butting the rear wall of my wardrobe. This shakes loose a pair of my hefty pole dancing shoes with killer heels out of their box where one of them thwacks him squarely in the right eye, and then he is still.

"No, no, no, no, no, no! Joshua, Joshua!!" I cry, bordering on hysteria as I now launch towards where Joshua lies motionless in a heap in my walk-in wardrobe —the stray pair of knickers still wrapped around one of his ankles.

Leaning in to see if he's breathing, I feel his hands grasp my arms, holding me firmly in place as his eyes snap open and the biggest grin spreads across his face.

"Gotcha," he says before gently pushing me onto my bedroom floor and kissing me. "I came here to say that I can't and won't stay away from you any longer." Joshua then stands and holds a hand out to me, helping me to stand.

Speechless, and unable to deny the fierce attraction of my own towards him, I'm relieved when he takes my hand to lead us both out of my bedroom, because if he wanted to get hot and heavy between my sheets, I'm not so sure I'd be able to resist with how I'm feeling—especially now after that explosive kiss.

"Hang on; let me get some ice for your eye," I finally manage to get out as I break out of our hand-holding embrace to run for the freezer. "Won't everyone be missing you back at your place?"

"Thank you for reminding me," Joshua says, pulling his mobile from his pocket. "Hey, Eva, can you shut down the party in about thirty minutes? Where am I? I've just gone to get some fresh air...yeah, difficult phone call with Mimi and my folks. Cheers, Eva. See you tomorrow."

"Here you go," I say, handing Joshua a cooling block wrapped in a tea towel.

"Cheers. Ah, where do you think you're going?" he murmurs, pulling me to him so that I fall into his lap—my heart all but erupting from my chest.

We're kissing again.

"Wait! This is ludicrous. How can this—we—possibly happen? I'm '*blow job girl*' remember?"

"Stop it! Don't do that!" Joshua demands quite directly, with a tone that hits me squarely in the chest.

"Do what?"

"Put yourself down. Max and I have cleared your name; the tabloid press won't print anything like that on you ever again, and before long it will be *yesterday's* news. Now be a good girl and make us some coffees. We can curl up watching James Bond movies while we get to know one another better."

Yes sir! I think obediently, doing as Joshua asks. *However, if he thinks I'm some sort of submissive pushover he will be surely mistaken.*

For the next few hours, we chat a lot about everything we like such as music, TV programmes, food, hobbies, and some family history about ourselves. I find myself opening more to Joshua than anyone before—what happened with *Busy Bee's*, my grandparents, Mum, ex-boyfriend. Joshua, in turn, shares of happier times with his family, the whole Stella affair and chaos that came with that, but he doesn't really offer anything up about how Mimi's disappearance affected him or the fact she was alive the whole time. This will be something I feel I will have to work on with Joshua, because at the way his mood swings stand—if they don't improve—I can't promise to devote myself to him, as I've already been with a man who showed the charm and then the aggression later, unable to express feelings or emotions in healthy ways instead choosing to use me as a punching bag over fucking eggs and chips!

Joshua feels like he has been talking to an old friend he's known for years. Not once has Darla interrupted him while speaking, which he is finding truly refreshing. It is only on looking down at his lap where her head now rests that he can see she is fast asleep.

That explains the no talking part then, he thinks humorously to himself.

Grinning, Joshua carefully manoeuvres himself off Darla's sofa to carry her to her room and put her to bed. She feels light as a feather in his arms, and before putting her beneath the covers, he unties the robe, which reveals pyjamas that have different types of emojis all over.

Silently chucking to himself, Joshua pulls the covers up and over her. Before making an exit, he lies next to Darla and takes a photo of his head next to hers. Binks, purring, comes over to greet Joshua, who says a swift goodbye to the little fuzzball. Once out of the door to Darla's apartment, Joshua waits until he is in the car with Max before sending a message.

Night, night, beautiful lady. Tomorrow after the festival you are staying with me — NO argument x

He sends this with the photo of him lying next to her as she sleeps.

~ Chapter Forty-Six ~

The Fire Festival

Not long after Joshua had put me to bed (realising this only when I awoke an hour later) did we start texting well into the early hours of the morning. The sentiment of him carrying me to bed and taking a sweet photo of us has not been lost on me. Eventually, I must have nodded off again, because the next time I wake, it's to the sound of the music drifting in from my en-suite bathroom. Rolling over and checking my phone, I now see a flurry of un-read messages from Joshua showing in my notification feed. The last message is one of his reflections to me that I must have fallen asleep as he had no answer, so he wished me goodnight.

Knowing how busy it's going to be today, I whip up a breakfast of scrambled eggs, toast, sausages and cooked tomatoes while dancing to music by the Ronettes. Binks harasses me for something, so I give him a piece of sausage from my plate. Before long, it's time for me to leave once Brutus comes knocking for me.

Inside Pink Club, I am now heading straight for my dressing room to dress in my official belly dancing garb for the opening and closing ceremonial dances. A beautiful huge bouquet of different pink coloured roses now sits in a big crystal vase on top of my dressing table, they smell *divine*. The message on my card simply reads, **From your secret admirer x**

Realising I don't have long to fawn over the flowers, I begin to get dressed into my pink sparkly genie: Middle Eastern styled belly dancing garb. The place is a buzz with activity, which I view in increments through the two-way mirror systems as I head up to the dance studio using all the back corridors and lifts.

"Ooh, la-la! Hello, beautiful girl!" Blaze exclaims as everyone turns to look at me. "Ok, everyone—into your starting positions. We have but thirty minutes to rehearse before we're needed on stage for the opening to the Fire Festival, so come on and focus, please."

"You look stunning," Medley whispers as he joins up with Maryanne.

"Very pretty," Maryanne says.

"Thank you."

"Ok, hush now...and 1..2..3..1..2..3.."

My brilliant pink diamond star necklace from Mimi and Joshua glimmers in the lights as I twirl along with the many sequins all over my floor-length skirt and crop top, which allows for my full mid-riff to be on display (rather than my boobs!). We all flow and shimmy in unison from one move to the next.

Having heard from the horse's mouth how Joshua really feels about me—finding out how he is adamant that he wants to pursue this connection and we both have to see where it will lead—gives me a feeling of now being less alone, and this realisation lifts me up like helium inside!

"Well done, everyone. Let's give each other a round of applause then make our way down to the main staging area," Blaze announces, bringing the last of our rehearsals to a close.

As we walk en-mass past Joshua's office, it is here that he calls out to me. Now I could potentially pretend I didn't hear him and keep going, but then he all but barks my name, earning me concerned glances from my dance crew and Red Velvet Ladies.

"Its fine, I'll catch up. Don't start without me," I call

to Blaze jokingly. She just rolls her eyes to Heaven, waving her hands at me and looking exasperated.

Once happy they are out of view, I push Joshua's door open, which was already slightly ajar. I am unprepared for when he gently pulls me inside, shutting the door firmly behind me and then leaning in to kiss me. I don't resist; I want this just as much as he does.

Thank goodness for smudge resistant lipstick! is all I can think as our lips get busy dancing a tango of their own.

"Am I still coming to yours tonight?"

"Yes, unless you want me at yours. Wherever you're more comfortable."

"Ok, yours it is then."

"After your first dance, I will be spending the day with you, showing you off to all our best members and guests. We need to build Pink's profile back up again now that it is mine and Mimi's brand of business."

"You sure that's not just another excuse to spend yet more time with me?"

"Why, Miss Pebble, I do believe you are a mind reader."

I simply find myself glowing from the inside out in Joshua's company.

Arriving just in time to the basement for the stage to be raised along with the final curtain call, I get glares and worried glances from my dance crew and the Red Velvet Ladies as I'm ushered to the centre of the stage. We are a rainbow of bright coloured delights. All the women are wearing vibrant rainbow colours, and my dance crew are topless but wearing top hats that match their black sequinned bottoms. Around each hat is a band of sequinned material that matches their dance partner's costume colour. Blaze dazzles in bright amethyst tones, Diane in lemon yellow, Viva sparkles good luck in green, Sheila is in turquoise and Maryanne finishes off our colour spectrum in orange alongside my vibrant pink outfit.

Here is some trivia for you: pink is not really my favourite colour, so to be surrounded by it and wearing it on a regular basis makes me appreciate that perhaps I should allow for some pink to eventually bleed out into my wardrobe at home. I've never been one for being a 'girly-girl' but always a tom boy. Maybe I need to femme up a bit.

"Now, remember to relax, breathe and move in time with the beat," Blaze says in a hurried whisper to everyone.

Good lucks are thrown around until, once again, someone in the darkness says a sensible 'break a leg.'"

Thoughts of Joshua and our explosive kiss we just shared in his office replay in my mind, confirming to me that *it's on now!* just as the stage reaches its highest point and the lights and music come on, signalling the start of our dance. It's nice to be dancing in bare feet again, feeling the music throughout my body, channelling the rhythm as I've been taught.

Flicking my metal fans open, I begin the intricate and ornate movements, as they are now alight. Below the stage, a circle of well-trained fire dancers start their routine just on the outskirts of where the edge of the safety floor mechanism sits (should one of us be unfortunate again to stage dive over the edge). I catch glimpses of them on the huge screen and it's hard not to get entirely captivated, but I know I must focus so as to not falter my footwork. It's always hard to spot audience members with the bright lights, but from what I can see, it is a sea of fiery-coloured costumes and outfits. People are cheering and clapping. When our segment ends, the soundtrack portrays a booming clap of thunder just as a rain machine makes it look like the heavens have opened on top of us. I was at least forewarned, this time, of the added special effect giving us all a light sprinkling of water.

Cheers, applause and feet stomping erupt around us as we take our obligatory bows before being lowered back down into the basement where we are now dried off by staff navigating us towards a temporary drying station that's been set up. Big fans blow warm air that dry off our dancing costumes within mere minutes.

~ CHAPTER 48 ~

"Darla, I need to borrow you for a few photographs and autographs with the punters," Eva says, spilling into view. Today she is wearing a fierce coral blouse that matches her nail polish, black suit jacket and trousers with coral kitten heels on her feet.

"Ok, everyone—don't forget to meet back here on time for our closing segment. Enjoy the festivities. And ladies, remember we are still guests here at Pink Club, so *behave* yourselves," Blaze tells us, addressing the rest of the Red Velvet Ladies.

Pink Club's professional on-site photographer has a station set up for photos that guests can purchase before leaving. Everyone has, so far, called me Cosmic or Cosmic Storm, and I think perhaps Joshua is right: I'm yesterday's news already as *Darla Pebble*. This thought helps me relax as one Cam Ruise comes into focus, sidling up beside me for a photo and giving me a smile and a wink before heading off to mingle.

"Hey, Cosmic," a familiar voice shouts to me from somewhere within the latest collection of guests and members. As before, not only am I giving autographs but also asking for some myself.

Mimi's beaming face comes into view. She's wearing a mask, but I'd know her voice anywhere. Taking in her outfit I see she's wearing a fiery orange crop top which looks to have been made with dragon scales—I'm guessing this because the mask is a dragon-styled one. She is also wearing a mini dark brown leather skirt and matching knee-high boots that have been specially designed to make her look like she's walked off some fantasy medieval movie set.

To get everyone's attention, Mimi removes her mask and, of course, all focus is aimed at her. I shrink away from the photographer to allow her space to set up where I was just sitting. Turning to leave, or make myself otherwise occupied, Mimi's hand suddenly shoots out as she draws me close to whisper, *"Joshua wants to see you. He's in the Pelican Brief."* I feel myself looking stunned at this admission. I notice how Mimi just winks at me before pulling her dragon mask back down to pose with guests and members.

Eventually, I manage to muscle my way through to the Pelican Brief bar, but on entering, I'm amazed at how different the place now looks. Different styled chairs and tables stand in place of the original dark wooden ones. Now there are golden chairs with round tables that have a faux red marble effect on the top. The bar has been dressed in fiery toned pennants; the staff are wearing costumes that make them look like they just walked off the set of *Xenia Warrior Princess,* and the guests inside blend very nicely in their varying degree of reds, orange, brown and yellow tones.

Feeling very much like a deer in headlights here, as I see no one I recognise—not even Eric, the usual bartender—relief floods me as a gentle hand pulls me round to face the owner of said hand. Joshua.

"Hey, sexy," he says cheekily, making me turn positively scarlet.

"Hi—err—are you sure this is a good idea?"

"What? Letting people know we have a 'connection?'"

"Yes—isn't that one of Pink Club's strictest rules?"

"Oh, that. Well seeing as my sister and I are now the correct owners of Pink Club, we may have decided to change some, if not most, of Stella's rules!"

"I see."

Unable to think of anything to say, I gladly follow Joshua as he leads me to a table with two more people sitting down, a very smartly-dressed man and woman who are both wearing masks.

"Darla, I'd like you to meet my parents, Pandora and James Glass."

Wowzers!

"It...it...it's lovely meet to you," I stutter, thinking, *thank you verbal diarrhoea!!*

"The pleasure is all ours," Joshua's mother Pandora

responds, smiling warmly to me; his father less so—more of a grimace.

"What can I get you to drink, Darla?"

"Oh, nothing alcoholic for me, please. You know, with the dancing later and everything." *Why am I acting so kooky?! Oh, I know why; maybe it has something to do with meeting my new love interest's parents before we've even had a chance to COPULATE!!*

"I think I know just the drink you'll like. Our menus are all different for today. Hang fire; I'll be right back."

It's not like I'm going anywhere fast!

As Joshua disappears to order me a *whatever* to drink, Pandora starts to open up the conversation. "This place really is something special; doesn't it make you feel proud of our children, darling?"

"It's certainly unusual, that's for sure," James Glass grumbles. He stands, excusing himself from the table to go in search of a bathroom.

"Gosh, you really are very pretty," Pandora says, looking directly at me.

"Hey, Mum, where's Dad? Here, I got us all some fire Phoenix non-alcoholic beers to try. The catering companies Eva got in seem to be doing a good job and have been a real hit with everyone."

"Wow, that's gingery!" I exclaim.

"Ohhh, and spicy, but I like it," Pandora adds.

"Cheers," Joshua says as we clink our tankards. (Yes, these are served in ye olde English styled tankards.)

"Your dad's just popped to the loo. He'll be back soon, I imagine."

"Hi, guys. Wow, this festival is amazing!" Mimi says, plonking herself in a free chair between Joshua and me.

"I thought I'd show Darla around all of the rooms and stalls."

"What a good idea! You two go and explore. I'll look after Mum and Dad here," Mimi says, winking at Joshua.

~ Chapter 49 ~

"Mimi seems in good spirits," I comment as we exit the Pelican Brief bar.

"There was a big family session in Tuscany. Now that the real healing can begin between us, Mimi's journey to recovery seems to be going from strength to strength."

"I'm really pleased for you all. Your mum and dad are lovely."

"Really? I thought Dad came across as rude and abrupt. They never approved of Mimi and I doing something *artsy*—as my dad always put it—as a career. No, they wanted children who grew up to be lawyers or doctors."

"Perhaps he realises he may have misjudged your business venture and now needs time to process?"

"Hmm, maybe. Anyway, no more talk about my folks. First stop is the Fire Village."

"Sounds exciting."

"It is, trust me."

The Fire Village is set up in the 1920's styled ballroom. Everything has been changed and set up to look like a ye olde English outdoor market. The pillars, walls and floor have been covered in faux stone materials; the stalls themselves are wooden and straw huts. There are tribal clothes, a hot yoga stand with hot stone massages available, exotic-looking trinkets at a jewellery stand with all handmade jewels. Then there is the glass stand with expensive ornate glass blown paperweights, vases and other various works of art developed from glass.

"Would you like something from here? Please choose whatever you'd like."

Deciding to indulge Joshua, I head straight for the glass stand, picking up a pink glass ballet slipper paperweight which has caught my eye. However, on seeing the price and noticing it's *very* expensive, I rapidly place it back on the table.

"Mr. Glass, your date is very pretty. The lady seems to like the ballet slipper. Can I tempt you with a special offer?"

"You know I love a deal, Samuel."

As the men barter over the glass ballet slipper, my eyes wander and lock onto a pink glass star.

"Wait! Here—this is what I want...please," I say just as Joshua is about to seal the deal on the slipper.

"Tell you what; buy the slipper from me, and the lady can have the star for free," Samuel the seller says.

"Actually, I'd like to buy the slipper for a friend. You

may buy me the star as a gift," I say, turning to Joshua, feeling happy in my decision.

"Who, pray tell, is this *friend*, hmm?" Joshua asks me quizzically.

"A lady who knows a thing or two about *golden* slippers," I reply cryptically and winking.

"Oh, that friend. Yes, I'm sure she will indeed love this. Good choice, Cosmic."

"Wait a minute...*this* is Cosmic?! Oh, please may I have your autograph? Here, I insist on gifting you one of these handmade bracelets with glass pebbles in it," Samuel says, holding out a small notepad and pen to me.

Finishing up our business with Samuel and his amazing artistic glass creations, Joshua then steers me out of the ballroom-come-market and off towards the rest of the rooms that have been transformed to give a festival vibe inside them. We go to the Fairy Fantasy room where all the lights and tones have been switched from purple hues to that of a more reddish pink. Madame Scarlet is out of her indoor gypsy caravan today and doing readings on the table just to the outside of where she normally does her business.

"Fancy having your fortune told?" Joshua asks, which makes me shiver.

"No, thank you. I'm a staunch believer in the old *ignorance is bliss* analogy." *Especially after the last time of 'hold on tight' followed not long after by my topless stage dive! What the eff?*

"Very well. Come on. We've got lots more to see before we have lunch with my folks and Mimi."

"Lunch...together...just the four of us?"

"Darla, please relax. I don't mind that anyone knows we are *courting* one another. I'm 50% boss man, remember? You have the other 50%'s blessing."

"You TOLD Mimi about our *arrangement?*"

I'm not so sure if this is a dream or nightmare scenario.

"Apparently, my sis seems to have a knack about these things. Madame Scarlett better watch out, as I feel Mimi could give even her intuitive insights a run for their money."

My stomach is now well and truly in knots—thank you, Mr. Glass!

~ Chapter 50 ~

Venturing round, I see the rooms transformed to feature a decorative theme to match the Fire Festival vibe. There are an array of fantastic products and services ranging anywhere from scented candles to homemade herb packets—some of which you can mix with mayonnaise to make up spicy condiments for the purpose of accompanying any salad or cracker biscuit. Then there are body products such as homemade bath bombs, soaps, lotions and potions, and even a spicy chocolate stand which I definitely indulge in.

The Area 51 room had been changed into a mini day spa! Now, I know what you're thinking: "Wouldn't this have been better off in the Pink Flamingo room with all the Jacuzzis?" But in there today they have fire-breathing and dancing performances going on for the guests in swimwear. How crazy is that? Getting a fire show while enjoying a nice relaxing soak! #jealous! I wondered if I might hire them to come home with me for my own bath time, but Joshua wasn't too impressed with this idea.

Last on our way round is the Frankenstein Room, which has temporary bookshelves showcasing an array of exotic books on sale by varying top authors, who are here in the flesh, promoting and signing their new releases. The subjects range from self-help guides—teaching how to turn up heat in the bedroom—to the more wide-ranging romance fictional novels going from vanilla level to full-on BDSM extreme style. Then there is the company *'fluffy bunny'* displaying sex toys, underwear and *other* products. Dancers and performers wow the revellers on podiums and in cages. There's a lot of bare flesh on show—PVC, leather, whips and chains. I'd say this has certainly been the *hottest* room on show for me in Pink Club today.

Joshua leaves me for a moment (*gulp!*) but fortunately, as he does this, I spot the chef Maurice (who, if you remember, was the clever clog responsible for giving Eva that *marvellous* idea for having me dance on New Year's Eve for my birthday) and head on over to catch up with him.

"Well, hello my favourite cake muse," he announces on spotting me.

"Hey, this is certainly an *interesting* space today."

"Eurgh, tell me about it. I'll be thankful when I can go home after my shift. Do you know I've had to make cakes in the shape of the female and male genitalia?! Eva insists that 'sex sells' and was adamant that we had to push this *niche* market today for our more colourful in-house guests. Yes, quite frankly I'll be thankful when the whole sordid affair is over," Maurice states, throwing his arms up, sounding exasperated.

"I take it you're not a fan of the BDSM scene or best-selling book series 'Seventy Sordid Sides to Susan' then?" I say, chuckling slightly at how, when I tried to read the first book in the raunchy series, it was just way too OTT for me.

"Pah-*lease* don't tell me you read such drivel, Darla."

"I may have dabbled on recommendation from a friend (Bonnie), but yeah...not for me."

"You, darling Darla, are as sweet as vanilla sponge; don't you ever change that!" Maurice says, leaving me to venture over to where some of his *designer* cakes are being distributed. Apparently he needs to *make an appearance.*

"Right, shall we go?" Joshua says, making me jump slightly as he walks up to me from the side.

"Everything ok?"

"Sure! I just caught up with Madame Tout-Sweet. She helps Eva organise our big book signing events alongside managing her own erotic fiction business. Here—she gave us both copies of the latest bestseller."

"Wow...erm...thanks," I say perhaps a bit too enthusiastically, which elicits a coy smile from Joshua. *Don't you get any ideas, buster! I'm a vanilla queen all the way.* I suddenly start fretting, wondering if Joshua is super kinky!

I'm glad the book Joshua hands me is in a nice black sparkly bag and well hidden. This will be going in a box in my wardrobe right at the back. Kink in the bedroom really isn't my scene. I'm vanilla through and through, and if that makes me boring, then tough luck; I am who I am.

Walking back into the Pelican Brief bar, Joshua and I spot Mimi chatting very animatedly to Psyche—and no one else in sight.

Ugh, oh!

A dark cloud passes over Joshua's features on seeing the pair 'cooing' over one another.

"Hey, Mimi, Psyche," I greet, announcing our presence as we join them at the table.

"Psyche," Joshua says, looking at my newest dance crew member with a look that could actually kill.

"Mum and Dad went to mooch about," Mimi says quite cheerily.

"You didn't think to chaperone them?" Joshua snaps.

"It's ok. Eva has taken them for the 'grand tour.' I can't believe they actually agreed to come this time. Maybe I played a bit on my 'vulnerabilities.' Mum was easy to coerce, but Dad...took a bit more time."

"Haven't you got somewhere to be, Psyche?" Joshua asks, not hiding his irritation at having him fawning over his sister well at all.

"Psyche is with me. Shall we order something to eat?" Mimi says and, I all but feel as if I'm in the middle of some awkward tennis match on words.

Before anyone can say anything further, Pandora and James Glass arrive at the table. They look happier, and at least James is smiling now.

"This place is so much *fun!* Look—your dad and I got our faces painted, and here...matching tribal bracelets," Pandora all but squeals with delight, which I notice elicits looks from both Mimi and Joshua as if their parents have both had head transplants.

"I have to admit I am very impressed. You have done a great job—both of you," James says. Mimi jumps up to hug her dad.

Pandora begins a conversation with Psyche, and when I glance up at Joshua, I'm thankful to see he looks a little less constipated—or like he needs to have an angry poo!

"Oh, this is a pretty bag. What's inside?" Pandora states excitedly, picking up my black sparkly shopping bag.

Oh god; I think she thinks it's Mimi's!

Before I can stop her, she's pulled out my copy of *Putting a 21st Century Guide for Karma Sutra Lovers on Steroids.* There is, let's just say, a photo of a big black man being 'pleasured' by his female counterpart on the cover.

"Well...this is certainly...interesting." Pandora's voice comes out as a high-pitched squeak as she says the last word.

"Joshua got it for me."
WHAT THE HELL!!!!!

I can't stop the words coming out; they just leave my mouth on automatic impulse, as if through sheer embarrassment, I feel the need to confess my sins. Pandora turns bright red as does James. Mimi spits her mouthful of drink directly at Psyche, who just looks stunned.

"Relax, everyone. I was given copies of Tout-Sweet's latest book, so as to not appear rude took them graciously. She helps Eva arrange our book signing events," Joshua explains very dead pan.

James begins to chuckle, which turns into a deep belly laugh, then before we know what's happening, all of us are literally falling about the place in hysterics. Tears fall, and my sides hurt by the time I recover myself.

"Thank you for making my folks laugh. We haven't had a happy family meal like this in...forever. I owe you," Joshua whispers, which makes me buzz inside.

"I'll make sure I collect what I'm owed at yours later," I whisper back.

"Kinky," Joshua whispers, which elicits an eye roll from me and a head shake.

~ CHAPTER 51 ~

Pandora and James finish lunch with us before making their excuses to leave. With the evening rolling in, James wants to take his wife on a romantic stroll. Pandora, looking positively giddy with excitement, claims her husband hasn't been this attentive to her since...but stops mid-sentence to not bring up Mimi's disappearance.

"Right, we'd better go and prepare for our closing ceremony dance," Psyche says, excusing us both from the table.

I see a *look* passes momentarily between Mimi and Psyche, but I don't draw any attention to it, having clearly seen how displeased Joshua is seeing his sis hanging out with Pink Club's newest dance member.

"Don't forget our meeting in the dance studio. I've decided to get back into dancing, isn't that exciting?" Mimi says, an angelic look to her features.

"Indeed, this is very good news. I will be sure to send

Octavia up with you as well. She is, after all, our best choreographer."

"Did you forget, Joshua? Today is V's day off," I remind him, jogging his memory.

"Ah, well, then…"

"We had best be off. Come on, Psyche, before Blaze has our guts for garters," I say, quickly taking Psyche's arm to lead us both to the door.

I've managed to slip a note to Mimi while Joshua wasn't looking, letting her know my apartment will be free this evening. I doubt even Mimi knows where I'll be instead, but she's a smart cookie, so I'm sure it won't take her and Psyche long to work it out.

By the time we've reached the basement to set up on the stage, the bell is already going to alert members and guests to take their seats before the final performance of the day is to take place.

"Where have you been?" Blaze demands in a tone much the same as a mother might use when scolding children.

"Sorry, we got waylaid —"

"With photos and autographs," Psyche finishes for me.

"How's the family?" Siren asks, which puzzles me for a moment until I realise that of course my dance crew and Red Velvet Ladies will have seen where me and Psyche were.

"Hush now! Positions please; we're about to begin," Blaze hisses, ending all and any awkward conversation.

Thank heavens for small mercies.

Max is driving Joshua and I to his apartment. We are currently sitting side by side, holding hands. Mimi had indeed gotten my message, so I left my apartment key in my dressing room, letting her know by text where to find it. I really hope she and Psyche have a good time; she promised already to take care of Binks for me, and I'm in no doubt she will.

"Ah, bit of a press problem here. My team and I can get you both in safely, but it means Darla will be photographed," Max informs us, looking back to Joshua, an intelligent man seeming to know something is definitely up between us.

"That's ok, Max."

"What? But...my identity!"

"Will still be covered by your make-up, and...this mask. You can walk in with me mask-free, but it's up to you." Joshua's eyes burn into mine as he says this.

"I'll go mask...free?"

"Excellent," Joshua says, taking me and, I think, Max back a bit, swiftly opening the car door and taking me with him.

Flashes go mad at the pair of us; people yell and ask for us to stand and smile and look at them. Max has run around to us with two more of his men and he looks a bit peeved.

"Evening, everyone," Joshua greets, holding a hand up to wave at the paps. My stomach clenches as fear grips me around the waist like a snake.

Out of nowhere, someone grabs me around the waist and I lose my grip of Joshua's hand. They lift me effortlessly, laughing with a few friends as if it's a joke. Joshua looks murderous as Max decks the man, causing me to fall to the ground, grazing my hands and knees.

More security appears, and soon the paps and idiots among them get pushed far enough away so we can enter Joshua's building.

I'm sure Joshua must be saying something to me, but I'm unclear. I'm in shock and shaking like a leaf. Max brings me back to focus by making eye contact and instructing me to pop a glucose tablet that he hands me. He has managed to get a bottle of water from somewhere —a vending machine, perhaps. Taking the lift to Joshua's floor, I chew the glucose tablet and sip on the water bottle, making it more apparent that my hands are shaking.

"Don't worry; it's just adrenaline and it will pass," Max says, as Joshua holds me close. His body heat takes the edge off my chill.

Entering Joshua's apartment, my thoughts drift back to the final dance and the goodbyes I said to the Red Velvet Ladies, Blaze reminding me that I would be seeing her before the next Fire Festival, that it was just Sheila and Maryanne who are returning to Egypt once their tours for the first half of the year are finished, which would be in a few weeks. My dance crew were going to an *after party* at *Lucifer's Haven*. I didn't have the heart to tell them it changed hands; I'm sure I'll get an update the next time I see them.

"Everything's all good. I'm going to retire for the night unless you need me for something else," Max says, approaching. He has already checked Joshua's apartment. The tired rings of fatigue are ever-present on his face.

"We are all good I think, Max. Thanks as usual for a job well done."

"No worries. Goodnight."

It's now just Joshua and me.

"Good evening, Joshua. Will the lady be requiring me to set up the guest bedroom?" Joshua's housekeeper greets as she enters from…somewhere.

"That won't be necessary. Thank you, Fiona."

"Very well. I shall excuse myself for the rest of the night. Goodnight," Fiona says, while collecting her keys from kitchen counter before seeing herself out.

~ Chapter 52 ~

It is the morning after, and as I lay here in Joshua's huge four-poster bed, I stretch as my senses fully awaken. All I wanted was for him to ravage me, but he insisted on waiting, much to my inner goddess's horror. I'm horny as hell and Joshua was the perfect gentleman—except now my perfect gentleman is nowhere to be seen.

Wandering around his apartment, I notice that Max is not here either. Wanting to leave but realising this will be a challenge, I take a few moments to think who can get me out of this tight spot.

Dante!

Quickly, I locate my old friend's number and don't hesitate to call him.

"Hello?" Sarah's voice answers.

Crush stealer, my green monster thinks.

"Oh hey Sarah, sorry, accidental phone call. Tell Dante I said hi," I say, hanging up the call just as Max and

Joshua enter. "Where have you guys been? I was worried."

"Breakfast! I gave Fiona the morning off so you and I could enjoy breakfast in private," Joshua explains, holding up two paper bags and take away coffees.

"Cheers, Max. Hold all my calls, won't you? If it's Eva, only let the call through if it's urgent. I'll be in my study."

"Certainly," Max says, taking his own food and coffee downstairs to his living quarters.

Entering his study, which is the room with antique furniture and amazing bookshelves, I choose a comfy squidgy brown leather chair to sit in as he perches on the edge of his desk. I'm wearing some of my crazy pyjamas. Taking a bite of my bacon roll, the quick hit of endorphins over how good it tastes takes my simmering disappointment from no sex with Joshua down just a teeny amount.

"Well...looks like the cat's officially out of the bag—you're officially my new *mystery* woman," Joshua says, throwing the paper down that I had missed was under his arm. It lands open to a huge photograph of him and I. The headline reads "One of London's wealthiest nightclub owner's comes home with gorgeous mystery blonde on his arm."

"That is a really good photo," I say, appreciating how high definition it is.

"Sure is sexy...sure is," Joshua says, again stirring my inner sex goddess with that smouldering look and '*come to bed eyes*' that feel as if will set me on fire any minute.

Passionately, we kiss each other in the middle of Joshua's study before he lifts me up to sit my bottom on top of his desk.

Do we make love in his office? Maybe we do; maybe we don't. You'll just have to wait to find out.

See you soon...

To Be Continued...

About the Author

Emma Bruce is a feisty 30 something Sagittarian who lives by the motto "Never give up" She lives with her family, the love of her life Matthew and their four beautiful children.

Her first book 'Pink Club' was received so well by the general reading population that there was a sudden big demand for her to complete the second book in her mini series to which she has aptly called "Dreams in Pink".

Emma (When not chasing after her children, picking out stray Lego bricks imbedded into her feet, cleaning pen from the walls with a magic sponge, among a plethora of other jobs being a mother and housewife entails), enjoys in her quieter hours both reading books as a form of escapism and relaxation alongside working on her own written projects.

For more information please check out Emma's website

www.emmabruceauthor.com
http://pinkclub.site

Acknowledgments

Proofreading by Agent M.

Email agentmproofreader@gmail.com

Professional bio: A qualified proofreader and beta reader. Agent M can proof your thesis, dissertations, fiction and non-fiction manuscripts. She is also available to discuss plot and character development. Agent M will also type up handwritten manuscripts if you provide a data stick for the finished project.

Personal bio Agent M is a fifty something coffee snob who likes nothing more than curling up with a good book on a cold, rainy day with her tortoiseshell cat Blaze beside her. Hobbies include baking and debating the merits of a Victoria sandwich cake over a fruit cake when reading a historical murder mystery. Agent M enjoy's many different genres and can be found in her local coffee shop, people watching while reading a good book.

Also by Emma Bruce

Pink Club series

Pink Club

Dreams in Pink

Coming Soon

Book 3

Printed in Great Britain
by Amazon